"DID HE THINK HE WAS GOING TO END UP IN YOUR BED?" DANIEL ASKED.

"I don't know and I don't care." She stared at him, willing him over to her.

They stood very close together, not touching, just having an eye to eye confrontation.

"Did you want to stay?" Daniel asked.

"What do you think?"

His lips were like fire, burning down on hers, and creating a sensation of excitement and abandon that seemed to have been buried for quite some time.

She wasn't aware of the clothes slipping from her body. But she was aware of the way his fingers traced every outline of her form, creating exquisite electric shocks of ecstasy.

She struggled to get his clothes off. Tore at his shirt, ripped the zipper on his trousers. "I want you so, so badly," she murmured. "I've wanted you for months and months. It seems like forever."

He touched her breasts, played with them gently, fingered her nipples until she wanted to scream. She wanted to beg him to make love to her . . .

Novels by Jackie Collins

Lovers & Gamblers
The World is Full of Divorced Women
The Love Killers
Chances

Published by
WARNER BOOKS

JACKIE COLLINS

The World is Full of Divorced Women

WARNER BOOKS

A Warner Communications Company

I would like to thank the following women,
Divorced, Married, or Otherwise . . .

JAN
HAZEL
JOAN
EVIE
LUISA
SHAKIRA
JOANNA
CHRIS
CAROLYN
ADRIENNE

and

JOHNY!

The World
is Full of
Divorced Women

Chapter 1

"Are you bored with sex?" Mike had asked the other day.

"Bored?" Cleo James had replied, her voice guilty, "of course not." But she was bored by him, by the way he always made the same predictable moves, by the way he always touched her in exactly the same places in exactly the same way.

It was the beginning of summer in New York, a time when it is still pleasant to walk in the streets. Cleo stood in a fitting-room at Saks and stared at her reflection in the mirror. She had discarded her own clothes and was trying on a beige suede dress. The dress had been altered for her the previous week and it now fitted perfectly; but still she stared in the mirror, seeing a slim girl with long straight dark hair, big eyes, a wide mouth.

Cleo wasn't really thinking about the dress. The

dress was fine. She was thinking about her husband, Mike. She was thinking about him *screwing* that other girl.

At the onset of their relationship, sex with Mike had been fantastically exciting. Now he seemed stuck in some strange set ritual.

He never wanted to try anything new.

He never wanted to do anything different.

Marriage had changed him.

He did not turn her on any more, and she never had been good at pretending.

They didn't row much. In fact, hardly ever. They had discussions where they talked things out, and analyzed situations.

Mike was an executive with a record company. He was thirty-six, seven years older than Cleo. Attractive in a free rangy style, with his Che moustache and come-on eyes. They had been married four years. A modern marriage where infidelity certainly shouldn't be the end of the world.

"Did you fancy her?" How many times had Cleo asked him that question, her stomach in knots waiting for his reply.

"Sure." Mike would laugh and make a joke of it. "I even fucked her a few times."

Ha, ha, not very funny, Cleo thought, and she never questioned further. She didn't want to know.

Now she knew. She had seen him.

Mike was her second husband, the first a vague memory when she was eighteen. She loved Mike, but not the white heat of love she had felt when they were first together.

"It looks great, huh?" The salesgirl popped her head around the door.

"Yes, it's fine," Cleo replied. But it wasn't fine that she'd caught Mike today. It wasn't fine that his lean naked body had been bent in such obvious enjoyment. It wasn't fine that the busty blond beneath him was one of her best friends.

She unzipped herself out of the beige fringed suede and handed it to the girl to take away to wrap.

Are you bored with sex? Why had he asked her that? She wasn't doing anything different. Were her sexual moves as predictable as his?

Perhaps the gradual lull in their sex life was her fault. But she knew it wasn't. It was Mike who had changed.

She had been unfaithful once. One man, one time. It had been beautiful, but at the same time sordid. She had made sure it was only once.

They had money, not vast amounts, but enough to satisfy most material demands. Mike was successful. Cleo worked for magazines as a freelance interviewer. They didn't need the money she made, but she enjoyed working, she loved her job.

She dressed slowly, dark brown gauchos, Sonia Rykel sweater, Biba boots, Gucci leather belt, Oliver Goldsmith brown-tinted sunspecs to cover her prune eyeshadowed eyes.

She collected her package and walked out into the Fifth Avenue sunshine. She was supposed to meet Ginny for lunch and it was too late to cancel. The last thing she felt like doing was having lunch with Ginny—Ginny of the baby blue eyes, blond curls, and vast sexual appetite.

"Ginny's a bird brain," Mike had said many times. But then he always had disparaging comments to make about most of her friends—including Susan, the blond wriggling about under him that very morning.

Maybe he had also had Ginny. It wasn't an

implausible thought. Ginny was a notoriously easy lay, but she was also the last of the great talkers, and if she had been with Mike full details would be all over town.

"I think you stink!" an old woman hissed at Cleo as she passed on by, and Cleo took no notice of the old biddy who launched away up Fifth Avenue waving a flowered parasol before her. New York was full of nuts, and you just ignored them and hoped that one day you wouldn't get raped or robbed or attacked or shot. New Yorkers were immune to the violence among them, only the tourists moved uneasily. Cleo felt like a New Yorker, although she had only lived there for the four years since marrying Mike. She was actually from London, a place she had hardly moved out of before—only as far as Europe for a weekend tan.

She wrestled with a blue-suited businessman for a cab, and won. Then she sat back and tried to untense herself. She didn't want to arrive at lunch in a neurotic state, ready to pour out the whole stupid story to Ginny.

The whole thing was so goddamn ridiculous. Why did she feel so bad about it? It was just one of those things that went on every day. It was perfectly understandable.

But screw him for choosing one of her friends. And double screw him for letting her catch them at it.

She half wished she had never met Mike, and she definitely wished she had never married him. Mike had been the one that had insisted on getting married, Cleo would have been happy just living with him. Her whole attitude upset him, he was used to being with girls whose ultimate goal was the thin gold ring on their wedding finger. He couldn't un-

12

derstand the fact that Cleo didn't care. It was a blow to his ego. He insisted that they get married. If they weren't married now it would all be a lot easier. She had one bad marriage behind her, she didn't want to make it two. . . .

The restaurant was small and noisy. Ginny was already there, sitting at a table sipping a Martini and exchanging glances with a well-known actor who was close by.

"Boy, would I like to handle him!" she enthused as Cleo sat down. Ginny was an agent, thirty, plumpish, divorced, not unattractive in a girly way. "Hey, you look very good today. I like the boots, where did you get the boots?"

"The Biba Boutique. I had to go back three times to get my size. Who's the extra seat for?"

"Susan said she'd try to join us. I had the most fantastic night last night; went to that new disco down in the Village with Bob, and *guess* who came in. Cy Litva. You remember what that bastard did to me last time—well, I tell you when I saw the little fink I went hot and cold—but I was cool, just smiled, y'know. I looked very good, had on my Saint Laurent shirt, and a darling pair of hot pants, and were they ever hot! Well . . ."

Ginny talked a lot. She told of each sexual encounter in detail and with great enjoyment. She didn't notice that Cleo was hardly listening.

Cleo was thinking—Susan will not be joining us, Susan would not have the nerve to join us, because even if Susan hadn't seen her walk unexpectedly into Mike's office, Mike certainly had.

She remembered the morning yet again. She had been near his office, and decided to pop in and surprise him. His receptionist was not there, so she had just walked right through. She had surprised him all right. They were on the large studio couch. Susan was naked, lying with the back of her head toward the door. Mike, astride her, stared right at Cleo.

She just stood there unsure of what to do. It seemed like hours. It was actually only a few seconds before she turned and walked quickly away. Mike never broke his movement. What a bastard! The least he could have done was climb off.

". . . so we had this really fantastic scene, one of those slow wild things that just builds and builds and goes on for ever, and—hey—here's Susan. Let's order, I'm starving."

Susan White was a tall girl with thick long blond hair which hung in a heavy curtain past her shoulders. Her hair, and her large accommodating breasts, were her best features, and she was well aware of that fact. She wore a soft pink angora sweater tucked into trousers. She was an actress, not really successful, but she worked quite consistently in off-Broadway productions.

It struck Cleo with much irony that Mike hadn't told Susan about their being discovered that morning. That would be just like him, weak, frightened of a scene. Either that or Susan was a better actress than Cleo had ever given her credit for, because she was approaching the table full of smiles. "Have I had a morning!" she announced, flopping down in her chair. "Two auditions, both on opposite sides of town. I'm exhausted!"

"Those auditions must really take it out of you," Cleo murmured, "all that taking off of your clothes."

"Huh?" Susan stared.

"I mean it is another nude role, isn't it?" Susan

14

had recently been in a play where she had had to strip off and simulate masturbation. The play had only run three nights.

"I'm not *typed* you know" Susan said irritably, "anyway actresses don't have to strip at auditions. It doesn't matter what your body is like, it's the play that matters."

"Oh sure," Cleo said. "Susan, I never thought I'd hear *you* coming out with that tired Hollywood claptrap."

"Let's order for crissakes," Ginny interrupted; "if I have a salad for lunch does that mean I can go mad tonight and gorge myself? Cy's taking me to eat Russian, and I *love* eating Russian. Hey—that conjures up a mental picture of a guy's dick covered in sour cream. Delicious—do you think he'd dig it?"

"Your conversation always reminds me of a college girl who finally got it for the first time the night before," Cleo said coldly.

Ginny shrugged. "It's always the first time for me," she giggled.

"How's Mike?" Susan asked, a shade too casually.

Cleo fixed her with green angry eyes, but her voice was even. "What the fuck sort of childish game are you playing, Susan? If this is the best acting ability you've got I can understand how you ended up playing with yourself in some fleapit off Broadway."

"What's going on?" Ginny asked blankly, putting down the menu. "What's with the insults?"

Susan muttered, a dull red flushing her face, "I don't know, I only asked how Mike was, I . . ."

"Oh, cut it out, baby," Cleo said, rising from the

table, "fuck my husband if you want, but don't take me for an idiot. Sorry about this, Ginny, I'll talk to you later."

Susan said, "But . . ."

Cleo didn't wait to hear. She was out of there. She was in the street. She was walking with tears blinding her eyes. She was cursing because her eyelashes were falling off.

I have blown my cool, she thought. Not only have I blown my cool but the whole of New York will know about it because of Ginny Sadler's big big mouth.

Where has all my women's lib good sense gone to?

Live and let live.

Fuck and let fuck.

Well, it was probably all for the good. It had certainly shaken Susan up.

What a fool Mike was not to have told her.

What a fool Mike was period.

She composed a letter to him in her mind. "Dear Mike—While we have lived together and loved together for several years I would now like to terminate this agreement. I feel that I have outgrown you, both mentally and physically, and we have nothing left to offer each other except a future of indifference. I wish you much happiness with Susan's big boobs. Sincerely yours—Cleo.

P.S. I never knew big tits were your hang up.

P.P.S. I never knew you liked girls who played with themselves.

P.P.P.S. I guess I just never knew."

Her tears had stopped, and under cover of her shades she peeled off the falling eyelashes and wrapped them in a tissue.

She would go home and repair her make-up,

16

bathe and change. She would also pack. She had been due to leave the following morning on an interview assignment in London, but she would leave tonight. She would take the coward's way out and stay in a hotel for the night and not face Mike. She didn't want to see him, he would only lie. She wanted time to think.

She ran for a cab, lost it, and waited for a bus.

Chapter 2

The girl had blond hair, bubbly and curly and streaked with little patches of orange.

Her face was very pretty, very painted.

False freckles abounded. Little brown dots painstakingly sketched on early in the morning.

Each extra eyelash was fixed individually. China blue eyes were surrounded by China blue eye shadow.

Her own eyebrows had been shaved off and replaced with clever arched strokes of soft brown pencil.

Full pouty lips were made more so by two different shades of pale lipstick, and over the top liberal helpings of lip gloss.

Clever shading fined her slightly plump cheeks down, and her skin was softly burnished all over by an out-of-the-bottle sun tan.

She wasn't very tall, only about five foot three, but the enormous clogs she was wearing added a good six inches. They were green with red stripes, and she wore them with bright green tights and rolled up to the knee faded blue jeans. She had a tiny waist, slightly exposed as the skimpy halter top sweater left a gap of four inches. She wore no bra, and her breasts, perky and upright, bounced engagingly through the thin material.

She strolled through Harrods, swinging an outsize canvas bag in one hand, and stuffing chocolates —Maltesers—into her ever open, every moist mouth.

Her name was Muffin, but all the photographers called her Crumpet.

She was twenty, and had found fame as a respectable nude model. Respectable meaning that her nude or semi-nude poses advertised everything from bras to men's shirts in all the best magazines and newspapers.

Muffin was oblivious to the stares, she was used to it.

She stopped at the sunglasses counter and tried a pair on. They were large and round, pink tinted.

Muffin liked them. She glanced surreptitiously around, no one appeared to be watching, so calmly she walked away from the counter, glasses stuck firmly on her nose.

She jammed some more Maltesers into her mouth, crumpled the empty packet and let it fall to the ground. Then humming softly to herself she went out of the front entrance and asked the doorman to get her a cab.

It was raining in London, but Muffin attracted a cab immediately. She lived on the top floor of a large house in Holland Park. She shared the studio apartment with her boyfriend, Jon Clapton. He was the photographer who had discovered Muffin when she was seventeen, and had moved her in with him as soon as they had persuaded her parents in Wimbledon that it was O.K.

"We're going to get married," Jon had assured them, "just as soon as I get my divorce."

"Anybody home?" Muffin called, as she let herself in. Scruff, the mongrel dog she had found wandering the streets, barked confirmation that he was indeed home.

"Want to go out for a walk, fella?" Muffin inquired. She looked on the message pad by the phone to see if Jon had left her any notes. He had been asleep when she had left that morning.

"*Terrazza*—nine o'clock," he had scrawled, "get tarted up, it's the Schumann calendar deal."

Muffin screwed up her face in distaste. She hated all the business dinners that Jon got together.

"We *have* to do them," Jon would patiently explain. "It's the personal touch these old geezers like. So what if they touch you up with their eyes, they're going to see all of you in the photos anyway."

"Photos are different," Muffin would argue.

"All right, forget it. Be just another dreary little model girl with nice tits. I'm making you a *personality*, a *star*."

Muffin had to agree that he was right. She was being offered money now that a year before she had only dreamed about.

Jon handled everything. They had a joint account and all monies that they both earned were paid into that.

Jon was a successful photographer, and on deals they did together they got paid a lot.

The calendar deal was important. Schumann Electronics put out a fabulous calendar each year using twelve different girls. Jon's idea was that they just use Muffin, with him taking the photographs. Twelve incredible naked Muffins.

The deal was nearly set, but Klauss Schumann was in London and wished to meet Muffin before the contracts were signed.

"Forget about the walk, doggie," Muffin sighed, "mama's got to start gettin' it all together."

Jon Clapton arrived at *Terrazza* at eight. He was tall and skinny, twenty-six years old, with long dirty blond hair and surprisingly innocent good looks. He had found the innocent look extremely useful when dealing with people. Underneath the clean-cut looks lurked a brain of crystal cunning.

Klauss Schumann waited in the bar, a middle-aged German in a shiny blue suit.

"Hello," Jon said warmly, "you're early and I'm five minutes late, sorry about that. What are you drinking?"

Klauss was drinking vodka and bitter lemon. Jon ordered rum and coke.

"Muffin will be a bit late," Jon explained, although actually he had told her not to be there until nine. He wanted some time alone with Schumann. "In the meantime I thought you might like to flick through these."

Jon handed Klauss a leather folder containing a series of photos of Muffin.

There was Muffin on a swing, coyly crossing her legs, naked.

There was Muffin bending down, bottom in the air, naked.

22

There was Muffin on the beach, in a car, on a boat, all naked.

There was Muffin in a large hat and nothing else. Muffin in fine black tights and nothing else. Muffin in thigh-length white boots.

"She's a lovely girl," Klauss said thickly.

"Yes," Jon agreed, "and she always looks so wholesome. Even the women love her. There's nothing rude about her, that's the great thing."

Klauss nodded, and flicked through the photos again.

"We have to have a final decision by tomorrow," Jon said quickly. "Other important clients are after her and I must let them know."

"Of course. Of course. I know you have worked out all the details with our PRs. But I thought as I was in town I should meet with you both. However, I'm sure the answer is yes." He picked up the photo of Muffin in the white boots. "Such a charming girl . . ."

Yeah, Jon thought, a charming littler raver, who if it wasn't for me would be finished by now, or perhaps would have never got started.

He remembered how they met. At a skating rink of all places. Jon was doing a series of picture articles "Birds around London," and Muffin had been at the skating rink, plump and spotty and toothy. She had been wearing an orange sweater, and Jon had thought, "great pair of knockers," so he had done a few photos of her. They had turned out all right, and he had taken her down to Brighton to do some bikini shots. She had just left school and was taking a typing course.

"Waste of time," Jon had told her, "woman like you stashed behind a desk."

She came to his studio to see the prints, and he suggested there was a lot of bread in nude modelling.

"My parents would be furious," she had giggled. But in no time at all she was out of her clothes, and he shot five rolls of film, and then in no time at all she was in his arms and they made it on the floor and he had asked, "What's a nice little girl from Wimbledon doing being so experienced?"

"I've had five fellas," she had announced, "one boyfriend a year since I was twelve!"

Within two months Jon had left his wife, and Muffin had lost her spots and ten pounds of baby fat.

Within six months Jon had started Muffin's career rolling, and she moved in with him.

They had an understanding relationship. From the start Jon had told her, "Look, you're young, lots of good things are going to happen for us together, so don't let's blow it."

"You're not exactly old," she had remarked.

"I know," Jon agreed, "but I've got a wife and two kids and I know what it's all about. Here's the situation, either of us want to screw around it's cool. Only there's a rule. One time only with the same person. Understand?"

Muffin had nodded.

"Oh, and we tell each other about it. O.K.?"

Muffin agreed. It sounded like a terrific rule.

And it worked. In the two years they had been together Muffin had slept with three men, one time with each, and she had told Jon all about it.

In turn he had told her about three girls he slept with. Actually there had only been one other, but he didn't want Muffin becoming too sure of him.

"Ah, this must be the young lady now," Klauss announced.

Jon turned to watch her entrance. Smiling, pretty, everyone turning to look.

Muffin had come a long way from the plump, spotty girl at the skating rink.

Chapter 3

Cleo went home, packed, bathed and changed, and was back at the office by four.

There was an urgent message for her to call Mike, and two calls from Ginny. She didn't return either of them. She checked through arrangements for her trip, and made a few business calls.

At five Russell Hayes sent a messenger to see if she was free to come up to his office. Russell was the owner-editor of the magazine *Image* that was sending Cleo to Europe. He was a thin nervous man who had a disconcerting habit of biting his nails—two or three at a time. He wore pink shirts and cramped Italian suits, and after three wives he had settled for a parade of statuesque girlfriends who called for him at the office.

" 'Lo, Russ," said Cleo. She was feeling very down. "What's going on?"

"Just wanted to know if you had any problems."

"Everything's under control. I'm all packed and ready to go. In fact, big surprise, I've got my suitcase with me and I was wondering if there was any chance of getting a plane tonight?"

Russell tapped a silver pencil on his desk-top. "Don't mess up my plans for you, sweetie. They're all set to take very good care of you tomorrow, cars are arranged both ends, also I am superstitious— *never* change a flight. Anyway, I want you to come to the Richard West party with me. You did promise."

Cleo had forgotten all about it. *Image* Magazine had bought the serial rights to Richard West's book.

Russell smiled a quick bunched-up smile. "The West book will be a winner—you see. *Sex—an Explanation*—what could be a better title?" He added pointedly, "*I* thought of it you know."

"I know," said Cleo with a smile. She liked Russell, they had a good business relationship, although at one time he had tried to make it more. Cleo had joked him out of it, and now she felt they were real friends.

"Is Mike coming to the party?" Russell asked. He and Mike were also close friends

"Why?" Cleo countered.

"What do you mean—why?"

"No, he's not coming."

"Is everything all right with you two?"

"Now that you ask . . ." she hesitated, "no it's not. Everything stinks."

"I've been through three, I know the signs." He walked around the desk and put his arm around her.

28

"It makes me feel such a failure," she said help-lessly.

"Tell me about it."

She shook her head. "If I talk about it I'll probably start crying. Anyway, it's over, and I've moved out, and oh God, that reminds me. I've got to book into a hotel for tonight."

"You can stay with me if you want."

"We're friends, right? I need friends, so a hotel will be better."

"I'll have my secretary fix it, don't worry about a thing."

The buzzer on his desk rang and the reception-ist told him Dr. Richard West was downstairs.

"Send him up," Russell said. "Cleo, you can meet him, and we'll all go over to the party in my car. How's that?"

"Fine. Can I use your bathroom?"

"Help yourself."

Cleo shut herself in the little oak-pannelled room adjoining Russell's office and stared at herself in the mirror. Her make-up was perfect, having only been freshly applied that afternoon. She added a touch more prune eyeshadow, it made her oval face paler.

"You've got the most incredible skin," Mike had told her the first time they met.

She combed her long dark hair and remem-bered the first time Mike had undressed her. The original hang-up was purely sexual, and when the sex stopped being exciting the rot set in.

How long could a relationship like that last? For how many years did one have to pretend it was the greatest thing in the world? Oh, sure it was great, but there were other things, things that Mike

29

didn't want to know about. Children. Cleo sighed.
She had always loved kids, and she had always
imagined she would have plenty. It had seemed
sensible when Mike had said they should wait. She
wasn't one of those women who relished the thought
of all those dreary months blown up like a balloon.
So when he said let's wait, she agreed with him,
thinking in terms of a year or two. It gradually
dawned on her that Mike didn't even like children,
let alone want any of his own.

When she asked him one Sunday, in bed, after
making love, he said, "Yeah, sweetheart, I can't say
I'm overboard about the idea. Like some little monster interfering in our lives—who needs it? And I do
not get horny over pregnant ladies—they turn me
right off." Had that been the moment when things
began to go sour?

Cleo went back into Russell's office and he introduced her to Richard West. "You don't look like
your picture on the book," she said.

He nodded agreeably. "I know. But if the picture on the book looked like me we'd have trouble
giving the book away."

She smiled. He was O.K. Not a neurotic. She
hated neurotic authors.

He was a man of medium height, slightly too
heavy, with thick sandy hair cut too short. The suit
he was wearing was horrible, and the matching shirt
and tie didn't help. In spite of it all he was attractive in a way he obviously wasn't aware of. She
wanted to tell him he had lips like Mick Jagger,
thick sensual lips on the face of a middle-aged sex
expert.

"I think we should go," Russell said.

They were the first there. Just them, and a room
full of waiters.

Russell fussed around magazine displays, re-arranging.

Richard frowned. "I hate these things," he said, "they make me nervous."

Cleo smiled. "Just be nice to everybody, you never know who you're talking to. And throw in a lot of quotes—you know—kind of racy statistics."

"What constitutes racy statistics?"

"Well—figures. Like how many times a man can—er—make it in twenty-four hours. Things like that. Titillation for the potential reader."

"Couched in more professional terms I take it?"

Cleo laughed. "Oh yes—*much* more professional."

Ginny was one of the first guests to arrive. She made a straight line for Cleo who was talking to a book reviewer.

"Can I interrupt?" she asked brightly.

"Sure," said the book reviewer. "I must go and find Dr. West. There are several points I want to discuss with him."

"I bet!" Ginny replied, tossing blond curls and looking around the room. "Who's here? Anyone I have slept with or should sleep with or might want to sleep with?"

"Is that what you barged in to ask me?"

"No. Actually, *why* didn't you return my call? I mean I just don't believe the scene at lunch with you and Susan, it's not like you to make scenes, and poor Susan was in a *terrible* state. She swears that nothing has gone on with her and Mike."

"Oh, come on, Ginny—she may bullshit you, but I am here to tell you I *saw* them together."

"*Saw* them together—what is that? Just because you saw them together doesn't mean the next step is a good healthy fuck. She did mention they had a coffee one day. But she swore to me on her mother's life that nothing went on, honestly Cleo, I think . . ."

"Will you shut up a minute. I *saw* them together —naked—screwing—at Mike's office this morning."

"Oh," said Ginny, and she was silent for the shortest of times, then—"That no good lying bitch! Swearing on her mother's life. Just wait 'til I see her . . . I just can't get over it. You must feel awful. I should have guessed you of all people wouldn't make a scene over nothing. I'm sorry, I'm really . . ."

"Enough, Ginny. I don't want to talk about it. It doesn't matter, it really doesn't matter. I have packed, and I'm leaving for London tomorrow. I just want some time to think things out."

"What does Mike say about it all? He can't possibly have a thing about Susan. Big girls were never his scene, and let's face it, great tits she may have, but the IQ of a five-year-old. In fact I think . . ."

"Ginny, I don't want to talk about it, and I'd appreciate it if you wouldn't discuss it all over town. Come on, I'll introduce you to Dr. West."

"Oh, all right. I always fancied comparing notes with an expert at the game."

They walked across the room.

"Richard, I'd like you to meet a friend of mine —Ginny Sandler. Ginny's an agent." Cleo smiled as she spoke. The smile was becoming weary on her face. She wondered if Mike had reached home yet and realized that she had moved out.

"Hello, Ginny," Richard said warmly, shaking her hand.

"I was thinking we might make a movie sale on your book," Ginny said as Cleo moved off. "They buy titles you know. *Sex—an Explanation*—it could be a sort of groovy skin flick—like educational. Or even a Julie Andrews starrer with her as a school marm. There's lots of possibilities. You're not represented, are you?"

Richard shook his head.

"Then I'm going to take you over and we'll grow rich together." She took his arm. "About that chapter on enlarged clitorises—there were one or two things I wanted to ask you about that."

Cleo felt suddenly tired. She had had enough of small talk, and smiling, and being nice to people who bitched as soon as you were two feet away.

She looked around for Russell. He was with a group of people, including the latest girlfriend, a redheaded giant named Florinda.

Cleo edged over. "I'm very tired," she whispered. "What hotel did you book me into?"

"Christ!" Russell banged his forehead with the palm of his hand. "I forgot!"

"Thanks a lot."

"Don't worry though, I told you I've got a spare room, lots of spare rooms in fact."

"Russell . . ."

"Surely after all this time you can trust me?" He acted offended. "I'll call my houseboy and tell him you're on your way. I won't be back until late, and unless you fancy sharing a bed with me and Florinda you'll be left very much alone."

Cleo felt too tired to argue. "Well, if you're sure . . ."

"Of course I'm sure. Your suitcase is already in

33

my car. I'll take you out to the chauffeur, he can take you to my place, then come back for me."

"If Mike turns up here . . ."

"My lips are sealed."

Impulsively Cleo kissed him on the cheek. "It's good to have a friend like you."

Russell laughed nervously. "I've told you before, if ever you and Mike split I'm very available."

Cleo nodded. He may make himself available, but he just wasn't her type.

Russell lived in a sprawling penthouse with incredible views over the city. Cleo had been there on social occasions and thought to herself what a great apartment. Now, seeing it devoid of people, it seemed like a set out of a movie.

The houseboy let her in, and showed her to an orange tented bedroom, adjoined to a bathroom that featured a sunken bath big enough for six. Silently the houseboy demonstrated how the bath could be turned into a thermal whirlpool. Cleo nodded. The last thing she felt like was a thermal whirlpool bath.

The houseboy pointed out various switches. One for music, or tapes, or TV.

It was one hell of a guest room, Cleo mused. She glanced at the piles of books piled neatly on the bedside table. *Erotic Art, The History of Erotica, Sexual Understanding*. She started to smile. Oh Russell! What a disappointment you turned out to be. Where was the stack of *Playboy* magazines?

Sure enough they were piled on a glass table near to the loo.

She pushed the button for the tapes, and Isaac Hayes came on at his most horny.

She wondered what Mike was doing now. He

would have arrived home. Would he realize she had gone? If he checked the bathroom he would. No more feminine clutter. If he looked in her closets he would. No more favorite clothes.

Perhaps she *should* have left a note. No. The hell with him. Let him wonder. By the time he got around to looking for her she would be in London.

She wanted to sleep, but sleep wouldn't come. Her thoughts were too active, darting this way and that.

Repeatedly the scene with Mike making love to Susan flashed before her eyes. If only he had stopped, rolled off. But no, he had just stared at Cleo, stared right through her, and just kept on grinding away.

What a bastard. Didn't want to spoil his fun. Fuck now—argue later.

Well she had screwed that little game. She just wasn't around to argue with; and Mike would hate that. Mike was a talker, a reasoner. Keeping it all to himself would choke him.

Good. Let him choke. Let him discuss it with Susan bird brain.

An hour must have passed when she heard her door open and someone tiptoed in. She clicked on the bedside lamp. It was Russell.

"I just wanted to check that everything's all right," he said lamely.

Cleo pulled the sheet up. "Fine. I just can't seem to sleep. What are you doing home so soon?"

"I was worried about you. Thought you might like a little conversation."

"Where's Florinda?"

"Sent her home."

"You shouldn't have done so on my account."

35

Oh Christ, Cleo thought, he's going to launch an attack.

Russell sat down on the side of the bed. "What do you think of this room?" he inquired.

"It's very modern."

Russell nodded. "You could stay here if you liked when you get back from Europe."

"That's very kind of you."

"You're a beautiful woman. Cleo. And what is more, an intelligent one. You and I could have a very fine relationship together."

We couldn't, Cleo replied silently, you bite your nails. She said aloud, "It's getting late, Russ. I think I'll try and get some sleep."

"You still love Mike, I know that, I'm not a fool. But you and I could have a different kind of relationship, a more mature one. Mike's not the man for you; he still has a lot of growing up to do." He leaned forward and kissed her, a practiced, insistent kiss.

She couldn't struggle, as under the sheet she was naked. So she accepted his kiss, and with both hands firmly pulled the sheet around her.

With a sudden movement he rolled on top of her. She wrenched her mouth away from his. "Get off, Russell, please!"

His body was moving up and down, his eyes tightly closed. He still wore the striped Italian suit, the pink shirt, the polished shoes.

Cleo lay rigid under the sheet.

At the moment of his climax Russell muttered, "I've always loved you, always . . ." He shuddered to a stop and Cleo couldn't help thinking about his suit, it must be absolutely ruined.

He lay still for a few moments, and then quietly

he clicked the bedside lamp off, whispered good-night, and was gone.

Cleo leapt out of bed and locked the door. She didn't know whether to laugh or cry.

The perfect end to a perfect day.

Chapter 4

"You were great!" Jon said, "absolutely perfect. The Schumann Calendar is going to be all ours by tomorrow. Takes care of our holiday problems this year."

Muffin giggled. "He didn't half give me a few funny looks. Honestly, sometimes I feel more naked than any of my photos when these old fellas gaze at me."

Jon patted her on the knee. "Doesn't bother you does it?"

"Sometimes it makes me feel a bit sort of funny . . ."

"Pie face, your little boobs are very famous, and they'd all like to have a grope. Enjoy it, revel in it. One day you'll be a little old lady in Wimbledon and then you'll be wishing you were a young piece of . . ."

"Jon!"

He put his arms around her and kissed the lip gloss off her full pouty lips. She snuggled up against him.

He pulled her blue denim frilled skirt up from behind and slid his hands under her tight-fitting bikini pants. "Beautiful bum . . ." he mumbled.

"Your hands are freezing!" she complained, but she didn't try to move them.

"I'm going to take your knickers off, little girl."

Muffin gasped, china blue eyes widened. "Oh please, sir! I'm just an innocent country maiden, please do not molest me!"

Jon peeled the pants off her. "O.K., country maiden, let me into your forest."

"But sir . . ."

The phone rang.

"Shit!" said Jon.

Muffin answered it, slowly unbuttoning the white camisole top she was wearing. "It's your wife," she hissed, sticking a small pink tongue out at Jon, and marching out of the room.

He picked up the phone. "Jane? What do you want now?"

He hadn't lived with her for three years but she still depended on him for everything. All right, he didn't mind supporting his kids, but why did he have to keep her and her layabout boyfriends?

She wanted more money. She always wanted more money.

He had bought her a little house in Putney, gave her twenty-five quid a week, *and* he paid all the kids' bills.

She was a rotten mother. He saw the children every weekend and they always looked filthy.

"Look after them yourself if you think your

little dolly bird can do any better," Jane would sneer when he criticized.

Jon would have liked to have taken her up on her offer, but there was no way Muffin could cope with two small children. Muffin was just a kid herself.

Plans for a divorce were well under way, but financial hassles kept on holding it up.

Jon agreed to send her another fifty. Fucking leech. So much for young romantic love. *Never* marry young. Even better *never* marry.

Muffin was at her dressing table carefully peeling off single eyelashes and placing them on a Kleenex. He ruffled her hair. "Get lost!" she muttered. Jane on the phone never put her in a good mood. It reminded her of the divorce that Jon had promised and so far failed to get.

Chapter 5

Mike James smoked long, thin, black cigarettes. They were better for you than ordinary cigarettes, and cheaper than cigars. Actually the main reason he smoked them was because they had style, and Mike always had been a man who liked style.

That was why he was mad that Cleo had caught him with Susan. If there was one quality Susan did not possess it was style. She was just a schlock with a great body. Sometimes the lure of a pair of sensational knockers proved too much for even the most discerning of men.

After being discovered by Cleo, Mike got rid of Susan quickly. She went with a smile and a wink. "See you again soon, honey."

Oh, the loyalty of women. The only thing you could trust them with was your cock, and that was only on a temporary basis!

He regretted the fact that he hadn't waited to ball Susan. Waited only a matter of days until Cleo was safe and sound in Europe. But his motto in life had always been "do not do tomorrow what you can do today."

He thought of a million "if only's."

If only he had locked the office door.

If only he hadn't sent his secretary out for coffee.

If only Cleo had knocked. Jesus, she *never* called in on him at the office; now she would think he spent his entire time there screwing.

Mike paced around his office. Cleo was certainly not going to take kindly to the fact that she had caught him with one of her friends. It would have been better if he had been straddling a stranger aboard the office couch. That would have been bad enough—but this . . .

Susan had been giving him the come-on for some time. He had lunched her the previous week, and they were both aware of what promises "come to my office for coffee" offered.

It was one thing your wife finding out about another woman, but actually catching you at it— well, that just wasn't a good scene. Not unless you had in mind a cosy threesome, and Cleo would never go along with *that*, indeed he wouldn't want her to. Sex with Cleo was beautiful. Cool, calm, satisfying. Sex with other women was different, more raunchy, rougher. He could use them in a way he didn't care to use Cleo. He had used Susan. It meant no more to him than a morning's fun.

From the very beginning things had been different with Cleo. She had come into his life at a time when he had decided that the life he led was perfect. He worked hard at a job he liked. He had a nice apartment. A Ferrari. A lot of different girlfriends. In fact he felt he was personally living out the *Playboy* dream.

Cleo came along and proved to him that it was just a wet dream after all.

She didn't want to get married. She was independent. She asked him for nothing. After six months of living together he insisted that they marry. "If you really love me you'll prove it by marrying me," he had said.

How many girls had said that to him in the past . . .

So they got married, and it was great. Four years of living with an intelligent, beautiful girl. A very modern marriage.

Surely Cleo had never imagined he was faithful? No one was faithful. She wouldn't expect him to be.

Of course *she* probably was, well naturally. Women *were* different, they didn't have such needs. Anyway he just knew that Cleo wouldn't deceive him with another man, it wasn't her scene. He kept her happy sexually. He kept her happy in every way. Anyway he'd fucking kill her if she ever screwed around. But of course she never would.

They had often discussed other women. He had often said he fancied this one or that one, and they had both laughed about it. Cleo was probably laughing now. When he got home later she would be laughing . . .

"Got no bloody taste, that's your problem," she would say. And they would talk about it, and laugh about it; and later they would make love . . .

Yes, Mike decided, that was the way it would be. Cleo was far too clever a woman to make a big deal out of this.

Maybe the best thing to do would be to not mention it. Just ignore the fact that it had ever happened. No—he wouldn't get away with that. Cleo would want an inquest. She was entitled to an inquest, and he was quite prepared to eat humble pie.

After all she was the woman he loved, and he was going to have to prove it to her.

Perhaps it was a good thing that he had finally been caught. Now it would have to stop, and maybe what he really wanted after all was a one woman relationship.

Chapter 6

Cleo did not feel safe until she was on the plane, in the air, on the way to London.

It wasn't crowded, and she sat on the aisle seat. The middle seat was vacant, and the window seat was occupied by a male singer that she vaguely recognized as Shep Stone. He was taking nervous swigs out of a Tiffany hip flask, and as soon as they were airborne he lit up a joint which he calmly smoked hidden behind a *Time* magazine.

Cleo was in no mood for conversation, and fortunately it seemed he felt the same way.

She was angry, humiliated, disgusted. Russell Hayes' behavior was really chickenshit. He had appeared that very morning like nothing had happened. He was smiling and dapper and full of business-like conversation. They had eaten breakfast together, silently as far as Cleo was concerned. But it hadn't phased him one bit. He had insisted on coming to the airport with her. Paid her excess baggage. Bought her ten new magazines and an ugly toy dog. When they parted he tried to kiss her, but she moved her face and he just got her cheek.

"Last night was wonderful," he whispered. What did you say to a man like that?

She tried to smile a goodbye, but after years of being fairly good friends she suddenly hated him, and her smile turned sour.

"Don't feel guilty, darling," Russell said reassuringly. "Everything will work out for the best."

Cleo boarded the plane in a mild fury. Christ! What an egotistical shit Russell turned out to be. Sweet, kind, funny old Russ. One of Mike's best friends. A hell of a best friend *he* turned out to be. A hell of a friend *Susan* turned out to be.

"Can I borrow one of your magazines?" Shep Stone leaned across and asked.

"Sure." Cleo dumped all ten of them on the middle seat.

"Going to London?" he inquired.

What a stupid question considering that's where the plane was headed. "Umm," Cleo mumbled.

"Been there before?" he persisted.

"Yes," Cleo replied coldly. What was it about planes that gave men the impression you were there for an immediate pick-up?

"Lovely city," he said. "I've been there many times. Are you a New Yorker?"

Cleo turned to stare at him. "Look, I have an awful headache. Do you mind if we sit this one out?"

"Huh?"

"Have a magazine, a hostess, anything. But

48

please, a little silence." She turned away, but not before he had managed a hurt expression.

Shep Stone was quite well-known as a singer of romantic ballads, but he had never really made it big. He was about thirty-five with brown hair and a nice smile. Not exactly an Andy Williams, but heading that way.

Cleo shut her eyes and tried to regain her thoughts. She was going to London to start on the series of interviews *Image* magazine had commissioned. It was to be headed "Who's Afraid of the Big Bad Wolf," and it was to be an in-depth, probing analysis, of five famous eligible male movie stars.

"You'll do the five most horny guys," Russell had said. "You'll do a great job, baby. We'll run it over five issues."

Cleo had liked the idea. She was good at interviews, although she was usually more into politicians or businessmen. "Actors are so overdone," she had said at first. "What more is there to say about someone who's said it all three hundred times before?"

Mike had encouraged her. "It'll be good for you, a change of pace is just what you need. Your stuff is always so serious."

So Cleo had said yes. The money was good. A couple of weeks in London at the Connaught. She could see her mother. A few days in the South of France, and maybe Rome.

"Did my smoking bother you?" Shep Stone asked anxiously. "If it did I'm sorry. I don't usually need that stuff, but goddam it, I'm scared of flying. Isn't that ridiculous?"

Cleo sighed patiently. She found it extremely

49

hard to be rude to people. In print it was easy, but in person she chickened out. "It didn't bother me, I guess I'm just tired."

"Would you like a drink? It will pick you up."

Cleo nodded. May as well give in, now the plane was on its way he was determined to talk.

And talk he did. All the way across the Atlantic. She heard about his career, his three wives, his two children, his financial position, his political beliefs; and finally, of course, his sex life. "I like women," he explained, "maybe I like them too much. I started making it when I was eighteen. That's late, isn't it? Well, anyway . . ." The plane ran into a sudden storm, and Shep ran into a sudden silence. "I hate flying," he said, producing a Tiffany hip flask and gulping mammoth slugs. At the same time he was fiddling around in his pocket searching for another joint.

The plane was bouncing around like a ping-pong ball. Shep lit up and took a couple of heavy drags. "Doesn't make any difference," he said morbidly, "booze, drugs. I still stay as sober as the pilot."

He offered Cleo the joint, and she took it. She inhaled deeply. Pot agreed with her, gave her a much better high than drinking. She and Mike had enjoyed the occasional joint together.

The pilot's voice suddenly came crackling through the loudspeaker system.

"Oh, my God!" Shep gasped, clutching the arm-rests tightly, "we're going to crash!"

The pilot apologized for the bad weather, explained that the weather was equally bad over London, asked everybody to fasten their seatbelts, and explained that they would shortly be landing in Frankfurt.

50

"Sonofabitch!" Shep muttered, and remained in a nervous huddle until they did land.

Cleo summoned the hostess and discovered that it would be a stopover for the night in Frankfurt. She didn't mind. She knew that Mike would be phoning her as soon as she arrived at the Connaught. This would give him another night of stewing.

Let him stew.

Chapter 7

Muffin and the Japanese girl stood back to back. They were of the same height, but every other detail of their physical attributes were different.

They were both naked, and both held aloft champagne glasses.

"That's terrific, girls," Jon said, adjusting his Nikon. "Hey Annie," he called to the assistant, "rub some more ice cubes on their nips, they're getting a bit depleted."

Annie rushed forward with a small ice bucket and rubbed an ice cube across the Japanese girl's nipples. They sprang erect immediately. Muffin stuck her chest forward. "Me next please, my thrill for the day."

John said, "Bum in a bit, Muff, right leg slightly more bent, I'm getting a flash of the fuzz. That's beautiful, darlings. Beautiful!"

He worked quickly, the sounds of Bobby Womack belting out over the stereo system. After six rolls of film he was satisfied. "That's it, girls."

Muffin yawned and stretched. "I'm beat!" She and Kamika, the Japanese girl, went into the dressing-room.

"Charlie and I, we get a divorce," Kamika said, slipping into a shirt and trousers.

"Shame!" Muffin said. "You've only been married—what? A year?"

"One year, seven days," Kamika said precisely. "He fart all day, he fart all night. No longer can I stand it."

"Yeah, well all fellas fart," Muffin said sagely.

"But not in time to music!"

Muffin giggled. "Sorry, Kam, but you're so funny!" She wriggled into skintight jeans and a sweater, and stuck her new sunglasses into her hair.

"Very nice glasses," Kamika remarked.

"You like them, they're yours." Muffin handed them over.

"No. I couldn't. Please . . ."

Muffin insisted. "Compliments of Harrods," she said with a sly laugh.

Jon was still working, photographing a tall blond who posed silently in a long slinky nightgown. Muffin kissed him on the cheek. "See you later, sweetie." She waved at the tall blond. "Hands off him Erica, he's taken."

She had the afternoon before her. It was a rare treat, most days she hardly had time for lunch.

There was a variety of choices. She could go home, and take the dog for a long walk in the park. Or she could go shopping. Or she could go to a movie.

Then again she could drift down to the *Carou-*

sel for lunch, there were bound to be a lot of her mates there. She could have a gossip and a chatter and find out who was doing what to whom.

Erica said, "You and Muffin are still going strong I see."

"Legs a bit more together, that's it, fine, lovely." Jon clicked away. "Yeah, we're still together."

"I'm amazed?"

Jon grunted. "Right leg forward a bit, not too much. Perfect! Why are you amazed?"

Erica shrugged. "I just never thought a girl like that would be a long-term prospect."

"Head back, and don't be bitchy."

Erica threw her head back. "Would *I* be bitchy."

"Yeah. You're the original bitch."

"You didn't think that when we were together."

"I gave you one four times a few years ago, so that doesn't make you an expert on what kind of girl I want to spend my time with."

"Jon Clapton, you're a liar! It was at least six times." She posed provocatively. "Want to make it seven?"

"You're a married lady, Erica."

"You were a married man the last time. This will make us even. Anyway, I'm getting a divorce."

"Thanks for the offer but no thanks. Be a darlin' and slip into the black satin job while I change film."

"Bastard!" Erica muttered. "You just don't want to blow your bread and butter. Who do you think the two of you are? Justin and Twiggy?"

"Belt up and get changed."

John lit a cigarette. Justin and Twiggy, that was

a laugh! He and Muffin were going much further than that.

The *Carousel* was packed. Muffin squeezed in with Jan and Brenda.

"Where you bin, girl?" Brenda inquired. "Want to hear my new song?"

"How's the boyfriend?" Jan asked. "I haven't seen him since Africa."

"He's fine," Muffin replied, biting on a stick of celery. "Ooh—who's that?" She pointed at a slight blond boy in skin-tight chamois leather.

"Forget it," Brenda said. "I've had it, and girl—it's quick and small!!"

They all laughed.

Muffin said, "I was working with Kamika this morning and she's getting a divorce."

"What's the matter, her old man gone off Japanese food?" Brenda laughed. "By the way, isn't it about time we were all dancing at your wedding?"

Muffin smiled. "Soon," she promised.

Jon better get his finger out. He had been promising to divorce his wife for long enough. If things went on for much longer she was going to look like a fool. Anyway, she wanted to be Mrs. Clapton. Mrs. Jon Clapton.

Chapter 8

"Take it easy. Calm down," Russell Hayes said. "I know she's a wonderful girl, but if it's not to be, it's not to be."

"I don't need your half-ass philosophies," Mike said shortly. "Christ almighty! All I did was screw some moon-faced blond, and Cleo vanishes off the face of the earth."

"If I had a wife like Cleo," Russell said primly, "I don't think I'd feel the need to screw around."

"Balls! You were married three times and you still tried to stick it into anything that moved!"

"Yes, but I wasn't married to Cleo."

"Keep it up, Russ, and I'll think you and Cleo had something going."

Russell sipped his drink and didn't say anything.

"I don't understand her," Mike said shortly. "To take off without even discussing things with me. I mean she's treating me like some sort of boyfriend. I'm her husband goddamn it! She can't just walk out on me without a word."

"Why not?"

"What do you mean—why not? She's mine. We're married. We're *tied* to each other in every way."

"Except sexually," Russell commented dryly. "Or so it would seem."

"Whose side are you on anyway?"

"I can see both points of view. My personal opinion is that perhaps you're not suited, perhaps this is the best thing."

"Bollocks! A quick fuck ain't gonna end *my* marriage."

Russell shrugged. "Perhaps the choice won't be yours. Anyway—you've been whoring around so long you were bound to get caught eventually."

"Oh, you're a great friend, very reassuring. Look, when I can *find* her, *talk* to her, everything will be all right."

"I hope so," said Russell insincerely, "I really hope so. But knowing Cleo I wouldn't count on it."

"What do you mean by that snide remark? If anyone knows Cleo it's me."

"Perhaps you don't know her as well as you think you do."

"Jesus, Russell, what is it with you? Anyone would think you were happy about what's going on."

"What will be will be . . ." Russell repeated sagely.

"Yeah—and I'll tell you what will be. I'll find

her, talk to her, and everything is going to work out just fine."

Mike went home. Russell really pissed him off with his slippery smile and pompous manner. What did he know about serious relationships? Three failed marriages had taught him exactly nothing.

He placed another call to the Connaught. Mrs. James had *still* not checked in.

He missed her. The apartment seemed so strange without her. He studied their wedding photo that stood in their one and only silver frame. Cleo. That face. Those eyes. That beautiful slim body with the smooth skin. Long legs. Small feet. Tiny hands. Everything about her was understated. Mike liked that, there was nothing obvious about Cleo.

The first time they had met at a rock party in London, there had been one of those instant sexual attractions that they were both aware of. He had wanted to drag her into the nearest bed and make love without exchanging so much as a word. She knew it. He knew it. Instead they had allowed themselves to be introduced, and they had chatted lightly whilst their eyes met, locked, and carried on their own private conversation.

Later, after the party, after a drink at a discotheque, he had suggested his hotel. Cleo had politely declined.

Mike had been prepared to wait. There were certain games to be played, rules to be followed before he was allowed into her bed. He understood. He waited.

When they became lovers she came to live with him in New York. It was a temporary arrangement, Mike was not prepared to settle for anything less than marriage.

So what had gone wrong? What had led him into other beds and other bodies?

There had been no other women when he and Cleo were living together. Three weeks after they married it had all started.

Mike had always found women were very attracted to him, and came on strong. He could not recall exactly how many others there had been but he knew it was a lot. He could remember only a few of them. Fanny, because she had given him a dose of the clap. Brook, because she was only sixteen and forgot to mention the fact until they were actually doing it. Linda, who claimed he got her pregnant and demanded a thousand dollars abortion money. And of course Susan, Cleo's good friend Susan.

Sex with Cleo was incredible, perfect. But somehow there were things he wanted to do that he didn't want to do with her. She wasn't some girl he was living with, she was his wife and deserved to be treated as such. Respect, an old-fashioned word, but a word he wanted to apply to his wife. He didn't want to make heavy demands on her, so almost as a service he turned to other women. It became a habit—like smoking— and like smoking he found he couldn't give it up.

Up until now he had always been discreet. What Cleo didn't know, Cleo couldn't possibly be angry about. He felt guilty, but only because he had the misfortune to be caught, and life was just not complete without Cleo. He needed her. He wanted her. And he desired her in exactly the same way it had been when they had first met.

So where was she? How could she do this to him?

It wasn't fair, didn't she have any feelings? How could she just leave him hanging? If she knew him at all she knew that he would want to talk, explain.

What she was doing to him now was punishment enough.

Angrily he picked up the phone again and dialled the international operator. "I want a person to person call to London, England. Mrs. Cleo James..."

Chapter 9

The hotel in Frankfurt was full of good old German efficiency. It was early evening and what with the drinks and the pot Cleo felt in fairly good shape.

Shep Stone became a different person when his two feet hit firm ground. At the airport he organized them a private car with one short phone call. At the hotel he said, "See you in the bar at eight." He took it for granted they would dine together.

Cleo took a leisurely bath and washed her long dark hair. She let it dry naturally and it surrounded her face with languid damp curls. To achieve the straight effect she had to dry her hair pulling it all the time with a brush. She couldn't be bothered, Shep would just have to accept her *au naturel*.

She put on a soft gray silk shirt and a pin-stripe suit tailored for her in New York. Around her neck she hung the jade horn Mike had given her last

Christmas, and on her fingers a mixture of thin ivory and jade rings.

"You look really terrific," Shep told her as he stood to greet her at the bar. He too was wearing gray, a suit with a strange short jacket piped with braid. Mike called them "bum freezers."

They dined in the hotel restaurant which was located on the roof and had good food and an awful cabaret.

Shep was charming and attentive. Cleo knew that he fancied her. She knew that at the end of the evening there would be the inevitable invitation for a drink in his room. She had already made up her mind to accept.

Why the hell not? When it came to discussing things with Mike she wanted to be on even territory. Shep Stone was an attractive man, so why not? Mike had screwed Susan. She would have Shep. Fair is fair.

Sure enough he went through the expected ritual of conversation. "How about a nightcap in my room?"

Somehow she would have preferred the more honest, "How about a fuck in my room?"

They took the elevator down and Shep summoned room service and ordered champagne. At least he had some class, although champagne always reminded her of the time Mike had opened a bottle of champagne on their water bed and had deliberately poured it all over her naked body and spent the rest of the evening licking it off her. She smiled at the memory and Shep took that as a signal to get started. He ripped off his "bum freezer" jacket, and gripping her tightly by the arms he started to kiss her. Long, hard kisses. They reminded her of Russell

64

and the unfortunate previous evening, and she wriggled free.

"What's the matter?" Shep asked offended. "I got bad breath?"

Saved by a short sentence. Cleo knew she could never go to bed with a man who asked "I got bad breath?"

"I've got a headache," she said. If he could say "come to my room for a nightcap," she could certainly say, "I've got a headache."

She thought he was going to be cool about it, but he suddenly unzipped his fly, and his cock, red and erect, popped out. "Just a little head," he pleaded.

Cleo was furious. Christ! Two of them in so many days. She stalked to the door and let herself out, nearly bumping into the waiter with the champagne.

Back in her room she called the desk. "Take me off the plane to London in the morning, please, book me on the first plane to Paris, with a connecting flight to London."

Shep Stone could shiver and shake his own way to London.

Chapter 10

Sunday lunch time with Muffin's family was a drag. Jon hated it, and it always managed to put the usually happy-go-lucky Muffin in a grim mood.

Lunch in Wimbledon at the small, neat, ever-so-respectable semi-detached house that Muffin had grown up in.

There was Mum, a plump youngish woman with worn hands and straggly curls. Dad, honest and jovial. Ben and Josie, ten-year-old twins. Penny, Muffin's twin sister, younger by eight minutes. And Penny's husband, Geoff.

It was the relationship between Penny, Geoff, and Muffin that caused all the tension.

When she was fifteen Muffin had dated Geoff a few times, then she didn't hear from him again. When Penny brought him home months later and announced the fact that they planned to be married

Muffin was furious. He had been pinched from right under her nose by her own sister. She had never forgiven her. She was a reluctant bridesmaid when Penny and Geoff got married. Shortly after, she met Jon, and moved out.

Muffin became a personality and Penny became the mother of one fat baby and another on the way. The relationship between the two sisters did not improve. Penny did not approve of her sister's nude modelling, she thought it was disgusting, and made a point of telling anyone who would listen, "Geoff and I may not be rich," she would say, "but Geoff would rather see me *dead* than stripping off in public."

Geoff remained silent on the subject. He was rather chuffed at having a famous sister-in-law.

Muffin took much pleasure in criticizing her twin's appearance. "You're too fat. Why don't you do something with your hair? If you had your front teeth capped you'd look much better."

Penny would reply maliciously, "Well, there's nothing we can do about our short fat legs is there?"

Reluctantly Muffin had to agree. Perfect boobs, pretty face, tiny waist, lovely little ass, but she was *still* stuck with stumpy legs. Anyway, nobody seemed to notice her legs.

Lunch was invariably stringy roast lamb, lumpy gravy, burnt roast potatoes, and watery peas. Muffin could remember when it was her favorite meal, that was before her taste buds had been developed at all the best London restaurants.

One of the newspapers had requested a fashion spread on Muffin with her family. They were all quite excited about it, that is all except Penny who had only agreed to be in the picture on condition she was paid. Jon had personally decided to pay her.

It would look a bit odd having photos of Muffin and her family without her twin sister.

In the front room there were suitcases of clothes. Matching jeans outfits for Josie and Ben. Sports casuals for Dad. A silk shirtwaist dress for Mum. Maternity outfit for Penny. And for Muffin full length calico, frilled and flounced, low cut and pretty. Lately she was in as much demand clothed as unclothed.

After lunch the entire family went off to get changed, and Jon started to set up his equipment. He would have preferred to work in his studio, but the paper had specially requested an at-home shot.

Geoff stood around watching, the two-year-old baby clinging around his legs. Although he and Jon were about the same age they had never had much to say to each other. They had nothing in common except the sisters. Geoff was a window-cleaner, apparently satisfied with his work. His only ambition was to operate a little firm of his own—an ambition he did nothing to achieve.

"You got a lot of gear," Geoff remarked. He was slightly taller than Jon, but not quite so thin.

"Yeah," Jon nodded, cursing privately that he hadn't though to bring an assistant.

"Me, all I need's a bucket and cloth and I'm away."

"Great," Jon muttered, fiddling with an umbrella he was attaching to one of his lights.

"I wouldn't have thought it would take all this larking about just for a couple of snaps."

Jon didn't bother to reply. Christ—if he and Muffin ever got married this moron would be his brother-in-law. A sobering thought. How the hell had Muffin ever managed to go out with Geoff in the first place?

"Caught a bird in the bath the other day," Geoff said cheerily, "mind you—I think she was looking to get caught, she *knew* I was in the house. I'm always coming across them in their knickers and bras. I could do myself some good if I wanted to. Little one the other day she . . ."

Jon tuned out. He wasn't interested in what he termed as wishful crumpet conversations. Muffin had told him that nothing had ever happened with her and Geoff. If it had, would he be jealous? No, he decided, the past was the past, even if it did keep on hanging around. Muffin came bouncing in. "Ready," she trilled.

Self-consciously the rest of the family trailed behind her.

"Cor!" exclaimed Geoff, "smashing looking group."

Penny glared at him. "This outfit is horrible," she complained. "The trousers are too long."

"You all look very nice," placated Jon, and he started to try and organize them into a family group.

It wasn't easy—everyone kept shuffling around, Penny kept complaining, and the baby clinging to Geoff started to scream.

Silently Jon vowed never to get involved in one of *these* scenes again. Muffin minus the family was quite enough thank you.

It was a long hard afternoon.

Later, at home, when they were in bed, Jon said to Muffin—"How did you ever manage to go out with that birk?"

"Who?"

"Your brother-in-law."

"Oh, Geoff," Muffin giggled, "well, he's very good-looking."

70

"Good-looking?"

"Yes. Well, he was, I guess he doesn't look so good now. Nagged into an early old age."

"Did he give you one?"

"One what?" she asked with wide, innocent, little girl eyes.

"Don't play silly buggers with me, fat ass."

"Don't call me fat ass."

"Why? Is it a sensitive spot? Here, give me a handful." Jon grabbed her roughly. She was wearing a shortie nightie with matching pants, and he ripped them off her.

"You swine!" She kicked him. "They cost me five quid at Fenwicks."

He pinned her down easily. "I'll give you a fiver," he spread her legs and entered her, "think this will be worth a fiver?"

"It's a good job you've got a big dick otherwise I'd be furious with you!"

Chapter 11

June in London is an unpredictable month. Sometimes cold, sometimes hot and sticky.

Cleo arrived in the midst of a mini heatwave. Heathrow airport was in chaos due to a bomb scare, and it was impossible to get a taxi. She travelled into the center of London on an airport bus sweating in the Gatsby-style suit that had been just right during the changeover of planes in Paris.

What a lot of trouble to have to go to just to avoid one idiot singer. She sheltered behind tinted glasses and surveyed the English in a heatwave from the bus window.

Every little patch of green they drove past was littered with half-naked bodies. Businessmen in rolled-up shirtsleeves and crumpled trousers. Secretaries in old-fashioned miniskirts and sweaters with bra straps showing. Long legs, short legs, hairy legs —they were all on show.

Mike had fabulous legs for a man. Long and straight, not too heavy, lovely curved calves with a light smattering of dark hairs. As a matter of fact he also had a fine set of balls, tight and hard.

Cleo couldn't help smiling to herself as she thought about Mike striding around their apartment naked. Men looked so vulnerable when the hard-on was gone, and so horny when it was there.

"I like your style," had been one of Mike's favorite lines to her.

"And I like your balls—figuratively speaking that is!" had been Cleo's reply.

The bus rattled and shaked its way toward the Brompton Road air terminal. It was late afternoon, another day past. Cleo felt like she had spent the last few days in limbo, as indeed she had. She wanted a bath, and a visit to the hairdresser. She wanted to unpack and phone old friends. She wanted to drop in and surprise her mother. She wanted to shop at Biba, Harrods, and Marks and Spencer. Four years was a long time to have been away.

There were numerous messages for her at the Connaught. Mike had phoned at least five times, and there was an international operator's number to call immediately she checked in. Russell Hayes had called twice. Ginny Sandler once.

There were flowers waiting from Shep Stone with a humble note of apology. Why had she ever told him where she was staying?

She stripped off her Gatsby suit and headed for the shower. She felt inexplicably horny. Was it the hot weather or just the thought of her unfaithful shit-faced husband's lovely legs and tight balls?

Mike had always claimed that the hot weather

turned her on. They had made love the previous week and it had been short and boring.

"I think we should pop down to Puerto Rico for a few days," Mike had said, "get some rest and sunshine."

"When I get back from my trip," Cleo had replied. Maybe in Puerto Rico they could talk about starting a family.

The phone rang and Cleo decided not to answer it. She was still wet from the shower and not ready to get involved in any hassles. Whoever it was would call back.

She dressed in plain trousers, a silk shirt, and tied her long dark hair back. Then she unpacked, realizing that if the hot weather continued she had brought all the wrong clothes.

After her clothes were put away, her make up and toiletries laid out, and her notepads and files and tape recorder stacked neatly on the desk, she felt better.

"You're so organized," Mike was always mocking her. He stepped out of his clothes leaving them on the floor. His desk was a clutter of junk. The bathroom awash when he was finished in there.

Cleo wondered wryly what their apartment looked like now after three days of her absence. The only thing Mike bothered to clean was his Ferrari.

"I love you," Mike had informed her one day, "'cos you're the only girl I know that cleans my toothbrush."

"An old English custom," Cleo had replied sweetly.

She too had been brought up to do nothing for herself. Middle class English family with a series of maids who picked up after her. Only child like Mike. Spoiled rotten like Mike. Then at eighteen a runaway marriage to a scruffy layabout who thought he had found himself an heiress. She had learned then. No maids to pick up after you when you're squatting in a derelict house. No one to spoil you rotten when you didn't have enough money to eat.

A year had been long enough to teach Cleo the facts of life. At nineteen she got a divorce and started to write for magazines. Within a couple of years she had got herself a good reputation and plenty of work.

She met Mike when she was doing a piece on an American pop group who were with his company. Mike came to London for their launching. They met at the press party.

At the time Cleo was sleeping with an extremely attractive disc jockey. He wanted to marry her. Mike was going through his rounds of different beautiful girls. They met and stuck. Cleo went back to America with him, he introduced her to Russell Hayes, and she became *Image* magazine's special lady reporter. She also eventually became Mrs. Mike James.

"You and I are going to make it work forever," Mike had told her on their wedding night, "just the two of us—forever."

The phone rang again, and Cleo picked it up hesitantly. "Yes?"

"Cleo? At last. Did you get my flowers? I thought we could have dinner."

"Who is this?"

"It's Shep, baby. Shep Stone."

Cleo sighed. Give, and they would take. Run, and they would follow.

"I'm sorry," she said, "but you have the wrong approach."

Chapter 12

"Shit!" exclaimed Mike James, and he banged the phone down yet again. Where the hell was Cleo? He was late for an appointment, and he grabbed his leather jacket and stormed out of the apartment. No breakfast. No fucking. This sort of life was not good for a man.

He rode the elevator down to the car park in the basement. He didn't usually take the Ferrari out on a weekday, but he was late, and getting a cab was impossible, and anyway he wanted to.

The Ferrari waited gleaming and shining in its parking bay. Nine years old and still looked like new. It was a Five Hundred Superfast, a great model.

Mike patted the bonnet lovingly and climbed in. He started the engine and magic sounds filled his ears. He relaxed. Whatever else, he still had his beautiful baby.

He pushed in a tape to listen to a new group, and steered his car carefully through the snarling New York traffic to his office. His thoughts were of Cleo. He was remembering the last time they had made love. It had been a very quick event. Short and sweet. It had been good for him—let's face it a come is a come. But how had it been for her? Maybe he should have spent more time at the beginning getting her in the mood, she hadn't been exactly ready. But she had been ready at the end, he could always manipulate her to a beautiful climax. And no faking—he always checked that out, there were ways to tell when a woman was faking.

Their sex life was pretty good; no, that certainly couldn't be the reason she had run off. He could understand it if she had caught him screwing Susan and she wasn't getting any herself. But he had plenty to go around. Plenty. Of course Cleo did have some hang up about having children, but they had discussed it, and she had finally agreed with him that it would be best to wait. God, he had seen what kids had done to other people's marriages. Anyway he was not yet ready to share Cleo with a small person who would infringe on their lives.

Hampton Records was a chrome and glass building filled with blue jeaned secretaries and bearded young men. Everyone was on first name basis from the boy who delivered the mail to Eric B. B. Hampton—president and founder of Hampton Records.

Mike went straight up to B. B.'s office.

B. B. consulted a solid gold watch. "Dragging your ass again," he commented.

"Fuck you," Mike replied cheerily.

"Ooh baby, that would be a sight to see!"

B. B.'s secretary brought in black coffee for Mike, and a huge chocolate milk shake laced with rum for B. B.

"Be a nice girlie, run down to Charlie O's for a selection of Danish," B. B. requested.

The secretary looked unsure. "Mary Ellen told me no, absolutely no. She said no food for you 'til after twelve-thirty."

Mary Ellen was B. B.'s girl friend.

B. B. picked up the solid gold clock on his desk and twiddled the dials until it read twelve-thirty.

"O.K. now, little smart ass? Make sure you include a few with cherries." He smacked his lips and leered at Mike. "I love those little ripe cherries, don't you?"

Mike grinned and nodded.

"Hey," said B. B., "the deal is this. With all the advance publicity working for us and Cassady out of it, I think we should bring the Little Marty Pearl Europe gig forward. I feel now's the time."

"Yeah," Mike said slowly, "be a good one for the new record. In fact the timing's great."

"Before I put my ear to the instrument I wanted to check out with you that you can go along on the trip. I think it's important you go."

Mike nodded. "I guess there's nothing I can't postpone. When?"

"Soon as soon. I'll let you have dates later today."

"Great."

Little Marty Pearl was Mike's own personal discovery. "Let's ride with the weeny bopper market," B. B. had instructed his five top executives a year previously. And Mike had obediently scouted around and come up with Little Marty Pearl. He had spotted him on a television commercial, liked the look of him, tracked him down, and been delighted to discover that Marty had a plaintive simple voice that all the little weeny boppers would love. Of course the voice was secondary, it was the looks that really mattered, and Marty got an A-plus for looks. He was every mother's idea of Mister Teenage America. He was medium height, with calf-like brown eyes, freckles, tousled blondish hair, and perfect teeth. Little Marty Pearl was supposed to be sixteen, but actually he was going on nineteen, a closely guarded secret.

Mike had guided him through three super hit records, and in American he was a big star. So far he had not yet cracked the European market, but they all had high hopes at Hampton Records that his new record *Teenage High* would be the one.

Mike smiled to himself. Convincing Cleo to come back was going to be a whole lot easier when he surprised her in London.

Chapter 13

"We're in, Muff!" Jon shook her awake, waving a contract in her face. "This came this morning, all it needs is your sweet little signature."

Muffin yawned and rubbed her eyes. Jon was already searching around for a pen.

"I knew we were in as soon as Klauss the German started eyeballing your fanny in the photographs. He was drooling. Timed the whole thing perfectly. The pictures, then you making your entrance late. Perfect! Here, sign where the cross is."

"I want to pee," Muffin said in a whiney voice, ignoring the pen that Jon was offering her. She wriggled out of bed and went into the bathroom.

Jon sat on the side of the bed and scanned the contract yet again. What a deal he had got for them!

In the bathroom Muffin splashed her face with

cold water and stared at herself in the mirror. The face that launched a thousand products. She stuck out her tongue at her reflection. Without make-up she looked disgustingly like her sister.

"Come on, Muff," Jon called, "I want to get this contract in the post."

Muffin emerged from the bathroom. "Jon," she said sweetly, "how's the divorce going?"

"What?" he questioned shortly.

"D I V O R C E," Muffin spelled it out.

"*You* know the problems."

"Yeah. Bread—right?"

"Yeah. Right. Why?"

"Well why hassle over money? We'll have plenty if I sign this contract."

"Sure."

"O.K. Settle with Jane, give her what she wants."

Jon sighed impatiently. "You know that's impossible. She wants fifty quid a week, the house, *and* all the kid's schooling, doctors, all that."

"If I sign we can afford it."

"Yeah, for a couple of months. But it's a lifetime deal. Who knows what I can afford next year."

Muffin narrowed her eyes, "I'm sick of waiting, I'll wait forever. I want you to settle with her, work it out. I want to get married. You *promised* we would get married. I'm not signing anything until you settle with Jane."

"Now listen, Muff, don't be stubborn, don't be silly."

Muffin climbed back into bed. "I mean it," she said, "and I won't be conned either. I want to see the papers from the solicitors before I sign anything."

Jon frowned. She had him by the short and curlies and she knew it.

"Look, Muff . . ." he began.

She replied by burying her head beneath the covers.

Jon knew when he was beaten.

Chapter 14

Butch Kaufman was the first actor on Cleo's list.

Butch Kaufman, a blond-haired, blue-eyed, all American, sexy film star.

He had achieved fame as the star of a long running TV soap opera. "Like being in um er prison for six years," was the way he put it.

He was twenty-eight and had starred in six major blockbuster box office smash hits in the last four years. Along the way he had collected and discarded two wives. "Never um er marry an actress," was the way he put it.

He was currently in England filming, and Cleo met with him at the studio on her first day in London.

A lunch was arranged by an anxious press lady with fluttery hands who obviously planned to join them until Cleo told her politely but firmly that she

85

only ever conducted interviews on a nobody else present basis. The press lady was put out, but *Image* was an important publication and she didn't want to blow it. She fussed round Butch, settling him in his seat, and then reluctantly she left with a departing whisper in his ear.

"What did she say?" Cleo asked.

"She um er told me you eat movie stars for breakfast."

Cleo smiled. "You're lucky then that we didn't meet for breakfast."

Butch laughed, and the ice was broken.

Cleo clicked on her tape recorder and started in with the questions.

An hour and a half later they parted friends.

"How long you um er here for?" Butch inquired.

"Just a week."

"Maybe we could grab a bite to eat one night."

"Maybe," Cleo nodded. He wasn't a super stud, he was a pussy cat.

She sat back in the studio car that drove her back to the Connaught and played the tape over. There was some good stuff, he was interesting and funny.

At the hotel the temporary secretary she had hired was waiting. "Transcribe this." Cleo tossed her the tape. When she had it all typed out she would select the best quotes and write the story.

"Your husband called from America," the secretary said. "Would you call the International operator."

"I have got to go out," Cleo replied, "if he calls again tell him to try again tomorrow."

She took a taxi to Eaton Square. It was four o'clock and her mother was expecting her for tea.

Stella Lawrence was an immaculate woman of forty-eight. She was groomed from her short, chic, ash blond hair, to her waxed, thin, perfect legs.

She greeted Cleo with an impersonal peck on the cheek. "Wonderful to see you, darling."

Stella had remarried rather well when Cleo's father had died of an unfortunate heart attack seven years previously. She had found herself a Greek shipping tycoon. It suited her that her twenty-nine-year-old daughter had gone off to live in America.

"You look magnificent," Cleo said dutifully.

Stella smiled distantly. "Do I? Do I really, darling? I'm such an old bag I'm amazed I'm still in one piece."

Cleo suddenly realized that Stella had indulged in a face lift. There were no visible scars, but Cleo knew, could tell. "How's Nikai?" she asked.

"Busy as ever. He wanted to see you, but he had to fly to Athens."

"Oh, I'm sorry." Cleo suddenly felt incredibly scruffy and unattractive. Her mother had always somehow managed to make her feel like that.

"What about Mike?" Stella inquired. "Is he going to join you here?"

It would be nice, Cleo reflected, to have the sort of mother one could confide in, but Stella wouldn't understand, she never had. Stella enjoyed men for their money, and their admiration of her. Stella wasn't interested in men as human beings.

"I don't think he will. Work pressure—you know"

Tea was wheeled in on a trolley by a uniformed maid.

Cleo found herself eating all the wafer thin sandwiches and three cream cakes, while Stella just sipped at a cup of lemon tea.

"You'll get fat, dear," Stella remarked disinterestedly.

Cleo wondered if she could leave right after tea. Stella gave her a massive inferiority complex.

Later, back at the hotel, Cleo wrote her piece on Butch Kaufman. It pleased her, she hoped it had bite and humor. She wanted reaction to it, so she decided to take it along with her that evening. She was dining with an old friend, Dominique Last. They had been out of touch for four years, and Cleo was looking forward to meeting her friend's husband, Dayan. Dominique had described him as "big and handsome and clever." He was an Israeli businessman, and they lived in a house in Hampstead, and had a baby of eighteen months.

Dominique looked as sensational as ever. She was a small compact girl with masses of red curly hair, and full seductive lips. They met in the bar of the Connaught, and Dominique and Cleo hugged.

"Show me a picture of the baby," Cleo demanded.

Dominique nudged her husband. "You've got the pictures." He shook his head. "Oh God, you're so stupid!" she exclaimed, and Cleo noted a look of anger pass between them.

Dayan was indeed big and handsome as Dominique had described him. But what about the clever? Married only three years and already clever had changed to stupid.

"I thought we would eat at Mr. Chows," Dominique announced over a Campari and soda. "Cleo, you look *so* well, and I do love your hair that way."

Cleo's hair was a mild freakout of curls as she had still not had time to get to the hairdressers.

"It's a mass of fuzz. What hairdresser do you go to now? I feel like such a tourist."

"Christine at Main Line. She's fabulous, you'll love her. Now tell me, I'm dying to know, how was Butch Kaufman? Is he divine?"

Cleo hesitated. Dominique seemed so different, sort of wound up and on show. She decided against displaying the Kaufman interview tucked safely in her Gucci shoulder bag.

"He was nice, sort of ordinary."

"Ordinary!" Dominique hooted with laughter. "You really are too much."

So are you, Cleo thought, I think marriage has changed you into a petulant bitch.

"We'd better go," Dayan said, "or we'll be late for our table."

"Go get the car, darling, we'll meet you outside." As soon as Dayan was out of sight, Dominique confided, "He's so bloody boring, I don't know what's happened to him. He makes me want to scream. I'm seriously thinking of divorce."

Cleo showed her surprise. "But you seemed so happy—"

"Happy," Dominique snapped, "with him? He's only interested in the baby and TV. In that order. He has no interest in me or what I think or how I feel."

"But you've only been married such a short time."

"Yes I know. But we can't all find instant sex and happiness like you and Mike. I mean it, Cleo. I'm fed up, absolutely fed up."

Dayan reappeared. "The car's outside."

At Mr. Chow's they were joined by Dayan's best friend, a thin, wiry man by the name of Isaac. Dominique and Isaac spent the rest of the evening in close conversation. Cleo attempted polite talk with Dayan, but the intimate looks flashing between Dominique and Isaac were creating an uneasy situation.

It was with relief that Cleo arrived back at her hotel. She lay on her bed and thought about her marriage with Mike. They had never reached that married limbo land of calling each other stupid in public. Indeed Cleo didn't think that Mike was stupid at all. Surely if you put down your partner as an idiot you were putting down yourself for marrying them in the first place.

She sighed. Maybe it was time to talk to Mike. Maybe it was time to work things out.

Chapter 15

The trip was all set. Jet out of Kennedy the very
next day. Mike James was pleased. Everything was
going to work out perfectly. He could do the business he had to, get that out of the way. And then he
and Cleo could spend a little time in London together. It would be romantic getting together again
in the city where they had first met. He took a
shower, and naked, started to sort out the clothes he
thought he might take.

The doorbell rang, and he knotted a blue towel
round his waist and went to answer it. Maybe it was
Russell dropping by to commiserate. Well there
would soon be nothing left to commiserate about.

It was Cleo's good friend Susan. Susan of the
big boobs and thick blond hair and unsuccessful
acting career.

"Mike," she said dramatically pushing past him, "I'm so upset, so distraught!"

He trailed her into the livingroom where she picked up a cigarette package from the coffee table and shook out his last cigarette. She placed it between quivering lips and turned to him for a light.

He wondered how she managed to walk around without getting arrested. Mammoth unbra'd bosoms in a faintly transparent white shirt.

"I don't want to be responsible for breaking up your marriage," Susan wailed, tears filling heavily mascaraed eyes. "Cleo is my friend, my dearest friend."

"Yeah, well . . ." Mike said lamely.

"I'm not a marriage breaker," Susan said primly. "I'm not even promiscuous."

No, you just like fucking a lot—Mike thought. And why not? Nothing wrong with it. The name of the game was not getting caught.

"You haven't broken up any marriages," Mike said kindly.

"I haven't? But I thought Cleo had left, gone."

"Only on a business trip. Everything is cool, Susan. Cleo's hip, she understands."

"Oh!" Susan sat down deflated. "I mean I heard . . ."

"Never believe everthing you hear."

"Ginny told me it was all over. I wouldn't have wanted to be the cause of anything so—well y'know —drastic."

"I guess we picked the wrong place, wrong time."

"I guess so," Susan flicked her hands through her long blond hair, "but it was nice, wasn't it?"

"It was very nice," And it had been until Cleo had appeared at the office door. God, the shock of it.

It was amazing really that he had been able to stay on the job.

Susan was wearing an unfashionably short skirt, and was it—Mike stared—yes it was—stockings and suspenders. He felt himself stir under the towel. And of course she immediately noticed, good little nymphomaniac that she was. Well, there was no hiding a hard-on under a towel. He remembered her body, ripe and luscious and juicy.

Susan licked full red lips. "I wish you weren't married," she said throatily.

Mike flicked the knot on the towel undone. "Be a good girl, everything off except stockings and shoes."

Susan smiled understandingly and stood up. Like a stripper she shed her shirt and skirt.

He had known she wouldn't be wearing any panties.

After all he was battling with Cleo about Susan already. One more time wouldn't make any difference. And anyway—he *needed* it, it was purely a medicinal fuck.

After, Susan demanded a cigarette. Mike slipped on some clothes and went downstairs to get some from the corner drugstore.

He felt physically refreshed, but he hoped it wouldn't be long before he could get rid of good friend Susan. She was like rich cream cakes, you wanted them when you saw them, and felt sick when you had had them.

God, what was it with him? Why did he have such insatiable urges?

When he returned—surprise surprise—Susan was fully dressed and ready to leave.

"You really are a motherfucker!" she said daintily. "Cleo phoned from London. It seems to me that she doesn't understand at all. She left you no message, and the message she gave *me* I wouldn't repeat." Susan snatched the pack of cigarettes from him and made a good exit.

Mike swore to himself softly, he had done it again. But then of course you couldn't expect a girl who wore no panties to have the intelligence not to answer other people's phones.

Chapter 16

Muffin posed prettily for the hordes of photographers.

Legs crossed, shiny lips moistened, sweet bouncy tits straining at the neckline of her red gingham blouse.

A crowd had gathered in the usually quiet English park to watch her being photographed.

"Who is she?" a nanny inquired of a young photographer.

"Muffin," he replied, as if that was explanation enough.

"She's got fat legs," the nanny muttered to no one in particular. "*I've* got better legs than her." She walked off pushing her pram disconsolately.

"Isn't she lovely," a travelling charlady remarked, pausing to watch.

"Cor, I don't 'arf fancy 'er," said a fourteen-year-old schoolboy to his friend.

"Yer," agreed the friend, "she looks a real wanker's special!"

"How about a few with the lucky lad," one of the photographers asked, and Jon was reluctantly pushed in to the picture. He felt like a right fool. Behind the camera was his scene, but anything to make Muffin happy.

"We'll announce our engagement," she had finally compromised, and signed the contract.

It had cost him six hundred quid for a lousy engagement ring. And God knows what it would cost him when Jane saw the engagement pictures. One thing he hadn't been able to change about Muffin was her stupid conventional working-class background. Marriage had been on her mind the moment they had moved in together. Christ, before you knew it she would be wanting kids.

"Smile," one of the photographers demanded, "you look dead gloomy."

Jon attempted a smile. Muffin snuggled close to him and gave him a secret grope. He felt dead gloomy. Who needed a divorce to be rushed straight into another marriage?

A woman reporter with red hair and glasses asked, "How does it feel to be engaged to every man's fantasy?"

"Great." Jon managed a smile. "Wait 'til you see the new calendar we'll be doing together. We're thinking of having a competition to find out what twelve fantasies your average guy in the street would like to have Muff portray."

"What a good idea," the lady reporter said. "Perhaps our newspaper would be interested in organizing it."

Jon perked up. "I'm sure we could work something out."

Muffin celebrated with lunch at the *Carousel* for a table full of mates. She didn't have what could be termed as any close friends, but a certain select group of models were the closest to her.

Kamika, on her right, said, "I hope it work out O.K. for you."

Muffin grinned, "I want babies, lots of babies!"

"You told Jon, darling?" inquired Erica. "I don't get the impression he's in line for another family just yet."

Muffin giggled. "I'll surprise him!"

Beautiful black Laurie hooted with laughter. "Some surprise, baby! Who *needs* all that crap. Nappies, washing, dirty little brats always buggin' you."

"Children can be more than nappies and washing," Kamika intoned primly.

"Bullshit!" exclaimed Laurie.

"Ladies, ladies," said Erica sweetly, "I'm sure our little Muffin knows what she wants."

"I had the most incredible new guy last night," Laurie announced, anxious to impart her news at the first opportunity.

"I didn't know there was such a thing as a *new* guy," Erica said.

"Maybe not to you, baby," Laurie retorted swiftly, "we all know you've been through everyone!"

Muffin smiled dreamily. Soon she would be out of all this bitchy competition. "Good key and lock?" she asked encouragingly.

Laurie laughed happily. "Fantastic! Good solid stuff!"

"Japanese say quality not size that matter," Kamika remarked.

"Yes, we all know that old wives' tale," interjected Erica, "if that was the case you'd still be married."

"I get no divorce because of *size*," Kamika explained patiently. "I divorce because of *farting*."

They all dissolved in laughter.

"Have I got a guy for you, Kam," said Laurie brightly. "He's got a prick the size of a cigarette, and terrific manners!"

Later Jon joined them, and they lolled around the restaurant until four-thirty, at which time Muffin insisted that they all come back to her place for tea.

"You can't even boil a kettle," said Jon in the car, "what's with the hostess bit?"

"I'm going to learn to cook," Muffin said excitedly. "I'm going to turn you on with tasty little gourmet meals. Hang on a sec, stop at Lyons and I'll pop in and get some tea bags and cakes."

Jon sat in the mini and waited. Jane had been a terrific cook. Great breakfasts, eggs, bacon, fried bread, the lot. Home-made teas. All the good cooking in the world couldn't hold a marriage together. Jane had turned from a free-thinking pretty young student into an unattractive nag. Four years and two kids and he had a changed woman on his hands. He had decided then that marriage was definitely not his scene. However, his hands were tied, so marriage it would have to be. He loved Muffin as she was, he just hoped a thin gold band on the finger wasn't going to turn her into a split personality.

"Got buns with sticky jazz on top," Muffin announced, bouncing back into the car. Passersby stopped to stare at her. The familiar face that they

98

couldn't quite place. "Why don't we buy some champagne instead of tea?"

"Easy on, I spent every last penny cash on the ring."

"We do have money in the bank, don't we? Let's made a check. Stop at Harrods."

"I feel like tea."

Muffin pouted. "You aren't half mean."

"Yeah. That's why we've still got money in the bank."

Erica had collected a boyfriend on the way, and Laurie asked if she could phone her fantastic new guy and ask him over.

"It's turning into a party," Muffin said excitedly. "I'm going to phone a few more people."

Jon made a face at her.

By six o'clock the place was jammed. Jon had gone out for half a dozen bottles of cheap wine, and a new Barry White record was blaring on the stereo.

Jane phoned in the middle of it all. Jon could hardly hear her.

"I've changed my mind about the divorce settlement," she screamed down the phone. "I just caught a flash of your little tramp's ring in the evening paper. Christ, you must be rolling in it, and I'm sitting here like a pauper. Go on, enjoy your party, don't worry about your kids, I can't even buy them winter coats. You rotten bastard, you stinking . . ."

Jon replaced the receiver.

Problems. Always problems.

Chapter 17

Cleo and Dominique lunched at *Rags*, a restaurant club in Mayfair. Dominique started the lunch with a vodka martini.

"Pretty good for a girl who didn't used to drink," Cleo remarked.

"I do a lot of things I didn't used to do," Dominique fluttered her hands nervously.

"So I noticed," Cleo said dryly.

"Well it's all right for you," Dominique was suddenly petulant, "interesting job, glamorous life in New York. You get out, meet famous people. How would you like to be stuck in a house in Hampstead, with a baby, and an au pair, and a husband that takes you for granted."

"Don't forget the lover."

Dominique reddened. "You always did know me better than anybody. But don't blame me. Isaac *cares* about me, Dayan wouldn't know the difference if I dyed my hair blue and posed naked for the *Sunday Times!* I gave up a terrific job to marry him, and now I feel I've wasted nearly three years."

"Hardly a waste if you have a lovely baby to show for it."

"I'm going to divorce him," Dominique confided urgently.

"What are you waiting for then?"

"It's not easy. Isaac doesn't have any money, and I don't know if I could get my old job back. What I really need is a super rich man to come along and bail me out."

"Charming! It's all down to economics now."

Dominique adjusted a curl and smiled at a nearby acquaintance. "I suppose it is. Listen, Cleo, Dayan doesn't even like sex anymore. Give him a choice—*Match of the Day* or me, and guess which he would pick. He was practically a sex maniac when I married him. Thank God for my afternoons with Isaac or I'd go mad."

"Cleo!" Shep Stone lay a triumphant hand on her shoulder. "Quite a coincidence." He stood by the table, a pleased smile suffusing his face. "Did you like the flowers?"

"Lovely," Cleo replied. Dominique was kicking her under the table, so she added, "Oh Shep, I'd like you to meet a friend of mine—Dominique Last—Shep Stone."

Dominique fluttered her eyelashes. "I've seen you on television, *loved* your last record."

Shep regarded her with sudden interest, his smile broadened. "I ain't Sinatra, but I manage to jog along." He shot a look at Cleo to gauge her reaction to the fact that he was indeed a star. She had taken to studying the menu.

"How long are you here for?" Dominique inquired, and without even a pause for breath, she added, "Why don't you join us?" She snapped delicately manicured fingers. "Waiter! Another chair over here, please."

The waiter rushed a chair over, but Shep still stood.

"I'm with some business associates." He stared at Cleo, hoping she might press him to be seated, but she resolutely continued with the menu. "Maybe just for a minute then." Shep sat himself down.

Cleo stood herself up. "I'm going to the bathroom," she announced.

In the sanctuary of the ladies' room she stared at herself in the mirror angrily. God, it wasn't enough that she had problems of her own—problems that might be eased if there was only someone who cared enough to listen. But on top of everything else she had been lumbered with the one man that she had absolutely decided she couldn't stand. She had a vivid picture of him in her mind, redfaced and pleading, unzipping his fly and demanding "just a little head."

Dominique had asked him to join them, let Dominique be the one to get stuck with him.

Mind made up, Cleo went to the reception desk and left a note to be sent up for Dominique. Called away on business. She would probably be furious, but that was just too bad. I am sick of being nice to people, Cleo thought, the nicer you were the more you got taken advantage of.

She left enough money to settle the bill and taxied off on a shopping trip.

Two pairs of Yves Saint Laurent shoes, three Biba tee shirts, one pair of Oliver Goldsmith sunglasses tinted green, and a Chloe dress later, Cleo felt a lot better. Ease the tension by releasing some hard earned cash, there was nothing like it.

All her life Cleo had wished to be slightly tougher with people. She was the one that got stepped all over. People did not respect weakness, they sniffed it out like aromatic coffee, and then they trampled all over you.

"Can't you *ever* say no to a party?" Mike had often admonished. "We never get any time at home, it's one goddam party after another."

"I tried to say no," Cleo would murmur, "but they insisted."

When pushed far enough she could be tough. In her writing she was tough. With Mike she planned to be tough. Christ! The nerve of him. She had hardly left the country and he had moved Susan big boobs in. Well let him keep her there. Let him hump her until his tongue fell out. It proved to Cleo that she had made the right move.

Divorce was on her mind. One quick simple divorce.

Chapter 18

"Geoff's coming over this morning to do the windows," Muffin announced.

"He's what?" Jon inquired.

"Coming to clean the windows," Muffin replied patiently, sticking out her toes and painting the nails in intricate white and green stripes.

"Why?"

"Because he said he wanted to. Said he was going to be in the district and would pop up and do them."

"Jesus!! Don't know why you want *him* up here. He's verging on being a complete moron."

"He's quite nice really."

"Oh, he's quite nice really," Jon mimicked her, "and was he quite nice when you were going out with him?"

"I only went out with him a couple of times."

"Oh yeah, that's right, your sister whipped him from under your nose." Jon finished dressing. He was unaccountably angry.

Muffin sat cross-legged on the bed intent on the art job she was doing on her toes.

"You'd better get dressed," Jon said irritably, "can't greet your window-cleaner in your baby dolls, or is that the whole idea?"

Muffin giggled. "Don't be silly. If I'd known you were *jealous* I would have said no."

"I'm not jealous."

"It's just that the windows haven't been touched for ages, and I thought it was sweet of him to offer."

"Sweet," Jon said morosely. He had other problems to worry about. Jane. Their agreement. She was taking him to the cleaners, and because of Muffin's stupid insistence about marriage there was nothing he could do except agree.

"I'm off then," Jon said. "Thanks for breakfast."

Muffin bounced off the bed. "Why didn't you say?"

"You knew I had to be at the solicitors at ten o'clock."

"I'll make you something now."

"Haven't got time." He relented and kissed her on the nose. "Get dressed," he admonished, feeling under her shortie nightie, "and put on knickers."

When Jon had left, Muffin resumed painting her toes. When they were finished she got out her make-up case and started on her face. She was just dotting on the last of her freckles as the doorbell rang.

Scruff started to bark, and Muffin quickly inspected herself in the bathroom mirror. She ran a brush through her orange-tipped blond curls, and sprayed on some Estée perfume. Then, still in her skimpy nightie, she answered the door.

Geoff stood there looking slightly embarrassed. He wore blue dungarees with a bib front, a check shirt, and he carried a ladder and large bucket.

"Morning," he said. "This is your friendly neighborhood window-cleaner."

"Morning." Muffin grinned. "You'd better come in."

She had arranged the whole thing. She had phoned Geoff and complained about the fact that their windows were in a terrible state and that they just couldn't get anyone and could he possibly come over and not to mention it to Penny as she would only think it was a liberty to ask.

Geoff had agreed. Muffin had said Tuesday morning would be perfect. She knew that Jon had an early appointment with his solicitor. She had worked the whole thing out carefully.

It still hurt the way that Geoff had used her. She had been fifteen, an impressionable age. He had picked her up in a cinema queue, bought her a ticket and a packet of crisps, chatted her up. Sat next to her and caressed her breasts, stuck his tongue in her ear, tried to explore under her skirt. The excitement of necking in a cinema at fifteen was hard to beat, especially with a good-looking older man. Geoff at the time was twenty-two. He had walked her home, and arranged another date.

Again the cinema, again the hot sticky unbearably exciting groping. He had undone her bra, practically got her knickers off. After, they had gone for a Wimpy, and he had said, "Tomorrow night, John Wayne."

With hammering heart she had met him the next evening. The back row, the same routine. But when finally he managed to jam a finger inside her she had whispered, "I'm only fifteen, I'm a virgin." He had moved his hand rapidly, then a few minutes later he had said he was going to get some chocolates.

That was the last she saw of him until Penny brought him home as her prospective bridegroom.

The agony she had felt at that time was secret and private. She had never told anyone. Then Jon had come along, and when he made love to her the first time he didn't even realize she was a virgin. She had told him she had had lots of boyfriends. He had liked her. He had rescued her.

Moral. Girls who fuck are more popular.

Muffin had worked on it.

She became an extrovert. She became famous. She fell in love with Jon. Now they were to be married, but before that, well there was just one little matter to be resolved. A matter of pride. "Cup of tea?" Muffin inquired.

"Never say no."

She moved around the small kitchen aware of the fact that her nightie was almost transparent.

Geoff sat awkwardly on a chair and remarked, "Nice little dog—come 'ere, fella, come on, boy."

"How is Penny?" Muffin asked sweetly. She remembered her sister on her wedding day saying "Geoff says he never even kissed you, is that true?" And she remembered herself replying "Yeah. True. He did stick his fingers in my drawers though." Penny had stamped off to the altar red-faced and furious.

"She's fine," Geoff said cheerily, "fat and fine."

"I wish she'd do something about herself. After the baby she should go on a strict diet."

"I expect she will."

Muffin yawned, "Oh—I had such a late night. Lots of wine and lots of love." She smiled softly. "Know what I mean?"

"Yeah." Geoff grinned. "I think I do."

"I get letters from complete strangers wanting to make love to me. They carry on about my face and my body." She sat down. "Hey, remember John Wayne?"

"Did *he* write to you."

"No, stupid. John Wayne. The back row. Please, sir, I'm only fifteen."

"Pardon?"

"Us."

"Us?"

"When I was a silly little kid."

It finally dawned on Geoff. "You mean when I took you out. Cor, when I see your picture all over the newspapers it doesn't seem real."

"It was real. I didn't half fancy you."

Geoff took a loud gulp of his tea.

"Did you fancy me?" Muffin persisted.

"'Course I did."

"Then why did you run out on me?" She whined plaintively, her bright blue eyes suddenly and unexpectedly filling with tears.

Geoff stared down at his tea. "You was fifteen, only fifteen. Know what a bloke can get for interfering with a girl of fifteen?"

"But Penny was the same age," Muffin accused.

"Yeah, well that was different, wasn't it? I never touched her, never laid a finger on her until we was married."

"Charming! What was I, the trailer?" She tugged down her nightie angrily, then blurted out,

"You know you're not nearly as good-looking as you were then. You used to look like Steve McQueen, now you look like Michael Caine gone wrong."

Geoff stood up. He was very tall. "I never thought I'd have a chance with you," he announced, "not after you became famous and all that." He was edging around the table toward her. "Jon's a nice bloke, I wouldn't want to take any liberties." He grabbed hold of her. "Give us a kiss, darlin', give us a little encouragement."

As his hands started to explore under her night-dress she sat perfectly still. This was it. This was the moment she had been waiting for. This was the man who had given her the first orgasm she had ever experienced while fiddling around under her sweater in the local Odeon.

He was at it again. Fiddle. Fiddle. Fiddle. His technique hadn't changed much. Muffin squirmed more with aggravation than excitement.

"Take it easy," she complained, "you're not tuning a television!" She noticed the bulge in his jeans and it didn't look that big. Jon was big. Jon had a terrific technique.

"I think you're a smashing little woman," Geoff was mumbling, "a real little darlin'."

Muffin pushed him away. Poor Penny, she hadn't got hold of any big deal. Businesslike, Muffin stood up. "I'm going to get dressed," she announced. "You'd better start on the windows, Jon will be back in a minute."

Chapter 19

Ramo Kaliffe, Arabian film star extraordinary. Dark curls tipped with gray, olive skin, broody black eyes, and a voice tinged with Eastern promise.

Cleo met him in the bar at the Dorchester. He clutched her hand, stared into her eyes, and muttered, "You are very beautiful."

She had her opening line for the story. Ramo Kaliffe has a voice that sounds like hot molasses buried in sticky treacle. His eyes are as hot as desert sands, red-tinged like the sunset.

Cleo smiled to herself, and he took it as a sign that she liked compliments and launched into his full display.

How she longed to say, "Shall we cut out the bullshit, Mr. Kaliffe, and get down to a really interesting interview?"

Butch Kaufman had told her that underneath

the Desert Arab lurked a thoroughly likeable, very Westernized, amusing man.

An hour and a half later she found him, and soon he was telling a series of funny stories against himself.

When finally she clicked off the tape recorder and said she had enough he insisted that she join him and some friends for dinner. She agreed. He was nice, he was funny, and he was devastatingly attractive, bloodshot eyes and all.

It had been a confusing day. Mike and Susan were on her mind, and she couldn't shake off the feeling of disappointment. One lay with a girl like that—O.K. But moving her in? Definitely not O.K.

Dominique had phoned, she was delighted, in fact she didn't even mention the fact that Cleo had absented herself in such a fashion from lunch.

"Shep Stone is the most exciting man I have ever met," Dominique enthused. "He's so vibrant and strong, and so down to earth for a star."

"I take it you like him." Cleo's sarcasm was ignored.

"I think this is the man I have always been waiting for. I did something with him today that I have never done before."

"What was that?"

"I slept with him!" Dominique announced dramatically.

"You've done that before."

"Not an hour after meeting," Dominique said coldly. "The vibrations were too strong, neither of us could resist. We were both helpless. We went to his hotel and fell upon the bed like two people possessed."

"It's not called possession, it's called frustration."

"I didn't think you would understand. It's probably never happened for you like this. I'm leaving Dayan."

"What about Isaac?"

"What about him?" Dominique said irritably. "He was just a passing fancy. Shep means everything to me."

"My God, you sound demented. Are you sure Shep feels the same way about you?"

There was a pause, then, "I think so. I'm almost sure. I mean nothing was said, but after, he had to rush and I had to get home. It was too beautiful to spoil with words. That's why I'm phoning, Dayan will be home in a minute and I can't seem to reach Shep, so I thought that maybe you could phone him and say I'll meet him for lunch tomorrow."

"I'm not phoning him. If you can't reach him leave a message."

"Thanks a lot. I thought you were a friend."

"I am a friend, not a message service. And take some advice from me, don't leave Dayan until you check out with Shep that he wants you to. I suggest you also ask him about his current wife and the two that went before."

"You're jealous," Dominique accused. "I wondered why you disappeared at lunch. Couldn't take the fact that he fancied me and not you. Really, Cleo, since you got back I find you very changed, I..."

"Oh for Christ's sake!" Cleo slammed the phone down.

Had she changed? Maybe for the better if it meant getting a clear view of someone like Dominique.

Ramo's friends for dinner included Butch Kaufman with a frizzy-haired girl, and a small Danish blond who eyed Cleo suspiciously and hung tightly on to Ramo's arm.

They went to *Trader Vics* and feasted on spare ribs and Indonesian lamb roast. Navy Grogs were the drink of the evening, and Cleo soon felt that very special glow that one gets from good food, interesting company, and turn-on booze.

Ramo divided his attention between Cleo and the small blond, likewise Butch and the frizzy-haired lady.

Cleo thought—it's time to even up the score. Butch or Ramo? She liked them both. They were both attractive in different ways. Neither as attractive as Mike though. Mike had the most amazing eyes, and the most amazing balls.

I'm drunk—Cleo thought—no rash moves while I'm drunk.

But later, when they all went to *Tramp*, crushed against Ramo on the dance floor she decided she would have one of them. Like a man she felt horny, and like a man she would pick a suitable mate and screw just for the sheer sensual pleasure of screwing. No strings. If Mike could do it and enjoy it she saw no reason why she couldn't.

The only problem was which one. Ramo was fun, but a little obvious, and not too particular. He had already had the small blond earlier in the day, a fact that the small blond had insisted on confiding.

Butch was a more promising proposition. He had a stud reputation, but if you wanted to screw what better than a stud?

The girl with the frizzy hair was so stoned that she wouldn't even notice if Butch vanished.

Ramo asked her to dance, and pulling her toward him with a firm grip he suggested a threesome. "You, me, and the little Dane."

Cleo declined, "Not my scene."

"You a married lady?" Ramo questioned.

"Why?"

"Married ladies usually love threesomes."

"Including their husbands or not?"

Ramo threw his head back and laughed. "I like you. Shall I get rid of the blond and make beautiful love to you?"

Cleo couldn't help smiling. Here at last was a truthful man.

Back at the table Butch was throwing her moody looks, and his frizzy-haired friend was dancing by herself on the packed dance floor.

"You going with lover boy?" he inquired.

"No, I'm coming with you."

Butch nodded. "Great. Let's go."

Butch was renting an apartment in Mayfair. It was all plush leather and dimmed lights.

"Not my um er style," Butch drawled. "In L.A. I've got this great beach house at Malibu. Sea swirling about at your front door, sun, sand. You get up in the morning, straight in the ocean for a swim, jog along the beach, barbecued bacon for breakfast. Can't beat it. Do you smoke?"

Politely he offered her a joint. Politely she accepted it.

"My stand-in scores the best grass in town," Butch said proudly, "good huh?"

Cleo nodded. It was good, very good to just relax and let all your tensions hang out.

"I guess you're always being told how beautiful you are. When you came to interview me you blew my mind. How come you're not into the model actress bag?"

"Why should I be? Are girls with looks supposed to all follow the same ballgame?"

"Nope. Guess not. Prettiest girl I ever knew was a schoolteacher." Slowly he leaned over and undid the buttons on her silk shirt.

She leaned back and drew strongly on the joint, letting the smoke drift in a slow swirl toward the ceiling.

Butch undid her bra which clipped at the front, and she shrugged it free. Then she stood up and unzipped her St. Laurent trousers and stepped out of her brown lace bikini pants.

Butch stood up too and stripped off his clothes.

They smiled at each other, then Butch pulled her very close, and quietly with their hands they explored each other's bodies.

They made love standing up until both their bodies were covered with a thin film of sweat.

"You've got to be fit to do it this way," Butch gasped.

Cleo's eyes were shut, a half smile hovered round her lips.

"Hey, baby? What do you think? Together?" Butch asked.

Cleo arched back even further. A purely physical fuck. Like Mike she could enjoy it too. "Any time you're ready."

Together they came, then collapsed on the floor laughing.

"Jesus!" Butch exclaimed, "you are too much. No sobbing and moaning and I love yous."

"Did you want them?"

"Hell no."

She dressed. "It was lovely, I'm going home now."

Butch shook his head in admiration, "Miss Cool. Will I see you again?"

"Around."

She took a taxi back to the hotel. It was true. A woman could enjoy it as much as a man.

She felt free, high, very confident.

O.K. Mike. If we've got anything left to work out let's work it out on equal terms.

She ignored the phone which had begun to ring, and went to sleep.

Chapter 20

The weeny boppers were out in full force at Kennedy airport. Small, sweaty, pubescent little figures darted here and there, screaming and wailing. One tiny little blond stood quietly sobbing.

Mike reviewed the scene with customary amazement. He had seen it many times before but it never failed to amaze him. Where did they all come from in their minis and their boots and their Marty Pearl emblazoned sweaters? What about school? What about their parents? What kind of life did they lead that they could just forget everything and spend a day running around Kennedy airport hoping for a glimpse of their idol?

They were all so young. "I'm eleven," one little girl had lisped proudly when he had inquired. Eleven! He was no stranger to the way these girls got treated if singled out for attention by any of the pop groups on their entourage. Eleven!

They were traveling by commercial jet. There was Marty. His backing group. His manager. His dresser. His publicity man. His mother. And of course Mike.

The hostesses were flashing bright smiles and serving drinks. Little Marty Pearl ordered a scotch and his manager laughed and said, "What a joker!" and changed the order to orange juice.

Lately, Little Marty Pearl was getting rather pissed off at still being sixteen.

When the flight was under way, and Omar Sharif was chasing Julie Andrews on the cinema screen, Little Marty's manager, Jackson, came and sat himself down next to Mike. He was a youngish guy with prematurely gray hair and watery blue eyes.

"The kid's getting impossible," he remarked glumly. "I try to isolate him, but what you gonna do—he's gonna be nineteen in two months."

"You're doing a great job. His reputation is clean as a whistle. Doesn't drink. Doesn't smoke. Doesn't fuck. What more do you want?"

"It ain't easy, Mike. One of these days I'm just not gonna be able to tell him what to do. Besides, everywhere we go we got groupies climbing up the wall. Caught one giving the electrician a blow job the other day in the hope that he'd take her over to Marty."

Mike laughed. "Maybe the time has come to find him an official girlfriend."

"She get torn to bits. Listen, the kid is getting very randy. I've thrown a couple of professional pieces his way in the last month and he's lapped it up. At least hookers keep their mouths shut. We can't afford a girlfriend yet—the fans just wouldn't like it."

Mike shrugged. Little Marty Pearl's sex life was really not his problem. Cleo was his problem. No way was he going to allow four years of a pretty incredible marriage to be swept out of the way like so much garbage.

He would go straight to her hotel. Surprise her. Make love to her. They would forget about the past. Mike would promise to be a good boy, and Cleo would agree that it would be stupid for a girl like Susan to come between them.

In future, Mike decided, if he felt like playing around he would be very very careful. Discreet, that was the word.

Jackson said conversationally, "Last time I was in London I had the best piece of ass this side of heaven."

"Oh yeah," Mike replied politely.

Jackson's watery blue eyes filled with emotion, "Fat juicy little redhead. Stoned shitless, but what a lay!"

"You going to see her this trip?"

"Naw," Jackson shook his head in disgust, "don't even know her name."

"Excuse me, Mr. Jackson," Little Marty Pearl's mother was standing in the aisle. Emma Pearl was a woman of forty who looked a great deal older. Her husband was dead, and Marty was an only child.

"Yeah?" Jackson looked her over with the resignation he usually felt for her requests.

Emma Pearl plucked nervously at the collar of her dress, "I was wondering if the accommodations arranged include adjoining suites for me and Little Marty. I was most disturbed in Philadelphia when I

121

found myself on a different floor of the hotel." Her voice started to rise. "After all, Mr. Jackson, *you* know that Little Marty likes me to be near. He *needs* me near him. He . . ."

"Sure," Jackson cut her off, "I'm sure it will all be fine in London. No problem."

"You know I don't like to be a bother, Mr. Jackson. You know I never cause trouble. But Little Marty likes me near him." Emma Pearl bit on her lower lip nervously. "He wants me by his side."

"Quite right." Jackson nodded reassuringly, and Emma Pearl went back to her seat on the plane. "Piss off, you old crow," Jackson muttered in her wake. "Jesus!" he exclaimed to Mike. "We gotta do something about her. Marty's bugging the crap out of me—get rid of her—keep her away—stop her following me. She still thinks he's fucking thirteen."

"Why is she on the trip then?"

"'Cos Marty ain't got the balls to tell her he's a big boy now. He expects her to come along and stay out of the way. And who's supposed to keep her out of his way? Guess who? Schmuck face, yours truly, that's who."

Mike nodded. "Relatives always turn out to be a drag. I guess a mother is better than a wife though."

"Maybe. The mother scene is bad enough. The wife scene I don't wanna even imagine! Gives me bad vibes, know what I mean?" Jackson tailed off, suddenly remembering that Mike was married.

In London it was raining and in spite of the fact that Little Marty had never had a hit record outside of America, there was a massive crowd of teeny boppers waiting to greet him.

"We set up 'bout a hundred," Jackson remarked enthusiastically, "but there seems to be nearly a thousand."

There was a fleet of cars to meet them, and Mike managed to push past the photographers and crowds, and commandeered a car to himself. He had plans to head straight for Cleo's hotel. There was nothing he could do for Little Marty, he was surrounded by people ready to deal with his every whim. Really Mike was only along on the trip to keep an executive eye on things. And of course, as far as he was concerned, to meet and make up with Cleo.

In the car he rehearsed his opening lines. Should he apologize? Explain? Lie?

Actions always spoke louder than words. He would give her some action.

Mike smiled to himself. He always had been known as the man with the answer to every problem.

Chapter 21

Jon Clapton was worried. He had committed himself. He had arranged to sign a large chunk of himself away in payments to his soon to be ex-wife.

One hundred quid a week she had finally demanded, plus the usual benefits such as children's school fees, doctor bills, dentist bills. He had baulked at holidays. Surely on a hundred quid a week she could scrape enough together to manage a couple of weeks in Brighton.

Cow! Bitch! Women!

It had been a long haul to pull himself up into the money, and now that he was nearly there Jane would be hanging around his neck like a financial albatross.

However. It would be worth it. Now he would be free to marry Muffin, and Muffin stood for money. Together there would be no stopping them.

The Schuman Calendar deal alone would take care of their monetary affairs for the next year at least. And after that, well who knew? Muffin had incredible potential.

He hadn't told her yet the full scheme of his plans for her. Dancing lessons. Singing lessons. Drama coaching. She had natural talent. With a little bit of polishing she could become a star. She already had the name. Everybody knew her. Her picture appeared in one or the other national papers practically daily. Comedians made jokes about her on television. She received hundreds of admiring letters a month.

Jon was confident she had what it takes to become much more than just a sexy body and a pretty face.

Today was an important day for Muffin. A journalist on one of the big daily papers had requested an interview with her. It was important that now she started to come across as a personality, and Jon had coached her in how she should behave.

"Anthony Private is a prick," he had warned her, talking of the journalist who was to do the interview, "he'll try to charm the knickers off you with his small chat, but just remember that he's a bitch, probably a closet queen, and jealous as hell."

"Will I fancy him?" Muffin had asked coyly.

"Only if you fancy skinny geezers with glasses and thin mean lips. Oh, and do me a favor, Muff, if he tries to give you one the answer is very definitely no."

"Yes," said Muffin.

"Yes?" questioned Antony Private incredulously.

"Yes," confirmed Muffin, "I was thirteen."

"That seems awfully young," Anthony mumbled unsurely.

"How old were *you* then?"

"Me?" Anthony Private coughed nervously. "*I'm* interviewing *you*. I don't think how old I was is really relevant."

"Just curious. I bet you were a late starter."

Anthony reddened and quickly changed the subject. "How do you feel about thousands of men ogling your naked body every day?"

"Chuffed."

"Pardon?"

Muffin openly yawned. She had spent an hour and a half over lunch with Anthony Private, and she was bored. He asked stupid questions in a stupid high-pitched voice, and she was amazed that this was the man who had a full page weekly in a national daily paper.

"If looking at me in the buff turns old geezers on then I'm chuffed. Like it's a giggle, right?"

Anthony threw her a disdainful look. "How does your father feel?"

"You have a cold sore on your lip," Muffin pointed out accusingly, "you know what that comes from don't you?"

"No, I don't," said Anthony irritably, "and I don't want you to tell me either. What about your father?"

"*He* doesn't have any cold sores; and I've got a lovely mum."

"Christ!" Anthony heaved a sigh of despair, and called for the bill. "What are you doing now?" he inquired of Muffin.

"Having lunch with you," she stated in surprise.

"I mean now—when we leave here. Are you going home?"

Muffin shrugged. "Hadn't thought. Why?"

"I would like to see where you live. Get a sort of background picture."

"Oh, all right. Come back for coffee. But I'm telling you now—no nooky."

"I can assure you I wouldn't dream of it."

"No, I didn't think you would!"

Over coffee at Muffin's Holland Park flat Anthony Private snapped, "Do you make a lot of money doing nothing?"

"Pardon?" Muffin asked. She was not used to people who were arrogant and sly and jealous.

"How much money do you make a year?"

Jon had often instructed her never to discuss the money that they made, so she said hesitantly, "I'm not really into money, my boyfriend sort of takes care of that side of things."

"Women's lib would love you," said Anthony dryly. "What do you think of your looks?"

"I should like to be taller, you know, sort of a Verouchka type lady. And I should like to have longer thinner legs."

Anthony Private stood up. "O.K.," he said, "I think I have everything I want."

Muffin smiled nicely. She sensed that he didn't like her, but she didn't want him to know that the feeling was mutual.

"Goodbye." She scooped up Scruff and walked her guest to the door. "See you again I hope."

When he was gone she burst into tears. She didn't know why, he just made her feel sad. After a while she recovered, and full of new energy she stomped off to Harrods. If you were into shoplifting, Harrods was *the* place.

Chapter 22

"Mrs. James," Mike told the receptionist confidently.

"Mrs. James checked out this morning."

"She can't have."

"I can assure you that she did."

"Where has she gone?"

"I'm sorry, sir. I'm afraid I cannot reveal information about our guests' movements unless they request that we do so."

"I'm her husband."

"I'm sorry, sir. Mrs. James left no forwarding address, but she will be returning to us on the 24th of this month."

"That's three days. You mean you have no idea where she's gone?"

"Sorry."

"Can I get a room?"

"I'm sorry, sir. We are fully booked."

"Jesus H. Christ!"

Mike deposited his suitcase with the hall porter, and made his way to the bar. What timing! A mad dash all the way across the Atlantic and she was gone. He didn't even know where to.

Russell Hayes would probably know. She had obviously taken off to interview someone. He had known that she wasn't going to stay in London the entire time, but he had thought at least a week.

Now he couldn't even get a room in Cleo's hotel. He would be forced to join the Marty Pearl entourage over at the Europa. A drag.

He swallowed two fast scotches to drown his disappointment. He was really starting to miss her. Badly. In fact so much so that if Susan hadn't presented herself at his apartment and made herself readily available then he wouldn't even have bothered to get himself laid. For the first time in years he was off casual sex. He was concentrating on building up one hell of a hardon for his own wife.

He took a taxi over to the Europa, and there were lots of little girls milling about outside. There was a suite booked for him, and he placed a call to Russell in New York. Then he got through to Jackson on the house phone to find out how everything was going.

"A breeze," Jackson informed him. "Gonna tuck Little Marty up for the night, and then I'm gonna find myself a nice tight little piece of English country. You wanna join me?"

Mike declined. He felt tired, a touch of jet lag. And besides he wanted to try and find out where Cleo was. Maybe she was somewhere near, somewhere he could join her at.

Russell Hayes did not call back for an hour.

"I don't know where she is," he informed Mike,

"as long as she mails her stuff in on time she's a free agent."

"Thanks a lot. You're a big help."

"If you find her have her call me."

"How can I find her?"

"I don't know, she's your wife. Call her mother, her friends."

"Thanks Russ. I can always depend on you for fuck all."

He didn't know where to contact her mother. He couldn't remember any of her friends. In fact her life before he had met her was a closed book, one he had never bothered to open.

He called down to room service and had them send up a menu. There was nothing he felt like. He certainly did not feel like sitting alone in a hotel room all night. He pulled on his leather jacket and went out.

In the hotel corridor a bizarre sight greeted him. Mrs. Emma Pearl .was sitting on a cushion outside the door to her son's suite. She jumped up nervously when she saw Mike.

"What are you doing?" he inquired incredulously.

"I am seeing that Little Marty is all right."

"Oh," said Mike, "I see." He paused for a moment, glancing along the corridor to see if they were being observed. They were not. "Why are you *outside* his room?"

Emma Pearl blushed, ashamed of her own eccentricity. "He doesn't want me inside."

Mike nodded. The woman was obviously mad. "Where's Jackson?"

"He has gone out for dinner. They have all gone out for dinner. They have left Little Marty alone, and frankly, Mr. James, I just don't think it's right.

Why, only five minutes ago a dreadful blond girl tried to get into his room. She said he had sent for her. Of course I knew she was lying and I sent her packing. If I hadn't been here she would have probably got in. Mr. James, he's only a young boy, and idolized by these stupid girls. He shouldn't be left alone."

"Mrs. Pearl, he's nearly nineteen."

Emma rolled her eyes wildly. "*We* know that, Mr. James. But to the world he is sixteen, and sweet sixteen he must stay."

Mike shrugged, and at that moment the door to Marty's suite was flung open and Little Marty himself stood there. He was a short boy with a cowlick of blondish hair falling on his forehead, and big brown eyes. Clad in a white towelling dressing-gown he had none of the strut of the boy who appeared on stage in skin-tight white leather and high-heeled studded boots. A rash of angry red spots were gathering on his chin. He had been about to scream abuse at his mother, but upon seeing Mike he quickly shut up.

"Hey, Marty," said Mike. "I thought you were having an early night. You've got a real bastard tomorrow."

"Yeh," agreed Marty, "I was." He glanced expectantly along the corridor. "Tell my ma to get off to bed, Mike."

"That's just what I was doing. Come along, Mrs. Pearl. Marty's going to get some sleep, he's perfectly safe." He led her off toward the elevator. He winked at Marty. "Get to bed."

Mrs. Pearl said in a tired disappointed voice, "I'm not even on the same floor. I *told* Mr. Jackson I wanted to be near my boy."

"Sure," Mike soothed, "you stay in your room

132

for tonight and I'll see what I can arrange for to-morrow."

He deposited her on the floor above, and then took the elevator down to the lobby. "Which is the young lady for Mr. Pearl?" he inquired at reception. They pointed out a blue-jeaned blond waiting for a taxi.

Mike went over to her. "It's O.K. now," he said, "Marty's waiting."

She gave him a toothy grin. "You sure? Some batty old lady is guarding his room."

"The coast is clear."

"Thanks, sugar."

She wiggled her way over to the elevator and Mike admired her ass.

Poor Little Marty. What use was it being a pop star if you couldn't even get laid in peace?

Chapter 23

The flight to Nice was very pleasant. Cleo made sure that she didn't sit next to any unattached men. Instead she found herself next to a very pretty lady who was celebrating her divorce by taking a holiday.

"I had seven years of misery," she confided to Cleo, "just me, him, and his bloody mother. I saw more of *her* than I did of *him!*"

At Nice Airport Cleo hired a car, a small gray convertible. She had wanted to drive along the coastal road but the summer traffic was so bad that she changed her mind and switched to the highway.

Just under three hours later she arrived in St. Tropez. Hot and dusty she checked into the Byblos Hotel.

She had a cold bath and put on the bikini she had purchased in a hurry before leaving London.

She attempted to phone the office of the film company whose star she had arranged to interview. There was no one there who seemed to know anything about it, so she decided to phone back later.

She felt embarrassed going out to the hotel pool alone. Women on their own always seemed so vulnerable. Other women summed them up as potential rivals, and men summed them up on their probable bedability. Baby—you've come a long way was bullshit. Women were still the second classes of the world. Judged on their looks. Judged on their morals. A man who screwed around was "clever old Fred." A woman was still an old scrubber.

Ten minutes after settling on a mattress, applying sun tan oil, and ordering a long cool drink, the first man appeared. He was short and extremely hairy.

"Just arrived?" he questioned in English tinged with cockney.

"No," replied Cleo coldly.

"Oh. I thought you had." He squatted down next to her. "Want a drink?"

"I have a drink." She got up and dived in the pool and left him squatting. She stayed in the pool until he left.

The next arrival was French with a deep mahogany oiled body. He didn't waste any time. "You like to have good evening dancing tonight?"

Cleo ignored him.

He made a face and drifted off, to be quickly replaced by a blond German who hovered beside her and commented on how boring it must be to have men chasing her all the time. She ignored him too, and word must have gone around the pool because after that she wasn't bothered anymore.

After two hours of sun she went inside and tried to phone the film company again. This time she got the publicity man, and an appointment was made for her to meet Sami Marcel for lunch the following day.

"Tahiti Beach, one o'clock," the pubicity man said. "We shall be filming there all morning, so if you want to· come by earlier and watch the action, just do so."

Great. St. Tropez. Alone. No desire to be with anyone. But what was there to do alone?

Female on her own. Instant pick-up. Already proved.

There was no alternative but a long and boring evening in her hotel room.

Sami Marcel was tall, sinewy, and ugly in a way that was devastatingly attractive. He had horse teeth, a large nose, fleshy lips, and he was the current heart-throb of France.

Cleo had taken the publicity man's advice and come down to Tahiti Beach early to watch them shooting. She and several hundred other ladies. The area in which they were filming was roped off, and Cleo had to literally fight her way through to reach the location. She used her school French, and the publicity man came over and helped her over the ropes.

"Sami's a great guy," he told her swiftly. "Got a reputation for being a pain in the ass, but believe me, he's a lot of fun."

The film crew was American. It was Sami's first American film, and as such quite important for him.

They were shooting a scene that involved Sami walking alone along the water's edge. He was wearing white trousers rolled up around the ankles. His chest was bare, and a large gold disc hung around his neck.

In her mind Cleo composed the beginning of the story she would write. "Sami Marcel looks like he should smell strongly of garlic. According to his legion of girlfriends he does."

It was boring watching the filming. Take one. Sami strolling along. Cut. No good. Break. Take two. Sami strolling along. Cut. Sami sneezed. Take three . . . and so on and so forth.

Cleo lay back on the sand and slipped her shirt off. The sun was hot, and she closed her eyes and enjoyed it. It would be nice to have come here with Mike. He loved the sun, he could lay unmoving for hours. She wondered if he would take Susan to the sun. She wondered if he missed her. Probably not as much as if he lost his bloody Ferrari.

The call came to break for lunch, and Cleo looked around for the publicity man. He came puffing up looking harassed.

Cleo put her shirt back on over her bikini. "We have an hour, right?" she inquired.

"Yeah, well Sami usually takes a short break before lunch, but I'll take you over to the restaurant, he shouldn't be long."

The restaurant was at the back of the beach. Wooden tables, striped umbrellas, and tight-assed waiters.

There was one long table in the middle set up for about twenty people, and the publicity man sat Cleo at it.

"Hey," she objected, "I have to interview Sami on his own, I told you that from London."

"Yeah, I know. We'll work it out. Sami has to be handled, he's been treated badly by the press."

"What do you mean—he has to be handled? I arranged to interview him and everything was supposed to have been set up."

The publicity man looked sheepish. "He's a difficult guy, he's moody. I'm sure when he meets you he'll give you some time."

"Gee, thanks a lot." Cleo's tone was cold with sarcasm. "I just don't work this way. I've come all the way from London for this interview and now I'm supposed to take my chances that he'll give me a few minutes."

"I'm sorry. I'm sure it will work out."

"Bullshit. You are just not doing your job properly. If Sami Marcel doesn't like interviews say so up front. Don't drag people down here on spec. It won't do you, the film, or Sami any good."

Some of the crew from the beach were sitting down. The director. The cameraman. The continuity girl.

Cleo was really furious. Oh God—was she going to do a scorcher on Mr. Marcel. If he thought he was badly treated by the press wait until *she* finished with him.

He arrived after half an hour. A brunette nymphet on one arm, and a curly blond on the other. Both girls were wearing just the tiniest bottom half of their bikinis. The brunette was compact and small, with boyish sun-tanned bosoms. The blond was more ample with bouncy breasts that still featured white marks from the recent confines of a bikini top.

On looking around Cleo realized that most of the females in the restaurant were topless, and there was a dazzling array of unfettered breasts. Big ones, small ones, perky, droopy. Take your choice.

Sami sat opposite her, his girlfriends clinging to

an arm each. His horse teeth were extremely white, and his eyes were black and broody.

The publicity man said nervously, "Sami, this is the lady I was telling you about. *Image* Magazine, remember?"

Sami ignored him. He listened to the whispers of the blond on his left, and absently stroked the shoulder of the girl on his right.

Cleo leaned forward. "Monsieur Marcel," she said firmly, "my name is Cleo James. I'm from *Image* Magazine, and it was arranged that I should interview you."

Sami's eyes swept over her without a flicker of interest. "Why are you all bundled up in a shirt?" he demanded. "Where are your titties?" He banged on the table, acquiring an admiring audience. "Put them on the table, woman, where they belong!"

Cleo felt the blush sweeping over her face like a wave. What a pig. She tried to ignore the blush, to keep her cool.

"Sami," the publicity man attempted a laugh that was stillborn in his throat, "don't joke about. Miss James is with *Image* Magazine. It's a biggie in America." Desperately he added, "A real biggie."

"And her titties?" Sami inquired, "are they— how you say—biggies too?" He roared with laughter, and the girls on either side of him laughed too.

Cleo had recovered her composure. "Monsieur Marcel," she said sweetly, "when you see fit to expose your balls maybe I'll join you and take off my top. Until that time comes why don't we just both keep our clothes on."

Sami narrowed his eyes. "A woman should not talk like that," he said sternly. "A woman should be

140

soft, pleasurable." He looked around the table to make sure everyone was listening, then continued expansively, "A woman should be feminine, sweet, quiet. A woman should be a mother when required, and a whore when required. Most women manage to combine those qualities admirably."

"Do they?" Cleo asked sarcastically. She had managed to switch her small Sony tape recorder on and was getting every word.

"But of course," he fingered the blond's bouncy breast and her nipple hardened under his touch, "women are beautiful playmates to be loved and to be kept in their place."

"And what—in your opinion—is their *place?*"

"Oh, at home, in the bedroom, the kitchen," Sami said vaguely. "They are decorative creatures, they don't belong in man's domain."

Cleo laughed, "You have the strong aroma of a male chauvinist pig."

Sami did not like to be laughed at. "You must be a lesbian," he stated.

Cleo laughed even louder. "Jesus! You really are too much. Is any woman who doesn't agree with your philosophies supposed to be a dyke?"

Sami stared at her, his thick lips pursed together with disapproval. "I think you are frustrated," he said shortly. "I think you need a man to make love to you. To fuck you properly."

"Fuck you, too."

Sami stood up from the table, his eyes flashing angrily. "You have a mouth like a sewer."

Cleo was unperturbed. "Just following the great master."

Sami's mouth twitched nervously, then with a sudden angry gesture he strode away from the table.

The publicity man was sweating. "You shouldn't have done that."

Cleo treated him to a look of scorn. "Listen, I *do* what the situation calls for, and this situation was caused by your incompetence." She stood up from the table. "Anyway, as it happens it all worked out O.K. I'm sure I have a most enlightening interview. Thanks for lunch."

She walked back to her car.

Monsieur Marcel look out!

Chapter 24

"He's a rotten, stinking, filthy swine!" Muffin screamed. "An uptight, stupid, limp dick idiot! I hate him, Jon, *I hate him.*"

"Stop screaming. Calm down."

"You'd be bloody screaming." Muffin picked up the newspaper she had flung on the floor in her fury. "Listen," she said shrilly. "Short, Fat, and Rich! And that's only the heading! How would *you* like to be described as short, fat, and rich?"

"I wouldn't mind the rich."

Muffin narrowed her blue eyes. "Can I sue him?"

"What for?"

"Well, detrimental treatment, damage to my character, *you* know what I mean."

"Don't be silly."

"Why is it silly?" Muffin thrust the newspaper in Jon's face. "Read it again, read the insults, and look at the picture, three years molding away in their files. *I don't look like that anymore.*"

"It's not *that bad*, Muff."

"Oh, isn't it? Isn't it?" She started to cry. "How can I go out and face people? How can I go to the cleaners?"

"The cleaners?"

"Yes, the bloody cleaners. They know me there, they cut out my pictures. How can I ever collect my suede skirt?"

"When you are in the public eye," Jon explained patiently, "you must expect all sorts of publicity. True. Untrue. Good. Bad. Just read it and if it's bad forget it. Everyone else does."

"I want to take out a full page ad in *Private Eye*. I want it to say Anthony Private is a Prick—in big black type. I *mean* it, Jon."

"O.K.," he humored her. "Although why waste the money? Anyone who's ever read his page *knows* he's a prick. They expect him to write like a bitchy college queen, that's why they read it. I did warn you."

Muffin stripped off her nightdress and stretched in front of the bedroom wall mirror. "I am *not* fat. Can *you* see any fat?"

"No way. Just a gorgeous pair of bristols and a grabable bum."

"What do you mean by grabable."

"Well, y'know. Nice. Comfortable."

"You mean fat."

"I don't mean fat."

An hour later they were both dressed, ready to leave the apartment, and not talking.

All the fury and hate and hurt that Muffin had felt toward Anthony Private had somehow maneuvered itself into Jon's direction.

"You're a shit," she hissed at him as they headed for the studio. "I don't even want to marry you anymore."

"Promise?"

"Yes, I bloody promise. And you can take your bloody Schumann Calandar deal and shove it."

"Great. I'll do it without you. I'll take some other little dolly on all the locations. Erica likes Barbados, maybe I'll try Erica."

"They want *me*."

"They'll settle for someone else."

"You're a bastard."

"Big word from such a *little* girl."

"I can understand why Jane hates you."

At the studio Jon busied himself with his equipment and his assistants.

Muffin put herself in the hands of the hairdresser, make-up artist, and fashion lady They were due to shoot a record album cover. Muffin and Little Marty Pearl. She had been most excited at the prospect of meeting him, but Anthony Private had spoiled all of that, and Jon had double spoiled it.

Muffin sulked quietly as her body was made up with a sponge and pancake make-up. She was fed up with taking her clothes off. Fed up with holding her stomach in, sticking her tits out, stretching on tiptoe to make her legs seem longer.

"That's nice, darling," said the camp boy, who was applying her body make-up. He was indicating her heart-shaped pubes. She had shaved them into a heart shape for a magazine glamor shot.

"Thanks," said Muffin glumly.

The boy bent down. "Be a sweetie and open up your legs, don't want patchy thighs, do we?"

Muffin stood with her legs apart while the boy fussed around with his pancake and sponge. Good job he was a fag as he had a bird's eye view.

"Have you seen Little Marty yet?" asked the boy, a note of excitement creeping into his voice. "I hear he's gay."

"Cor blimey, according to you everyone's gay!" exclaimed Muffin. "You'll be telling me about Prince Philip next."

"Oh. Is he?"

"Don't be daft."

Little Marty arrived with his mother and Jackson.

He was dressed from head to toe in white fringed buckskin. He immediately disappeared with the make-up artist to have his spots covered.

Jackson approached Jon, shook him by the hand, and said, "This is gonna be great, absolutely great."

Jon agreed. "Terrific idea," he said. "Muffin's never been on an album cover before. Was it your idea?"

"Yeah, sort of." Jackson forgot to mention it had all been arranged by the English P.R. whose firm handled Marty's records in England.

Muffin emerged from the dressing-room. She was wearing thigh length very high-heeled white leather boots, and a white Stetson cowboy hat. That was all.

"Holy shit!" exclaimed Jackson.

Mrs. Emma Pearl shot out of the chair at the back of the studio. "Mr. Jackson!" she complained in a shrill voice, "that girl is *naked*. Get her out of here before my Little Marty sees her."

Jackson's patience was wearing thin with Mrs. Emma Pearl. He took her firmly by the arm and led her outside to the chauffeured limousine. He placed her inside and instructed the driver to take her back to the hotel. She was complaining loudly. Let her bitch to Little Marty later. Right now he needed her out of the way.

He rushed back inside and quickly cornered Jon. Muffin had wandered back into the dressing-room.

"The piece?" Jackson asked breathlessly. "She put out?"

Jon laughed. "For me—yes. For you—no. She's my girlfriend, we're getting married."

"Oh, Jesus! I'm sorry, didn't know."

"Don't worry about it. I'm used to men falling about over her. She's terrific, isn't she?"

"Really something. She a model, actress, or what?"

"I thought you knew all about her. I thought that's why you wanted her on the album cover."

"Yeh, well, details—y'know. We just got in from the States yesterday. I knew they'd lined up a great broad for the shots—I didn't know she was *that* great."

Jon was pleased with the American's reaction. It proved everything he thought about Muffin. She had Instant Impact. Universal Appeal.

"Muff's *the* most famous model in England. She's a household name. This year we want to launch her out in other activities. TV. Movies. That sort of thing."

"You her manager?"

147

"Yes. I handle everything she does."

Jackson nodded. "Any contacts in the States yet?"

Jon shook his head. "Not yet. I was thinking of taking her over there later this year."

"Maybe I can help you. You gotta approach Stateside with a lot of clout. You gotta come in with balls. Know what I mean?"

"Well, when they see Muffin . . ."

"Not enough, take it from me, I should know. When I first got hold of Little Marty he was a farm hick. Nice boy. Nice looks. Nice voice. Without me he'd still be shoveling shit down on the farm. I gave him the works, made him a star. You and I should have a little talk about your girlfriend, I got ideas, money ideas."

"I'm always ready to talk about money."

Jackson clapped him on the shoulder. "Good boy, you've got a nose that sniffs in the right direction I can see. Why don't you and the girlfriend come along to Marty's reception tonight? After, we can have dinner. What ya say?"

"Terrific. We'll be there."

"Listen, kid, you don't want to be snapping pictures all your life. No offense—I know you're good, but I can steer you and the little lady right where the bread is. You stroke my balls, I stroke yours. You dig?"

Jon nodded. He didn't much like Jackson, but he sensed there might be a deal somewhere, and it would be good to have the right connections in America.

Muffin reappeared, and Jon introduced her to Jackson. She had thrown a silk shawl around her nakedness but it wasn't concealing much. She was still furious with Jon, and kept on fixing him with dark and moody stares.

"Hey," suggested Jackson, "maybe Muffin could bring a girlfriend along tonight."

"What for?" asked Muffin balefully.

"Sure," agreed Jon, who had got the message. "Any preferences?"

Jackson chuckled. "Just the usual."

Little Marty emerged from the dressing-room. He walked with a slightly put-on swagger. His boyish face was neatly blanked out with pale orange pancake.

Muffin shrugged the shawl off her shoulders and smiled.

Little Marty managed a blush that shone through his make-up.

"Hello," said Muffin.

Little Marty's voice cracked suddenly, "Hello."

"What a great couple!" Jackson enthused. "Don't they look perfect together?"

They did match very well indeed. Both short, in spite of mutual high-heeled boots. Both young. Both pretty. Jon had arranged a plain backdrop, and Little Marty was to stand face on to the camera, while Muffin, beside him, stood with her back to the camera, just turning her Stetsoned head.

"Fanfuckin'-tastic!" exclaimed Jackson. "Just right, sexy without being obvious. Just the image my boy needs."

Muffin left the studio before Jon. He had another photo session to do, and she wanted to go home, wash her hair, and generally prepare for the party Jackson had invited them to.

She looked forward to the party with an excited

149

churning in her stomach. Little Marty Pearl. He was lovely!

"Can I see you later?" he had asked. "Why don't you sneak over to my hotel after the party?"

"I don't see why not," she had replied, "not a word to anyone though."

"Secret," he had said, putting a finger to his lips.

"Secret," she had giggled in agreement.

They had been posing for the record cover while this whispered conversation had taken place. As soon as Muffin had set eyes on Little Marty she had flipped. After seeing his photo in so many magazines, hearing his records, well it was a real thrill to meet him in the flesh.

She had remained bad-tempered toward Jon. That way it would be easy to pick a fight at the party and walk out.

Her anger about the Anthony Private interview had evaporated. Jon was right. It was nothing to get excited about, the poor guy was just jealous.

Humming softly Muffin let herself in to the Holland Park flat. What should she wear for the evening's activities? Something sexy. Something great.

The phone rang and she picked it up. Silence on the other end. Muffin banged it down. The secret wanker strikes again! Jon said that there was an army of secret wankers who phoned pretty girls.

"It's the only way some geezers can get it off," he had casually explained. If *he* picked up the phone and there was silence he would sometimes yell down the receiver, "Go on, my son! Have one for me!"

"You're disgusting!" Muffin would complain at

the time, but she couldn't help laughing, and it certainly took the fear out of obscene phone calls.

The phone rang again. It was probably Anthony Private—now he *looked* like a secret wanker.

"Mrs. Wilson's home for unmarried scrubbers!" Muffin said primly.

"Is Jon there?" It was Jane's voice, sharp and unfriendly.

"No." She *hated* having to speak to Jon's wife.

"Is that—er—Muffin?" Jane made it sound like a dirty word.

"Yes. Who is this?"

"This is *Mrs.* Clapton."

"Oh, Jon's mother?"

"No, his wife, dear."

"So sorry. I thought you sounded like his mother."

"That's perfectly all right, dear. I thought *you* were the daily."

"Jon's out."

"So you said. Tell him to give me a ring will you. Oh, and by the way, I saw your engagement pictures. What a laugh! You silly little girls will do anything for publicity. Jon's got no intention of getting married again—he told me it was only to keep you quiet. The divorce isn't even definite yet, did Jon tell you it was? Don't bank on it, dear, I might even change my mind. Bye-bye."

"Oh!" Muffin was left hanging on to the receiver as the line went dead. "Oh, you horrible old bitch! He does want to marry me—he does." She banged the phone down in a fury. What kind of a game was Jon Clapton playing with her now? She would show him.—Oh boy, would she show him!

151

Chapter 25

London was sunny when Cleo jetted in. She had spent the few hours on the plane writing an explosive piece on Sami Marcel. It was an indictment of all men who felt that women were just attractive objects to be used for men's pleasure. He had turned out to be the perfect male chauvinistic pig, and in a biting, sometimes humorous piece, Cleo had exposed Sami Marcel, and all men who were like him. She couldn't wait to get it typed up and sent off express to Russell.

She took a taxi to the Connaught, and although she was back a day early they were able to find her a room.

There were three urgent messages for her to call Dominique Last immediately she arrived. She phoned at once.

Dominique said, "Thank Christ you're back. Can I come over?"

"I only just arrived. I have some work to get sorted out."

"Please. It's important. I must talk to you."

"All right." Cleo wasn't enthusiastic, but that hard-to-say-no streak was still prevalent.

Dominique arrived an hour later. Her red hair was hidden beneath a scarf, and her red eyes beneath sunglasses. She had obviously been crying.

Cleo felt a sudden rush of sympathy, and she decided to forget the things that Dominique had said to her a few days previously.

"You look awful!" she exclaimed. "What on earth has happened?"

Dominique removed her sunglasses to reveal a heavy black eye. "Look what the bastard did," she said bitterly.

"Dayan?" Cleo questioned.

"No," Dominique snapped, "*your* friend. That creep you fixed me up with."

"Shep Stone?"

"That's the name of the impotent little bastard."

Cleo sat down. "I'm not really following this conversation. Last time I spoke to you he was the most exciting man you had ever met, and you were leaving your husband *and* your lover for him."

"Can I get a drink?" Dominique took off her headscarf, and shook her long red hair free.

Cleo consulted her watch. It was four PM. "I don't know if the bar is open."

"Room service doesn't close. I'd like a scotch, a double."

Cleo picked up the phone and ordered tea for herself and a drink for Dominique. "So?" she ques-

154

tioned. "Can I please hear what this is all about?"

Dominique sighed. "As I told you, Shep forced me to sleep with him that afternoon after you introduced us. I suppose I was a bit tiddly. He took advantage of me. If you had stayed and not run out on me . . ."

"Let me remind you, it was *you* invited him to join us."

"I thought he was your friend."

"If I had wanted him to join us I would have been quite capable of asking him myself. Actually I can't stand him."

"Well anyway, if you had stayed . . ."

"On the phone," Cleo stated pointedly, "you said you had a marvellous time with him, true love and all that, and that you were going to leave Dayan for him."

"Nonsense," said Dominique briskly, "you must have misunderstood."

"Bullshit!" Cleo exclaimed.

There was a discreet knock at the door, and a waiter came in with their order.

They waited for him to leave, and then Dominique said flatly, "Anyway, I lost my diamond ring at his hotel, and when I went there the next day to retrieve it he hit me."

"Just like that?"

"Yes. Just like that."

Cleo poured out her tea. She was speechless. Dominique should get some sort of award for liar of the year.

"So?" questioned Cleo at last. "What do you want me to do?"

"Arrange a meeting. I want to talk to him."

"Talk to him! What about?"

"I want to have a private discussion. If you phone him he'll come here to see you. You will be out, and I'll be here. Simple."

"Hey now, just hang on a minute. Why would you want to see a man that clobbered you? And much as I dislike Shep Stone, I never did imagine him as a woman beater. *Why* did he hit you?"

"I don't know."

Cleo shook her head. "Listen. Either be straight with me or let's just forget it."

"You mean you won't help me?"

"Help you? Help you do what?"

"What I said."

"Your story has more holes than a punchcard. Please don't come here and give me a bag full of lies and then try and use me."

Dominique shrugged. "I didn't think you would help me." She drained her scotch in one fell swoop, and stood up, then evenly she said, "You are a very jealous person, Cleo, you still can't get over the fact that Shep wanted me and not you."

"Oh, come on . . ."

Dominique put her sunglasses back on, and her headscarf. "You are jealous because I've got a home and a baby. You always were jealous of me. My hair, my figure. You always . . ."

Cleo stood up. "Bye-bye, Dominique." She walked in the bathroom and slammed the door. Christ! This whole thing was so unfair. She had always tried to be a good friend, but look where it got you.

Russell Hayes. Good friend Susan. Now Dominique.

If you knew absolutely nothing about your *friends* what was it all about?

The phone rang, and when Cleo emerged she

was glad to see that Dominique had left. It was Butch Kaufman ringing and he said, "There's a slew of parties tonight, and I thought we might um er visit them together."

"Great. I could do with some parties."

"I'll pick you up at eight. Then maybe later a party of our own. My stand-in handed me something out-a-site today!"

"Maybe."

"O.K., Miss Cool. See you later."

Chapter 26

Unable to decide which girl would be the most suitable, Jon finally rounded up both Erica and Laurie.

They all met at the Holland Park flat, and Muffin, who was still hardly speaking to Jon, greeted them with, "Has he got a travelling fireman for you!"

"It's travelling salesman," Jon remarked, "visiting fireman."

"Pooh!" Muffin stuck out her tongue, and bounced off to finish her make-up. She hadn't mentioned the phone call from his wife yet. She was saving that piece of information.

Erica was wearing a brown satin jump suit, slit down the front, revealing pale, interesting, small breasts. Her blond hair was parted in the middle and hung long and straight.

"You look lovely," Jon said admiringly.

Laurie had emphasized the dark ebony of her skin with a red gypsy outfit. Her hair was freaked out Afro style, and her make-up was bright and arresting.

"Very tasty!" said Jon. He was pleased. Both girls looked sensational, and one or the other was bound to appeal to Jackson.

Muffin appeared in a white frilled blouse, tucked into white jeans, tucked into white boots. She immediately made the other two girls look ordinary by comparison.

"Saw the piece Anthony Private did on you this morning." Erica smiled. "What a bitch!"

"Yes, aren't you." Jon took her firmly by the arm. "That's one subject we are *not* going to discuss. Let's go."

Muffin glared. Trust Erica to have seen the Anthony Private thing. Stupid old cow. She must be at least twenty-six, what did *she* have to laugh about. It had worked out well that Jon had wanted to bring Erica *and* Laurie to the party, they would keep him well occupied. Muffin had plans to enjoy herself, and those plans did not include Jon bloody Clapton.

She hummed a little song in anticipation of the good times ahead.

Mike James spent the day involved in one business meeting after the other. He wanted to get everything he had to do done quickly, so that when Cleo returned he would have nothing but time for her.

Free time. Talking time. Fucking time.

He was taken to lunch at a restaurant in Chelsea, and he amazed himself by not attempting conversation with any of the dozen or so very pretty girls who were also lunching there.

I am a reformed character, he thought. I can look a roomful of nookie straight in the eye and not give it a second thought. Well . . . maybe a second thought. But that was all. Thinking not doing. An improvement on his former lifestyle.

He had a long talk with Jackson about Little Marty Pearl's mother. "She's got to go," he said, "it's no good having her on this tour, send her back."

Jackson was in complete agreement. "It's as good as done."

In the evening he went to the Little Marty Pearl party. Stay loose, he warned himself, don't get involved, let's see if you can do it for once.

There were a lot of girls there. Fat ones. Thin ones. Smart ones. Tacky ones. He stayed loose, he made idle chat, he even turned one smokey proposition down.

He felt proud and self-righteous. A faithful husband. A man who was saving himself for his wife.

"Hey," called Jackson, when the party was in full swing. "You gonna come to dinner with us?"

"I don't know," said Mike, and he inspected the two girls on either side of Jackson. The blond appealed to him, so did the black girl.

"You met Jon—er Jon . . ."

"Clapton," supplied Jon.

"Yeah. Clapton," said Jackson. "Jon photographed the album cover today—he's a good guy—great guy. This is Mike James, Jon. Mike's a top exec at Hampton Records, a good guy for you to get to know."

They shook hands, and Mike turned expectantly toward the blond. "I'm Erica," she said, extending her hand and holding on to his for just a moment too long.

Jackson whipped a quick arm around Laurie, claiming ownership for the night. He knew about Mike James' reputation in New York.

It wouldn't matter, Mike reasoned, if he got laid again *before* seeing Cleo. It wouldn't count. Anyway, she would never know, and what she didn't know she couldn't mind about. . . .

"So where are we going for dinner?" Mike inquired.

"You—as usual—look like an um er gorgeous person."

Cleo sighed. "Thank you, Butch. But I don't feel it. I feel uptight, and angry, and hurt."

"Not with me?"

"Of course not with you."

"Well, then?"

"Don't want to go into it, it's boring and dull. I just want to have a lovely enjoyable *selfish* evening."

"I couldn't agree with you more. Together we shall be decadently selfish. Shall we forget the parties?"

"No, let's go. I feel like noise and music and watching people."

Cleo was wearing her new Chloe dress. It was silk jersey, and it draped its way in beguiling curves down her body. She also wore black silk stockings, and very high heeled strappy shoes. It made a change from always being in trousers. She knew that Mike would love the way she looked, he was always complaining that he never saw her legs. "You have the best legs in New York," he would nag, "and you keep them hidden like a Portuguese nun!"

Thinking of Mike made her narrow her eyes in anger. He had stopped phoning. Just like that. No messages. Nothing. It didn't take *him* long to accept the fact that she had gone.

She would have to start sorting out her future. She had two more actors left to interview for the series, and then what? She wasn't sure if she wanted to go back to New York. She wasn't sure if she wanted to continue working for Russell Hayes and *Image*.

"First the Dorchester," Butch said. "I promised I would show my face at the party for Little Marty Pearl. If you play your cards right I'll introduce you. He's sixteen, a virgin, and prettier than you!"

Jackson and Jon watched like the proud parents as Muffin and Little Marty posed for pictures together.

"They make a cute couple," Jackson remarked.

"Yeah," agreed Jon absently. He was thinking it was a shame that he and Muff had announced their engagement, because a trumped-up romance between her and Little Marty would have been fantastic publicity. Also it had not helped the situation between him and Jane.

"You've got to watch out for my mother!" Marty whispered.

"Pardon?" whispered back Muffin.

"Just wait in the lobby. I'll call down for you when it's safe."

Muffin giggled. "Very cloak and dagger."

"I really like you," Marty said seriously. "Do you like me?"

"'Course I do!" she squeezed his arm, smiled for the photographers, and stuck out her incredible bosom.

Mike held on to Erica's arm and said, "What is a beautiful looking girl like you doing getting herself fixed up with a dude like Jackson?"

"Jon's an old friend, I thought it might be fun. My, what horny eyes you have!"

"All the better to stare you down."

"Down where?"

"You name it."

"Naughty, naughty!"

"I like your blouse."

"Blouse is such a sweet old-fashioned word."

"I used it because I can see I'm with a sweet old-fashioned girl."

"Ha Ha."

"How would you feel about skipping out on the mass dinner and going off somewhere on our own?"

"Sounds like a good idea."

Mike winked. "I shall fix it. Just a quick word with Jackson and we shall be on our way."

"My, what a fast way you have of doing things!"

"You ain't seen nothin' yet!"

"So," said Butch, "when the movie is finished, it's back to the beach house and um er flake out time. If you're around L.A. you are more than a welcome house guest. I've got a girl that sort of lives with me there, but I can always move her out for a spell, she'll understand." He helped Cleo out of the car. "What do you think?"

"I've got no plans right now, Butch. I'm just going to wing it."

A gaggle of girls sprang forward to get Butch Kaufman's autograph, and Cleo walked on inside the hotel. She stood in the lobby and watched a man approaching from a distance through the lounge. He looked very much like Mike. He had the same rangy walk. He was holding on to a tall blond, and as they got nearer Cleo realized with a stomach lurching throb that it *was* Mike.

He had been talking to Erica, light sexy conversation designed to warm her up. Then he had spotted a pair of incredible legs, and as his eyes had travelled up to inspect the face of the owner of the legs he had realized—shit—it was Cleo!!

He abruptly stopped walking, but it was too late, she had seen him also. He pulled his arm away from Erica, and a man he recognized as the film actor Butch Kaufman entered the hotel and took *his* Cleo by the hand.

"Jesus!" exclaimed Mike.

"What's the matter?" asked Erica. "Why are we stopping?"

While Mike tried to decide what to do, Cleo took the matter into her own hands, and came walking over with her escort.

"Hello, Mike," she said briefly. "Glad to see you're making out O.K."

He opened his mouth to reply, but hand in hand with Butch she was strolling off calm as you please. Bitch!! He had flown all the way across the Atlantic for *this!*

"Who was that?" asked Erica.

"Just my wife," said Mike bitterly.

Chapter 27

The desk clerk looked at Muffin suspiciously.

"I'm waiting for Mr. Marty Pearl," she said grandly.

"So are a lot of other girls," he said, scratching his head and peering goggle-eyed down her neckline.

"Mr. Pearl has invited me. I'll wait in the lobby, when he phones will you please let me know. My name is Muffin."

"What?"

"Muffin. M-U-F-F-I-N."

"You can't hang around in the lobby all night. Why don't you go outside with the other girls?"

"I am not a fan," Muffin said crossly. "I am a personal friend. Kindly let me know when he telephones for me to come up." She flounced off to a seat where she could watch the desk, and let out a sigh of relief.

It had not been easy. After the photographic session with Little Marty at the party she had wandered around cleverly avoiding Jon. There were lots of people there who knew who she was, and so she chatted to this group and that, until at last Jon had cornered her and said, "Come and be nice to Jackson, chat him up, throw on the charm. He could be just what we are looking for in America."

"No!" Muffin had snapped. "I'm sick of being nice to people. I'm sick of you with your deals. *And* your lies."

"Come on, Muff," Jon had pleaded, "this could be very important."

"Don't care. Leave me alone."

"You're being stupid."

"If I want to be stupid, I shall be stupid, and you can get stuffed."

They had glared at each other, and Jon had marched off back to Jackson, and Muffin had marched off to the front of the hotel and got herself a taxi.

Tomorrow she could make up with Jon *if* she felt like it. And if he had a good explanation for Jane's phone call. Tonight she planned to do something *she* wanted to do for a change.

The desk clerk was beckoning her over. "Suite 404," he said, "fourth floor."

"Thank you. I *told* you he was expecting me." She made her way over to the elevator. She had butterflies in her stomach. Ridiculous really! She could not remember the last time she had been *nervous*.

Little Marty was waiting for her at the door to

his suite. He had on a short white towelling bathrobe and nothing else. "Quick!" he whisked her inside, slammed the door, and locked it. Then he grabbed her and gave her a long and inexpert kiss.

"You make me *shiver!*" she exclaimed.

"You're really sexy!" he replied. "Come on in the bedroom and see my records."

They ran in the bedroom, holding hands, giggling. Laid out on the bed was an array of record albums all featuring Little Marty on the cover.

"I've made ten albums," Little Marty claimed proudly, "two of them golds."

"Fabulous. Shall I take my clothes off?"

Little Marty watched in fascination as Muffin shed first boots, then trousers, then top.

"You're so pretty," he said, reaching for her perky upright breasts.

She undid the belt on his bathrobe. "You've got a smashing John Thomas!" she exclaimed.

"John Thomas?"

"You know—your what not!"

"Oh. Gee, thanks. Shall I put a record on?"

"Yes. Terrific."

Little Marty put on *Teenage High,* and Muffin squealed with delight.

"Shall we do it?" Marty inquired.

"Why not?" said Muffin, and she lay on the bed and parted her legs expectantly.

Carefully Marty climbed aboard. Verbally Muffin encouraged him.

He came quickly, but then so did Muffin. So they put *Teenage High* back on, and started again.

Within an hour they had repeated the performance four times, and Muffin gasped, "You are superman! You are wonderful! I love you!"

And Little Marty said, remembering his previous sexual experiences with three dismal hookers, "I think we should get married."

"Yes," said Muffin, the idea appealing to her. "I think we should. Let's play sixty-nine and discuss it!"

Chapter 28

Not being an avid drinker Cleo decided that the time had come to get very very drunk. For someone whose entire alcoholic intake was limited to small glasses of white wine, she switched with a vengeance to double scotches.

"Let's go back to my place and get very very stoned instead," Butch suggested.

"I feel like getting good and drunk," Cleo insisted. "I am celebrating the end of my marriage, I want to do it with a bang."

"That's just what I had in mind."

"Sex maniac!"

They started the evening at the Little Marty Pearl party, then there was a drinks party in Fulham, then a film party in Mayfair where they bumped into Ramo, and he and two girls joined them.

By this time Cleo was well gone. The double scotches had moved on to champagne, and then brandy, and now, somehow, they were all back in Ramo's hotel suite, and someone was popping ammis under her nose, and she was trying to tell them that she *hated* the smell—just hated it.

Where the hell was Butch? Someone was trying to peel her out of her Chloe dress, and she finally realized it was Ramo, and somewhat unsteady she got to her feet, and insisted that she was taken home.

"But darling," explained Ramo, "Butch is in the bedroom with the girls, and so it is only you and me, and I want to make fantastic extraordinary love to you."

"No." Cleo shook her head, everything took off in different directions, and she felt filled with nausea. "I'm going home."

She wished that she had a home to go to. But the apartment in New York was no longer home, and until she got things sorted out it would have to be hotels.

She managed to make her way unsteadily downstairs, and was surprised to see it was almost light out. Christ! She had an eleven AM appointment with English actor Daniel Onel; she was going to be in great shape for *that*. She got a taxi, and concentrated on not throwing up. Outside the Connaught Mike paced up and down, white-faced and furious. "It's 5 AM!" he accused. "Where the hell have you been?"

One thing Mike had never been short of and that was balls. *He* was accusing *her*.

She paid the cab, and tried to ignore her soon-to-be ex-husband who was practically hopping up and down in fury.

"Well?" he demanded.

She squinted at him. "Something about you missing . . . Ah, I know. Shouldn't you have a blond draped around you? Doesn't look right, Mike, no blond."

"Are you drunk?"

"And tired. And I'm going to bed." She walked into the hotel and he followed her. "Go away," she said.

"I would like to talk."

"Go away and talk then, I'm not stopping you. I'm not stopping you doing *anything*."

"Cleo, baby . . ."

Anger struck. The lying, conniving, unfaithful shit. "Mike, baby . . . do me a favor and fuck off!"

She marched into the elevator, made it to her room, and promptly threw up.

So much for getting drunk.

The initial impact had been of the "fuck you" variety.

Caught with his pants down—figuratively speaking that is—it had taken Mike at least an hour to be fully outraged.

"Who was that?" Erica had asked, and when Mike had replied, "just my wife," he was suffering strong pangs of embarrassment at having been caught yet again.

It finally occurred to him that what the *hell* was Cleo doing hand in hand with a souped-up super stud like Butch Kaufman?

By that time he and Erica were sitting in the very same restaurant he had lunched in the previous day, and she was making conversations with various people at nearby tables who all seemed to be friends of hers.

"I wonder," said Mike, "if you'd excuse me?"

"Sure," said Erica, imagining he was off to the men's room.

He left the table, found a waiter, settled the bill, and left. He had no pangs of regret about Erica. She would be all right, she was surrounded by friends.

He taxied back to the Little Marty Pearl party, but it was sadly depleted. All that remained were a few drunken journalists getting a free skinful.

He wandered around the hotel's public rooms, but could find no trace of Cleo, so he taxied over to her hotel, and found that yes indeed she had checked back in that very afternoon, but at the moment she was out.

He then spent an exciting evening waiting in the bar until it closed. Waiting in the lobby until at 2 AM they politely asked him to leave. Waiting in the street until at approximately five minutes past five Cleo came wafting up in a taxi. Drunk. Sarcastic. Rude.

Now she had very nicely—oh yes, really stylishly, told him to fuck off. Language Cleo never used unless really pushed. Of course she was drunk, but what excuse was that when he had been waiting *all night long*.

Now she had vanished, gone to her room without even a goodnight. In the mood she was in he did not feel inclined to follow her. She was not in a forgiving mood. She was not in the right frame of mind for explanations.

Susan. Susan who? Oh *her*, well that was nothing, just a little slip, I felt *sorry* for her. It didn't mean anything.

Come back, Cleo. You looked sensational tonight. I saw your legs—Christ, but I get hard just thinking about you.

Back at his own hotel Mike restlessly paced the room. He would get a few hours sleep and go back to her. Maybe he would take her a present, she liked presents. Then, quietly, after she had forgiven him, he would find out what the hell she had been doing with Butch Kaufman until five in the morning.

Chapter 29

Somehow Jon found himself out to dinner with Laurie, Erica, and Jackson. Not the most ideal of situations. Not a scene that was going to drive Muffin mad with joy. Anyway it was *her* fault. She was the one that had run off like a bad-tempered teenager.

They sat in *San Lorenzo*, the four of them. Very cosy. Jackson had taken a strong fancy to Laurie, and he was engaging her in a secret whispered conversation which was producing much giggling on her part, and much groping on his.

Erica sat straightbacked and aloof, the original long cool blond. They had found her already there, unconcernedly tucking into a plate full of lasagne.

"Mike James did a vanishing trick," she explained, "but I stayed because I am absolutely starving."

San Lorenzo always had a scattering of spies for various gossip columns, and Jon knew that the next day there would be some snide mention of the fact that he was out with another girl. Not Muffin. Where was Muffin? Home in bed with an attack of the sulks no doubt. He would placate her later. Right now it was be nice to Jackson time. He was a key connection, a good guy to get in with.

"Where's Muff Muff?" Erica finally inquired, having finished the entire plate of lasagne.

"I don't know where you put it," said Jon, shaking his head in amazement.

"Oh yes you do! Or have you got a short memory?"

Christ! He could never forget his scene with Erica. She was stark raving mad when it came to sex. A true raver. He would never forget that one blazing moment when she had clicked those perfect white teeth hard down on his cock, and he had thought—oh no! She's going to bite it off. I *know* she's going to bite it off. Wrenching free had left him with some nasty scars, and a firm belief that you left the long cool blonds well alone. Of course that had been before Muffin.

He was glad that Jackson had not chosen Erica, although according to Muffin, Laurie had some wild sexual habits. Nothing violent though. Jon had discovered that Muffin and her girlfriends spent *hours* discussing their various sex lives. No details were spared. Who did what to whom. How big was it. Was a guy a good performer. Did he go down. Muffin seemed to know intimate details about every male in town. Second-hand details of course. Talk about equality. Muffin and her group could destroy any guy with one sarcastic chorus of —"Small!!"

"I asked where Muffin had gone?" Erica said sweetly.

"She was tired," Jon explained. "It was a long tough day, so I sent her home."

"Was she upset about that Anthony Private article?"

"Erica, would you be upset if you were the subject of a lead interview in a major daily newspaper? All due respect, my old sweet, you're a lovely model, but how often is your name mentioned next to your picture?"

"I don't need *personal* publicity. *I* never stop working."

"O.K. Great. But Muffin's going to be more than just another model. Much much more."

"You little Svengali you! You always were a terrific grafter. I believe you can do it, too.

"I can do it."

Erica tapped long fingernails on the table. "How about coming back to my place for coffee?"

"No, love."

"Home to your investment?"

"Nope. Just home to my girl."

Erica shrugged. "In that case I know you'll excuse me if I take off and join some friends over there." She stood up and smiled faintly. "When you change your mind, Jon, give me a buzz. I'll always have a soft spot for you—know what I mean?"

Jackson and Laurie were still giggling and whispering. Jon could hardly see the evening culminating in a big business discussion, so he tapped Jackson on the shoulder and arranged to meet with him the following day.

Jackson winked lewdly. "Thanks pally, tomorrow we'll sort some things out."

Jon nodded. Already he had decided what he wanted out of the American. He wanted know-all, and technique, and introductions to the people that mattered. After they had finished the Schumann Calendar photographs, America was the place to be. In America Muffin would become world famous, and Jon—with a little help from his friends—would be right there with her. He would offer Jackson a piece of Muffin—a small per cent—well maybe a medium per cent. Jackson did not look like the sort of guy that would do something for nothing.

In America Jon felt he would finally be able to get away from Jane. What a relief not to have to listen to that whiney nagging voice complaining about how terrible her life was. Of course he would miss his kids, but they could come over for visits. By that time he would be able to afford a nanny to bring them over. It would be great. A house with a pool. Several cars. Servants. Lots of parties.

Jon smiled to himself. Life was going to be really good. He planted a kiss on Laurie's cheek. "Be good to my friend," he instructed.

Laurie rolled her eyes. "You betcha ass, baby face!" she said with a laugh.

Well, it looked like Jackson was all set there. Jon hoped the American would remember who to thank.

He spotted Erica sitting with some friends and he threw her a cursory wave. He was quite flattered that she kept on propositioning him, but truthfully he just didn't fancy her any more. Home to Muffin. Pretty, cute, lovable, dumb, Muffin. Well no, she wasn't really dumb, that wasn't fair, she was just a bit childlike in her attitude toward life, and that was nice.

At twenty-six Jon was cynical toward women.

He had been screwing them since he was fourteen, and he had been through a lot. When he was married to Jane he had just been starting out on his own as a photographer, and it hadn't been easy. He soon found out it could be a lot easier. Mabel Curson was the middle-aged editor of a woman's magazine, and she was only too happy to put lots of work his way, and in return she wanted screwing at least once a week. In the fashion industry Jon found there were plenty of Mabel Cursons.

You could say he had slept his way up the ladder of success. Until Muffin. Muffin had been his passport to better things, and together they were making it work. It hadn't been necessary to service Mable Curson in two years.

Jon let himself into the Holland Park flat quietly. Let Muffin sleep on her grievances, she would feel better in the morning. He greeted Scruff, and gave him a saucer of milk. Then he took his clothes off in the bathroom and made his way stealthily to bed.

It wasn't until he reached out to touch Muffin that he realized she wasn't there.

Chapter 30

The phone woke Cleo early. She squinted at the clock and realized with panic that it was ten after ten. It had failed to sound its alarm bell at nine o'clock, or maybe she just hadn't heard it. Anyway, she felt terrible. An American operator was telling her to hang on, and she was parched with thirst, and had a raging headache.

"I can't hang on all day!" she snapped angrily down the phone, and when there was no response she slammed it down, got up, felt worse, forced herself into the bathroom and under a cold shower.

Her head cleared slightly and fragments of the previous evening came floating back.

Oh Christ! Ramo—naked and horny. Butch with two girls. Mike—or was that all a bad dream?

No time to wonder now. Eleven o'clock appointment. No time for breakfast. Fast make-up. Dress. Brush hair. Look shitty.

Gather up tape recorder, purse, notebook, pencils. Ten forty-five. Phone rings again. This time it's Russell Hayes loud and clear from New York. Wasn't it some unearthly time there?

"The stuff on Kaufman and Kaliffe is terrific," he enthused.

Yeah! thought Cleo, and I could give you more stuff on both of them that would blow your mind. For instance, Ramo Kaliffe has a foot-long cock, that she *did* remember.

"Thanks, Russ."

"I thought we'd use the Kaufman piece to open up with—going to send Jerry over to do the pics." He paused, then—"Have you seen Mike yet?"

She glanced at her watch, she was going to be late. "No. Listen, Russ, I . . ."

"Don't worry about anything. I'm here. I'm waiting, and if you want me to I can fly over."

Oh shit! "Everything is fine, no need for you to come over. I have to dash, I'm late for an appointment."

"All right, my darling. I just wanted you to know I'm here if you need me."

"Bye, Russ." She banged the phone down.

My darling indeed. Sadly, after this assignment it would have to be farewell to *Image* Magazine and all who sailed in her. A shame, but inevitable.

It would be starting all over again—in everything.

She rang down to the front desk and asked them to get her a cab. Ten fifty-five. If she was lucky she wouldn't be more than a few minutes late.

Daniel Onel lived in a small mews house in Belgravia. The front door was opened by a blond Danish au pair who smiled vacantly and ushered Cleo into an untidy living-room. "He won't be long," the au pair said in a thick accent. "You want the coffee?"

Cleo nodded. "Black. No sugar."

The au pair slouched off and Cleo took stock of her surroundings. A large room, very modern, with black leather chairs and couch, and chrome and glass tables.

Daniel Onel had obviously been entertaining the previous evening, for the ashtrays were all full, and dirty glasses abounded. Record albums were littered across the floor, and a vase of roses had been knocked over and lay in a damp mass on the carpet.

"Why do you want to include Daniel Onel?" Russell had questioned when she had given him her list for "Who's Afraid of the Big Bad Wolf."

"Because he's a very talented man, and women find him attractive. A guy doesn't have to look like Bobby the Beach Boy to be a stud."

"O.K.," Russell had agreed, "just asking."

But why had she decided on Daniel Onel?

Because she wanted to meet him. Because he was her favorite actor. Because even though he was on the short side, wore glasses, and was nearing fifty, he had a charismatic personality that appealed to women.

Cleo wished that she felt better. She wished that she could have stayed in bed all morning. Sometimes she almost wished she was like her mother and had never worked a day in her life.

In her marriage to Mike there had never been any question of her *not* working. Mike had always accepted without question the fact that she had her own thing to do. He believed in women's equality, and he didn't seem to have much respect for women who did nothing.

"Don't they get bored?" he had inquired about her married and idle girlfriends. "What the hell do they *do* all day?"

"Oh, they go to the hairdresser, shopping, lunch with the girls," she had replied.

"Scintillating!!"

Cleo had often wondered how he would feel when they had children—she wasn't about to give *her* babies away to a nanny. But of course that problem had never come up.

Daniel Onel came into the room. He was taller than she expected, and thinner.

He smiled, and said, "Sorry about the mess." He was wearing a paisley shirt open at the neck, black trousers, and white gym shoes. His normally dark hair was dyed henna red for a film. "You may as well know from the start I hate interviews," he announced pleasantly. "I find them boring for everyone concerned—you—me—and the poor schmuck who gets to read my opinions on everything from pot to sky diving."

"Well . . ." said Cleo.

He held up a hand to silence her. "However I read a piece in *Image* that you did on Senator Ashton, and it was so good, unbiased and fresh, that I thought it just might be interesting chemistry for you and I to get together." He took off his glasses and stared at her. "Verbally that is."

"Of course," Cleo stammered, suddenly unnerved by this strange man with his henna'd hair and white gym shoes.

"I must warn you," he said abruptly, "I do not want to discuss any of my wives except maybe the first one, and I do not have one solitary word to say on my last divorce. It was a terrible mistake—mind-blowing . . ." He lapsed into silence, and then bent suddenly to pick up the fallen roses and stuff them back in the vase.

The au pair came in with the coffee.

"Ah, Heidi," greeted Daniel, "have you met Cleo James?"

"We sort of see each other," said the au pair.

"Princess Heidi Walmerstein, may I present Cleo James," Daniel gave a mock little bow. "Here is a girl you could write about, poor little impoverished princess, arrived here with just the clothes she stood up in, and a few phone numbers of course, mine was one of them."

Cleo sensed sudden tension.

Heidi said, "Daniel, I go out now."

"Good," he said expansively, "spend a little more of my money, have some of the fun you say you're not getting with me."

"Oh Daniel!" exclaimed Heidi. "Do not always be to joking."

"Do not always be to joking," mimicked Daniel. "You've been here six bloody months. Can't you get your English straight?"

Heidi scowled. "I go now. Back in the later."

"Christ!" exclaimed Daniel, as he watched the small blond girl depart. "I don't know how I stand her. She's too young, too dumb, and can't even master the queen's English."

"She's very pretty."

"*Quite* pretty," amended Daniel.

"I thought she was your au pair."

Daniel roared with laughter. "You are forgiven for thinking that. Come to think of it she has got that fresh from Hendon look. But she *is* a Princess—I've met the family."

"How nice for you," murmured Cleo, and sipped at her coffee. It was unbearably strong. "Ugh!" she exclaimed.

"Tastes awful, does it? Come in the kitchen and we'll make some more. Coffee is not one of Heidi's strong points, expecially when it's for another woman. She nearly poisoned one of my ex-wives!"

The kitchen was in a worse disarray than the living-room.

"This place looks like a shithouse," announced Daniel.

"Don't you have a maid?"

"She comes and she goes. Right now she's gone as you can see."

"There's places you can phone and they send up out-of-work actors and people like that."

"Listen, love, if I had an out-of-work actor here do you think he'd be mucking around with a Hoover —no he bloody wouldn't—he'd be giving me an audition, wouldn't he?"

The phone rang, and Cleo was treated to a one-sided conversation—Daniel's side.

"She's driving me batty." Pause. "Well, of *course* I've told her." Pause. "She doesn't even *speak* it let alone understand it!" Pause. "I know, I know. I must." Pause. "Yes it is, it's the bloody same every time. If I wanted to be treated like that I could find a bird in Soho couldn't I?" Pause. "All right, old matey, maybe later." Daniel hung up. "I am going to tell little Miss Walmerstein to pack up her bags and get out."

"Look," said Cleo earnestly, "would you like me to come back later?"

"No, certainly not. I told you it would be boring. It will be just as boring later."

Cleo made the coffee; this time it was drinkable. Daniel produced a packet of digestive biscuits and they went back into the living-room.

"Tell me about Senator Ashton."

"You read all there was to tell." Cleo was really pleased that he had seen the piece she had done on the Senator. It was one of the best things she had ever done. A week in Washington following him around. Six hours of taped interviews—it was unheard of for him to give that kind of time to a journalist. Russell had said that the circulation of the magazine soared the week it appeared. Mike had been really proud, and a television producer had offered her an audition any time she liked for her own interview show.

"Are you married?" Daniel asked.

"Yes I am."

"Happily?"

"*I*'m supposed to be interviewing *you*."

Daniel threw wide his arms. "Interview me. Ask me what you like. Only don't ask me the usual bloody stupid questions."

"Why don't you just talk. About anything you like."

"What do I like? I'm not sure any more. I keep on getting stuck with things I don't like. Bad marriages. Bad relationships. Bad movies that I should never have done."

"What *do* you want out of life?"

"I want a beautiful great bird who only cares about me. A woman who is prepared to put me first.

189

A faithful woman. An unpossessive woman. A mother figure. A great lay. A fantastic cook. A lady with a sense of humor. Do you think she exists?"

"If she does I want the male equivalent!"

Daniel laughed. "Problems too?" he inquired.

"Who hasn't," sighed Cleo.

Daniel screwed up his face in a grimace of disgust. "Life would be so bloody simple if we didn't have to live it with other people."

"Is that another way of saying Garbo's immortal line—I want to be alone?"

"Perceptive little thing, aren't you?"

Cleo blushed. Little thing indeed! She was five-foot-six inches tall and twenty-nine years old. Daniel Onel made her feel about fourteen. "Why do you stay with Heidi if it's not the relationship you want?" Cleo ventured.

Daniel shrugged helplessly. "Habit. Loneliness. Have you any idea what it's like coming back to an empty house at night?"

"But surely you have plenty of friends?"

"Acquaintances," Daniel corrected. "Fair weather friends who are only too happy to spend time with you if your last movie was a big success."

"You must have close friends."

"Have you?"

Cleo thought of Dominique and Russell and Susan. "I think I know what you mean," she admitted.

"I have got a few close mates. People I have known from the beginning. But they have their own lives to lead. Their own families . . ." he trailed off.

"What about your children? You must be close to them."

"As they grow up they grow away in their own directions. I see Dick occasionally, he's eighteen

190

now—he's got his own thing to do. Listen, love, I'm on my own, that's it. I'm forty-nine years old and I've fucked up my personal life and now I'm stuck with some little Danish raver whom I certainly do not love. No, I don't love her, but it's good for the old public image—know what I mean?"

Cleo nodded. "I suppose so, but it seems such a waste. I mean, *somewhere* there is the right lady."

"Do you want to find her for me?"

Why did he make her feel so *nervous*. "I'm sure she's somewhere . . ."

Daniel smiled cynically. "Sure."

"Your sneaker's undone."

He bent to tie it. His hair was ever so slightly thinning. It didn't matter. Nothing mattered. He was the most attractive man she had ever met. He hadn't even noticed that she was a woman. To him she was a notebook, pencil and tape recorder.

Cleo cleared her throat. "Let's talk about your last movie," she suggested. "Is it true that you sent the producer a telegram saying that you would never work with him again?"

Daniel laughed. "Do birds fly?"

Chapter 31

Frantically Little Marty shook Muffin. "Wake up," he implored, "my Ma is at the door and if she sees you—like pow!!"

Slowly Muffin opened her eyes. Sleepily she looked around. Where was she? Oh yes. "Hi Marty," she said, snuggling further under the covers. She had been having this fantastic dream all about sandy beaches and photographs of her all dressed up in furs on the cover of *Vogue*. She wondered if Jon could arrange something like that—he was a very good arranger. Why did she always have to be naked with lots of tit and bum showing?

"Get up!" Marty hissed desperately. "We'll have to hide you, it will only be for a few minutes."

"Oh!" exclaimed Muffin crossly. "I'm so warm and comfortable."

In the distance, loud banging on the door could

be heard, and Mrs. Emma Pearl's piercing voice demanding to be let in.

"Come on!" Marty bundled her out of bed. "In the bathroom, lock the door and don't open it unless I say to."

"But I'm cold."

"There are lots of towels in there. *Please*, babe, just for me."

"O.K." She was still half asleep, and yawning. She allowed herself to be pushed into the bathroom.

Marty raced to the door of the suite. He opened it. Mrs. Emma Pearl came bursting in looking suspiciously around.

"Who's here?" she demanded.

"No one's here," protested Marty.

"Why did it take you so long to open the door?"

"I was asleep. Gee, mom, it's only eight o'clock, why d'ya wake me up so early?"

She peered through the door into the bedroom, and satisfied that it was empty, she collapsed sadly on to the couch.

"As if you don't know," she shook her head, "they are sending me back to America. A mother is bad for your image." Her voice rose to a plaintive shriek. "Since when has a mother been bad for *anyone's* image!"

"Yeah, mom." Marty studied the floor. "I have to go along with what they say—*you* know that."

"And who will look after you? Who will see that you eat properly? Get enough sleep? Wrap up warm after a show?"

"Gee ma, Jackson will take care of all that crap."

"Already you are using foul language and I haven't even gone yet. What about girls?"

"What girls?"

"Any girls. Just stay away from them, all of them." Mysteriously she added, "There are diseases so terrible that I would not even mention them."

"Yeah, ma."

Briskly she stood. "You are a good boy, Marty, in my heart I know that. I have to go now, but remember all that I have said."

"Yeah, ma."

She hugged him. "Think of your mother, and don't forget to brush your teeth *three* times a day. Teeth are very important to you. Do not eat candy. Remember to keep your eyes up in photographs."

"Goodbye, ma."

Tears were streaming down her cheeks, "Goodbye, son. It will only be a short parting."

Marty shut the door on her. Oh God! Freedom at last! Freedom to swear, eat candy, stay awake all night, and most important of all—girls!! Well—girl. Muffin. Sweet. Adorable. Gorgeous. Sexy Muffin!

Marty rushed to the bathroom and hammered on the door. "All clear," he yelled, "let me in."

Muffin had curled up on the bath mat and gone back to sleep.

"Let me in," pleaded Marty, "c'mon, honey, she's gone."

"I wish you wouldn't keep waking me up," Muffin mumbled, getting up and unlocking the door.

Marty pounced on her. "Gottcha!"

Mike woke late, swore, and called Cleo's hotel, but he had just missed her.

He shaved and dressed and brooded. He wasn't happy with the way things had developed. Not at all. In the past when he and Cleo had a falling out, they had sat down and discussed it, talked it out.

Always they would come to some mutually acceptable agreement. Cleo was by no means stupid, she was sharp and intelligent and what the hell were all these bullshit games she was playing?

O.K., he had fucked around. O.K. he was ready to take his punishment.

There was a knocking at his door, and for one bright moment he thought it might be Cleo, but on opening it he found it was Jackson.

"Congratulate me!" Jackson boasted. "Momma is at this very moment aboard a big beautiful jet bound for New York. I saw her on the plane *personally*."

"Very good," said Mike.

"And get a load of our coverage—not bad huh?" Jackson flung a pile of newspapers on the table, and a large picture of Little Marty with Muffin at the previous evening's party was on most of the front pages. "That little broad certainly helped things along," continued Jackson. "Looks good with our boy doesn't she?"

"Yes," agreed Mike. He really couldn't give a shit.

"Had a great piece last night," confided Jackson. "Hot English ass cannot be beaten—especially when it's laced with a little bit of Jamaica."

"How's the bookings on the concert?" Mike inquired abruptly. The last thing he wanted to hear about were Jackson's sexual adventures.

"Going great, should be a sell-out by this afternoon."

"What's Marty doing today?"

"I said he could sleep late, then it's lunch with some guy who's gonna do a full-page interview in one of the nationals. Then more publicity. Photos in the park, a couple of interviews for the music papers, then over and out for the concert. I'm gonna get him up now. You wanna come along to the lunch?"

"You're kidding aren't you?"

Jackson ambled off, and Mike finished dressing. His plans were set. Off to Cleo's hotel and wait for her, and this time things were going to get set straight. No more hanging around. He must have been mad to let her get away with sending him away. Fuck that type of treatment. No, this time it was all going to be different.

Humming to himself, Jackson knocked on the door of Little Marty's suite. He was pleased with himself. Pleased with getting rid of the mother. Pleased with the publicity coverage. Pleased with his evening of fun with the inventive Laurie—although he was a bit pissed off that Jon Clapton hadn't warned him the girl would expect to get *paid*.

"Can't you do it for love?" he had asked her.

"Fuck love!" Laurie had drawled laconically. "I don't get no money—you don't get no honey."

So he had paid her, laid her, and it had been worth it.

Marty came to the door and inched it open. Jackson attempted to enter, but Marty blocked him.

"Hey, kid, the coast is clear. Mommy's gone a-flying."

"I know," said Marty. "She came to say good-bye. Look—can you come back later?"

"Later?" Jackson consulted his watch in some surprise. "Listen, kid, it's past twelve, we have an appointment at one, and by the time you dress and we make it to the car . . ."

"I'll meet you in the lobby at ten of one."

197

Puzzled, Jackson stood his ground. "Don't you want to see the papers? You made every one."

Marty took the papers and started to shut the door.

"Hey, kid. What is goin' on? You got a little teeny bopper stashed under the bed in there?"

Marty reddened.

"Look, kid," Jackson spoke in a kindly tone, "flush her out and let's get it together huh? We got work to do. Let me arrange your sex life in future and then we get no morning stragglers. You point one out—hey, Jackson baby, I want the redhead— and I'll do the rest. That's what I'm here for, to look after you."

"I'll see you in the lobby," Marty muttered.

"O.K. If that's what you want. Wear the pale beige buckskin and don't be late. Oh and Marty, we'll let it go this morning, but in future all arrangements are down to me. We don't want momma back, do we?"

Chapter 32

A day spent with Daniel Onel was exhausting. Especially—Cleo decided—if you had a man-sized hangover and were also suffering from lack of sleep. She wished that she had spent more time on her make-up and choice of clothes.

She would have liked to have looked her best for Daniel. He was a complex, talented person, and she felt attracted to him, sorry for him, and strangely in sympathy with him. It seemed to her that here was a man who didn't quite know what he wanted, and yet was stretching out in all directions and coming up with all the wrong solutions.

Their meeting finally broke up when Heidi returned in the late afternoon with a group of her friends.

Daniel made a face. "I have to entertain the United Nations," he explained. "Heidi only ever brings home fellow Danes or the lower echelons of the chinless-wonder set. A real fun group."

Cleo smiled. "I only planned to stay an hour and I've been here all day. I've got lots of good stuff," she hesitated. "If you like I'll give you a ring when I've written it, and you can see it."

Daniel nodded. "That would be great. Do that." He took her hand and held it tightly. "I've really enjoyed our talk. I hope I didn't bore you too much."

"You didn't bore me at all."

He still held her hand and she didn't attempt to pull it free.

"Daniel," Heidi said petulantly, "where do you be keeping the champagne?"

"Well . . ." said Daniel.

"Well . . ." replied Cleo.

They smiled at each other, and he squeezed her hand before she extracted it. "I'll phone you," she promised.

"I'll look forward to it," he replied.

Of course I won't phone him, Cleo thought, in the taxi on the way back to the hotel. I must have been mad to suggest it. Any fool knew that if you showed an actor what you had written about him before publication he would want the whole thing changed. Egos were delicate, and constantly surprised at what other people thought of them.

As she was paying the taxi outside the hotel, somebody grabbed her from behind, covering her eyes with their hands.

For one blind moment of panic she thought she was being mugged, and then a high girlish voice was shrieking—"You're never gonna guess who this is!!"

"Ginny!" Cleo exclaimed, "what are *you* doing here?"

They hugged and Ginny said, "Supposedly working. But actually screwing!"

"Who?"

"I'm in love," Ginny said solemnly, "with a married man yet; and I think he'll probably have to divorce his wife for me," she giggled. "True love mixed with lust. I didn't think it was possible!"

"Who is it?" Cleo demanded.

"Shall we retire to the bar, and I'll tell you *all* in lurid detail. We're staying here, I tried to call you—did you get my messages?"

"When did you arrive?"

"Only today. I'm supposed to see Ramo Kaliffe about a package the agency is getting together. Do I look thin and beautiful? I've lost five pounds, does it notice?"

"Sure. You look great. Who's the guy you're with, Ginny?"

"Hold your breath and prepare for a surprise. Mr. Sex Expert himself—Dr. Richard West!"

"I do need that drink. Let's go up to my room and you can tell me all about it, or were you just going out?"

"I was going shopping—it can wait. I was only going to buy a long black sexy nightie—Richard's mad for me in black! So what is happening with you and Mike? Lovey dovey or daggers drawn? That Susan really turned out to be supercunt. What a liar!"

"It really is a lovely surprise to see you. How long will you be here?"

"Three days of suck and fuck! This guy wrote *Sex—an Explanation* and I'm having him explain it to me every inch of the way!"

Cleo smiled. Ginny Sandler really was outrageous. But she was a true original. "How did you and Richard West get together?"

"*You* introduced us, at that party for his book—remember? I guess we just sort of hit it off. I lured him back to my apartment, plied him with grass—his first time can you believe? Forty-six years old and a pot virgin. It was some thrill turning him on. I felt like a dirty old lady showing him my etchings! Anyway it all started that night, and here we are! He's doing some book promotion things, and as I said I'm here to grab Ramo Kaliffe on a deal."

"Knowing you," said Cleo laughingly, "that's not the *only* place you'll be grabbing Ramo Kaliffe."

"Cleo!" exclaimed Ginny in a hurt baby girl voice. "I told you I'm in love. I am even being faithful for the first time in my life!"

"I don't believe it!"

"It's true! Honestly!"

They arrived in Cleo's room, and as usual the switchboard had a varied assortment of messages for her. Mike had called three times.

Ginny was prattling on about New York, and her new grand affair, and the fact that she absolutely refused to talk to *that* Susan.

Cleo was only half listening. She really wanted to be alone. She fancied getting into bed with a good book to take her mind off *everything*. A full night's sleep was what she needed. Then in the morning perhaps her mind would be clear enough to think about Mike.

What was she going to do about Mike?

What did she *want* to do about Mike?

It was a difficult and painful decision, and one that would affect her whole future. Did she want to spend the rest of her life with a man that lied and cheated? Or did she want a chance to go it alone?

She just didn't know.

"Anyway," Ginny was saying, "I want you to have dinner with us tonight, y'know you can sort of slip Richard little items about what a marvellous girl I am and how kind and sweet and all that shit. He digs me, but like I want him to freak—y'know?"

"I'm sorry, I can't, Ginny. Maybe tomorrow, how would that be?"

"Great. Just great. Perhaps I'll try to fix you up with Ramo Kaliffe, how would *that* grab you?"

"Not at all. I have already met him, interviewed him, seen him in his full frontal glory, and that is enough thank you."

Ginny laughed. "You're such a kidder!"

Cleo smiled. If Ginny only knew! But she wasn't about to confide in her about Ramo and Butch. Confiding in Ginny would be like taking out a full page ad in *Variety!*

There was a knock at the door.

"Ah—the drinks," said Cleo. She opened the door and there stood Mike.

They stared silently at each other, and then Mike grinned and held out his arms and said, "Hello, baby!"

Cleo stepped back, avoiding his outstretched arms. He followed her into the room, coming to a stop when he spotted Ginny.

"Michael!" exclaimed Ginny. "Good to see you."

"I didn't know you were in town."

"That just goes to show you don't know everything! I'm part of the jet set you know." She fluttered her long false eyelashes at him. "You're looking as gorgeous and horny as ever."

Mike frowned. Cleo tapped her fingernails impatiently on the wall.

"I guess I'd better make a move," said Ginny reluctantly.

"No," Cleo was quick to reply. "I have some more questions." She turned coldly to Mike. "Ginny and I are in the middle of some business."

"I've hung around all day waiting to see you," Mike pointed out.

"That's not my fault. I never said I was going to be here."

"I think we should talk."

"I don't think we have anything to talk about."

"Oh come on, Cleo. We have everything to talk about."

"Look, kids," said Ginny, standing up, "I think perhaps I should split . . ."

"Yes," agreed Mike.

"No," insisted Cleo.

"Jesus!" exclaimed Mike, "when you want to be stubborn . . ."

"Stubborn? I'm just doing what I want to do. Isn't that the general pattern of our marriage?"

"I would like to talk to you—alone. I really don't think that's too much to ask."

"Fine. Don't just come barging in here like you own me. Make an appointment."

"Who with? Your fucking secretary?"

"If you're going to be sarcastic I don't think there is any point in us talking."

"You are not making this easy for me, Cleo."

"Oh I'm so sorry, what a shame."

"I'll come back later when you are alone. I don't think you're being fair to Ginny, she doesn't want to be involved in our problems."

"*Your* problems."

"I'll be back later."

"Don't bother."

"Christ! You can behave like a spoilt bitch at times."

"Fuck off, Mike."

Again. Yet again. Furious, Mike marched out of the room. Who was this strange angry woman who kept on telling him to fuck off? It wasn't the Cleo he knew. The calm beautiful woman he married. The lady with style. What had he done to conjure up a complete stranger? A person who was not even prepared to discuss things with him. All he had done was get caught in the act, and surely that wasn't a *crime?*

He went to the bar. He would wait an hour, give her time to calm down, get rid of Ginny. Then he would go back, and this time she would be reasonable, and they would talk, and everything would be O.K.

"Have you ever been to bed with Mike?" Cleo inquired casually as soon as he had gone.

"Huh?" stammered Ginny.

"It's a straight enough question. Have you?"

Ginny reddened. "Cleo, I'm your friend. How could you ask such a thing?"

"Easy. We both know you're not the vestal virgin type. You like guys, you like screwing. Mike's *very* attractive, I wouldn't blame you. Let's be open with each other. I won't be mad."

"I just don't know why you're asking me a question like that."

"Perhaps because I thought it might be fun if you gave me a truthful answer." She paused. Mike had called her a bitch—O.K., she would behave like

205

a bitch. "Listen, Ginny, Mike has done a lot of talking since he's been here . . . Isn't there something you feel *you* should tell me?"

"That sonofabitch!" Ginny exclaimed. "Jesus Christ, Cleo, the last time was *three* years ago. Three lousy years."

Cleo felt like she had been kicked in the stomach. A sudden hunch had turned into horrible reality. She had tricked a so-called friend into confessing something that she didn't even want to hear about.

"I don't know why he told you," Ginny resumed miserably. "It was never anything serious—just a quick screw for old times' sake. After all," she added, her tone becoming defensive, "you and I were hardly friendly then, and I had known Mike long before he even met you."

"So now it's you *and* Susan. What other good friends of mine has my darling husband been giving it to?"

"I don't know . . ." started Ginny.

"You do know. You know everything that goes on. I think you owe me at least a little information. I don't think you owe Mike anything—do you?"

"Oh God, I feel really bad about it. I mean I thought you knew about Mike."

"Knew what?"

"Well, let's face it. He likes to fuck around. I thought you knew all about his little flings and just turned a blind eye. I thought you got so mad because you caught him with a *friend*."

"He likes to fuck around," Cleo stated blankly, "and I guess everyone knows this, and I guess I'm like a schmucky wife in those TV soap operas who is always the last to find out."

"It doesn't mean he doesn't *love* you," Ginny

said desperately. "He's mad about you—everyone knows that."

"Oh great. Everyone knows that, and everyone knows he likes to fuck around. Beautiful!"

"You know how it is. Some guys can never get enough . . ."

"You're making Mike sound like a male verison of you."

"There's nothing wrong with that!" Ginny said defensively. "I am not ashamed of the fact that I enjoy sex."

"Goodnight, Ginny."

"Look, don't be mad at me, *I* didn't do anything."

"No, you're just a great big bundle of cute blond fun, and why don't I just give you a kiss and say thank you for humping my husband."

"Oh shit!" exclaimed Ginny. "I'm sorry if I have upset you."

Cleo stared directly at her. "*You* haven't upset me. You just surprise me. In fact I'm surprised at Mike's taste."

"I am not staying around for the insults. If you want to throw insults remember those three black girls Mike put under contract at Hampton. Dogs, all three of them, only Mike didn't think so. And remember Fanny Mason, tacky sloppy Fanny, well from her there was a little gift of the clap that Mike wasn't too anxious to bring home to you. Oh, and of course you remember . . ."

Cleo walked as calmly as she could into the bathroom and closed the door on Ginny's diatribe. She did not wish to hear the details of Mike's infidelities. It was enough that they existed.

She sat on the floor and mused on the fact that

this was the second time in as many days that she had had to seek refuge in the bathroom. First Dominique. Now Ginny.

Ginny yelled from outside the bathroom door—"I'm not surprised Mike had to fuck around. You're so cool it must have frozen his prick every time you did it!"

Oh it was good to have friends. Warm, honest, understanding individuals who were always around when you needed them. There was no one she could talk to. Not her mother. Not Dominique. Not Susan. Not Ginny. Not even Russell. Male friends had about as much loyalty as female friends.

In a fit of anger Cleo decided she would get on a plane, rush back to New York, and jump straight into bed with Russell. *That* would show Mike. *That* would be sweet revenge. But it was a childish thought, and one that Cleo soon dismissed.

Instead she went to bed. A night's sleep was what she needed. She told the switchboard no calls. She locked her door. She took two sleeping pills, and before long she drifted into a deep and uneasy sleep.

Chapter 33

Marty handed Muffin the papers. "We made all the front pages." Muffin squealed with delight, and studied the pictures with rapt enjoyment. Marty coughed nervously. "My manager is getting a bit uptight with me. I—er—don't want to tell him about us. He'll throw a stupid fit—you know the fans won't like it—that sort of stuff."

Muffin nodded understandingly.

"I've got a day of publicity, and then a big concert tonight. We could sneak off early in the morning and get married before they suspect. They can't do anything once we have done it. How do you get married here? Is it easy?"

Muffin giggled. "How should I know?"

Marty frowned. "In the States you need blood tests, you have to fill out forms, I think you have to wait."

"Let's phone Caxton Hall—that's where all the stars get married, they can tell us what we should do."

"Terrific idea!" Marty beamed. "Am I glad they got my Ma out of here, it would have been a real drag with her around—she follows me everywhere —even to the bathroom!"

He dialed the operator and asked for Caxton Hall. Muffin curled up on his lap. What would the girls say when they read about *this!* What would Jon say?

"Excuse me," Marty was inquiring, "can you tell me how one goes about getting married?"

"Well?" Muffin asked excitedly when he hung up.

"No sweat," responded Marty happily. "*You* need a birth certificate, *I* need my passport. You go along to your local register office and give notice that we want to get married—you put down we have both lived in the area for over fifteen days— then one day must pass—then like—yeah! So we can get married day after tomorrow!"

"Oh Marty, that's wonderful!"

They rolled about on the bed kissing and laughing.

"Gee!" sighed Marty, "I've got to get dressed and out of here. Now *you've* got to get it all together—think you can do it?"

"Of course I can do it."

"We have to be really careful no one suspects. Maybe you'd better go home and like cool it—then we could talk in the morning. I'll call you. If you could come back here tomorrow night then we'd be all set for first thing next morning."

"But what can I say to Jon?"

"Just boogie along. Don't tell him anything."

"You mean like nothing's happening?"

"Right on! We haven't seen each other since the party."

"I spent the night at a girlfriend's."

"You've got it. Now you have got to get to the register office and give notice. Isn't this wild?"

"Absolutely too much!"

"You'll soon be Mrs. Pearl."

"I don't know if I can last tonight without you."

"Maybe you can get Jon to bring you to the concert."

"I could watch you on the stage. I'd probably wet my knickers!"

"Gee, you're cute."

"Where the bloody hell do you think you've been?" demanded Jon. "I've been out of my head with worry."

Muffin bent to greet Scruff who barked with excitement.

"Well?" insisted Jon.

"Very well thank you," replied Muffin perkily.

"Cut that out," said Jon in an enraged tone. "I've even phoned the hospitals looking for you."

"I stayed with a girlfriend."

"Who?"

"None of your business."

"Don't be so childish."

"Don't be so nosey."

"I'm late for an assignment, and *you* were supposed to be at the wig place at eleven, you'd better phone them and get down there now. We'll talk about this later, but I am here to tell you that I'm really pissed off."

Muffin threw him a sulky stare.

"I'll be back at five," Jon stated, "and we might

have to meet with Jackson—he's big stuff in the States so try and be a little more charming tonight. He could do us a lot of good in America, look what he's done for Marty Pearl."

"Are we going to the concert?"

"I don't know."

"I'd like to."

Jon snorted. "Anything *you* want."

When he left, Muffin phoned her mother. "I need my birth certificate."

"Lovely pictures in the papers, dear. It's so nice to see you with your clothes on for a change. Daddy says . . ."

"Have you got my birth certificate?"

"Yes, dear. Auntie Hildy says . . ."

Muffin took a cab out to Wimbledon, and kept it waiting while she collected her birth certificate. Then she went straight to her local register office and gave notice of an impending marriage. High with excitement she kept the cab on to Harrods where she went on a marvellous shoplifting spree. Two pairs of tights. Blue-tinted sunspecs. A pair of stretch knickers.

For a grand finale she went in the record department and pinched the latest Marty Pearl single. Triumphant, she then went home.

"Tell me," inquired Anthony Private, "how do you feel about the eleven- and twelve-year-old girls who become completely out of control at your concerts?"

Marty glanced nervously at Jackson.

"We feel," said Jackson expansively, "that the kids are having a good time, y'know—letting themselves go."

"Marty," said Anthony Private pointedly, "how do you feel about it?"

"We feel," Marty's voice cracked, so he cleared his throat and started again, "well—like we feel the kids are having a good time."

"Yes, but don't you think that it could be dangerous? In fact it has been proved that it is dangerous. One young girl was crushed to death . . ."

"She wasn't at one of Marty's concerts," Jackson pointed out quickly.

"I know, but all the same . . ."

"If he thought," Jackson indicated Marty who was picking at a prawn cocktail, "that one little girl ran the risk of getting hurt, well he would just stop there and then. Give it all up."

"Would you, Marty?"

"Sure I would."

Anthony Private pursed his lips and scribbled something in a notebook. "What about sex?"

"What about sex?" boomed Jackson.

"I thought it might be fun if Marty told me about his first experience."

Jackson frowned. "This is a very religious boy. *Very* religious. He feels that he is too young to become seriously involved, in fact he doesn't even date yet. Marty's heart belongs to his fans."

"Are you saying that he's a virgin?" Anthony Private raised incredulous eyebrows.

"Is there anything wrong with that?" demanded Jackson.

"No, not at all."

Marty pushed his shrimp cocktail away. He couldn't eat. A naked image of Muffin danced before his eyes.

"Do you miss not dating?" Anthony Private inquired.

"Oh no, sir," replied Marty mechanically, "I have thousands of lovely girls who write to me and send me pictures, and their letters and love are more than enough."

"Yes," said Anthony Private, "of course."

Chapter 34

Ginny Sandler found Mike in the bar. She slid on to a stool beside him. "Just to let you know that I'm not a complete bitch, I thought I had better warn you."

"What about?" asked Mike shortly.

"I confirmed your story. By the way, thanks a lot, Cleo and I *were* friends you know."

"What are you talking about?"

"You and me."

"You and me?"

"You told Cleo—right? Why, I'll never know. Anyhow *I* told her the last time was three years ago. I don't think mentioning our fuck of the month arrangement would be wise. By the way, I want to terminate that arrangement. I'm in love—true love. I am going to be faithful. Order me a Martini will you?"

"You told her about us?" asked Mike incredulously.

"Yes. Didn't you?"

"No, you silly bitch, I didn't. She sussed you out, and of course you fell. You never did have any brains."

"But a nice cunt, right? You never objected to your little monthly visit there."

"Oh Christ!" Mike buried his head in his hands "Jesus Christ! She'll never forgive me for you."

"Boy oh boy—you and your lady wife certainly have a nice way of putting things. Forget the drink —I'm going."

Mike's mind was racing. Deny it. Deny everything. Ginny was just a troublemaker. A plump blond troublemaker. Cleo darling, would I even *look* at a woman like that? Yes I would, because I have been screwing Ginny Sandler since she was seventeen years old, and she is the most uninhibited fuck this side of heaven. A birdbrain. A fatso. A stupid cow. But an incredible fuck.

If he confessed that to Cleo what would she say? She wouldn't understand. Nor would she understand about the many others. And he couldn't blame her. So deny it was the only answer.

He went to the housephone and dialed her room. No reply. He went up in the elevator and hammered on her door. No reply. He wasn't surprised. He wrote her a note and slipped it under her door. Maybe tomorrow would be his lucky day.

Crowds of fans milled about outside the theater where Little Marty Pearl was due to appear. Young girls giggled and shrieked hysterically, some of them were wearing Little Marty Pearl T-shirts, some carried banners declaring their love for him.

216

Mike got out of his hired car at the front entrance and inspected the souvenir stands hastily erected. The latest records were displayed nicely, banked by a massive array of Little Marty Pearl posters.

Security seemed good, massive strong-arm men were everywhere.

Mike met with the manager, and had a short and friendly chat, then he made his way backstage.

Little Marty sat stiffly in a chair in front of a dressing table. His face was a mass of orange pan cake, and a spread of Kleenex were tucked neatly into the collar of his white satin jump suit to prevent staining.

"How's it going?" asked Mike.

"O.K.," said Marty. "I'll be glad when it's over."

"Sure kid," agreed Mike. He peered in the mirror at his own reflection. He looked terrible. Tired, strained, and uptight. He knew what *he* needed.

Jackson bustled in. "Mike baby, it's all lookin' good huh? Packed house, they love the kid over here. Wanna go to the press room for a drink, I got some guests. You gonna have dinner with us after?"

"What guests?" inquired Mike.

"You remember Laurie? Little black chicken I was tellin' you about," he winked, "and that photographer guy and his lady—the one in the pictures with Marty. Oh, and that blond you left sitting last night."

"Erica," stated Mike.

"I was never good at names."

"I'd like a drink," declared Marty.

"After the show," dismissed Jackson.

"Now," demanded Marty, "why not? My ma ain't here to complain."

"Oh shit!" exclaimed Jackson. "I knew I should have kept her around."

"Just a scotch and coke," pleaded Marty.

"Don't forget you can't take a piss in that outfit."

"I won't forget."

Marty got up. "Where are you going?" Jackson asked.

"To the press room."

"Sit down, *I'll* get you a drink."

"Can't I see the people?"

"No. After the show. You can come to dinner if you're not too tired."

Marty's face lit up. "Gee thanks."

Mike went along to the press room, and sought out Erica. In times of stress he found that sex was the only answer. "I have a headache," he informed her.

"You really are a shit," she protested mildly. "Why did you walk out on me last night?"

"Because I knew the chances were that I was going to rape you at the table, and I didn't want to put you in that kind of embarrassing position. Can I fuck you?" Honesty was going to be his new policy.

"My God, you certainly don't waste time."

"Don't believe in it. Well?"

"I think you're a little too direct."

"I think you're a very beautiful girl and a very modern girl. What's wrong with making love if two people want to?"

"Nothing. But . . ."

"But what?"

"But I didn't say that I wanted to."

"But you do."

218

"Do I?"

"You know you do."

"It's showtime folks," Jackson was saying, "let's go. Someone will take you out to your seats. C'mon everyone."

Mike put a hand lightly on Erica's arm. "We're staying here."

"Why?"

"Why do you think?"

"But I want to see the show."

"You'll see a show."

She laughed softly. "You really are a horny bastard."

"Isn't that the only kind?"

They waited until the room had emptied out, and then Mike locked the door.

"Hey," objected Erica, "there isn't even a sofa or anything."

Mike put his hands on her shoulders and peeled down the thin straps of her dress. She was wearing no bra and he bent his mouth to her small breasts and sharp pointed nipples.

Obligingly she unzipped his fly. "My God," she whispered, "it's jumbo jet time!" He pushed her to her knees. "I'll ladder my tights," she complained.

"I'll buy you some new ones," he soothed.

"The floor is hard."

"So am I baby, so am I!"

She opened her mouth and he pushed himself in. Oh, what a sensation. She had a way with her tongue, short feathery little strokes. He had to withdraw before it was too late.

He peeled the tights off her and the rest of her dress. Naked, she was very thin, with sparse blondish pubic hair.

219

"I want to be on top," she demanded, "you can have the floor."

He hadn't undressed so he didn't mind. He lay flat and she climbed on top of him, then she opened her legs suddenly, and he penetrated her deeply. She knew what she was doing.

"Are you ready?" she whispered after a few moments.

"Any Any Any time."

"Now!!"

Almost together, she was slightly ahead. And in the background they could hear the stamping and screaming of the teeny boppers.

"I always did like a big ovation!" murmured Erica.

Chapter 35

Muffin joined in the screaming, she couldn't help herself. All around her in the theater girls were freaking out.

On the stage Little Marty strutted and postured and made obscene movements with his guitar.

"This is one sexy little boy!" Laurie exclaimed. "Shakes that baby ass like a hot little piston!"

Jon remained unmoved. Jackson may have made this boy a star, but what did he have to offer? Good looking in an All American Boy Next Door way. A no talent, packaged in white satin and high-heeled boots. His voice you couldn't hear above the girls' screams, and his guitar playing was of the strum strum pause variety.

But the girls liked him, were obviously mad for him, and adulation was the name of the game.

It occurred to Jon that what would happen if

Muffin was put in the same position? She could hold a tune, she could be taught to strum a guitar. What a great idea! Boys would go mad for her. He would suggest the idea to Jackson, maybe they could cut a record. One guest appearance on Top of the Pops—it was a fantastic idea.

Little Marty was working up to his finale. The orange make-up was running in streaky rivulets down his face. The white satin jump suit was straining at the seams.

Muffin was bouncing up and down in her seat. Laurie was screaming with excitement.

Jon shook his head in amazement. He had never expected two girls like Muffin and Laurie to get carried away by this teenage corn flake.

At last it was over, and mob hysteria reigned while everyone yelled for more. The noise was deafening.

"Come on," hissed Jon, "let's get out of here."

"Where's Jackson?" pouted Laurie.

"I said we'd all meet at *Tramp*."

"Oh goody," enthused Laurie, "I love going there."

"Aren't we going backstage?" asked Muffin.

"And get involved in that mob scene. No thanks."

Muffin scowled. "I wanted to tell Marty how terrific his concert was."

"I'm sure he's got a dressing-room full of people telling him that. Anyway, Jackson said he's bringing him to dinner."

"Wow!" exclaimed Laurie, "I want to get my hands on that sexy little sweetheart!"

Muffin bit back a swift retort. Oh, wouldn't Laurie be jealous if she knew about the previous evening. Only a day to go and they would *all* be jealous!

She felt a bit guilty about Jon, but he would just have to understand. He would probably be quite pleased after he got used to the idea. Deep down she knew that he had never really wanted to get married again. Jane had just confirmed her suspicions. She had forced him into a commitment by withholding her signature on the Schumann Calendar contract.

Jon would still look after everything for her. He would still take all her photographs. They would be business partners. And friends.

Yes, Muffin decided, it would probably be a big relief for Jon in the long run. They had had fun together. Made it happen together. But now she had met Little Marty Pearl, and it wasn't *her* fault that they had fallen madly in love. It only proved that she hadn't really been in love with Jon in the first place—well maybe in the first place—but certainly not now. And anyhow Jon didn't want to marry her—and Marty did. It made a difference to a girl.

The restaurant at *Tramp* was bustling with activity; however, Guido had saved the big table in the corner for Jon, and he settled there with Muffin and Laurie.

"I hope I'm not going to get stuck with the check," Jon muttered to Muffin.

"Don't be so mean," she snapped back.

"I don't know who you spent last night with," said Jon peevishly, "but whoever it was they haven't sent you home in a good mood."

"I told you. I was with a girlfriend."

"I don't know why you insist on lying. We have

223

an arrangement. It's cool. One time with whoever you fancy." But it wasn't cool. He was secretly furious. Now that they were supposedly engaged, things should change. The arrangement they had was O.K. for two people living together, but it certainly wasn't going to be O.K. for his wife. When he got the business with Jackson cleared away, he and Muffin were going to sit down and have a long talk.

"Hey!" exclaimed Laurie. "Isn't that Butch Kaufman at that table?" They all looked.

"Yes," said Muffin, "very fanciable."

"Yes," agreed Laurie, "very."

"Do me a favor and try and spend tonight concentrating on Jackson," instructed Jon.

"I concentrated on him last night," pouted Laurie.

"Well concentrate again, and I'll do a whole set of new photographs for you."

"Oh, really? Just what I need. When can we do them?"

They arrived in a group. Little Marty, Jackson, Mike James, and Erica.

Jon maneuvered Jackson next to him, so *he* was happy. Muffin maneuvered Marty next to her, so *she* was happy.

"You've gone very quiet," Erica said to Mike. "Didn't you want to come?"

"Got to eat, haven't I?"

"That's charming! Very flattering."

"If it's flattery you're after you're sitting with the wrong guy."

She laid her hand lightly on his knee under the table. "If earlier was an example, I'm not with the wrong guy. I was thinking that perhaps you might like to spend the night at my flat."

Mike nodded. Whatever gets you through the night. And he wouldn't get through the night for thinking about Cleo if he was on his own.

Muffin enthused to Marty, "Your concert was terrific!"

Marty grinned and winked, and under the table they twisted their legs together.

"Gee thanks," he grunted. "The kids seemed to get a good buzz going."

Jon said to Jackson, "I've had this really interesting idea. Can you imagine Muffin on something like a TV special playing a guitar and singing?"

"Can she sing?" asked Jackson in surprise.

"Yes," said Jon confidently.

"Then it's a good idea. No problem getting her a guest spot. I think . . ."

Laurie suddenly threw her arms around Jackson's neck and kissed him long and lingeringly on the mouth.

Jon frowned. Not now, Laurie. Later. Concentrate on him later.

Butch Kaufman was approaching the table. Big, rangey, and blond, in blue jeans and a massive cable knit sweater.

"Marty, baby!" he greeted. "Great to see you. Hey, Jackson, it's all happening for you and the kid. Cannot pick up a paper without seeing that cocky um er little face."

"Who you with?" Jackson inquired.

"Couple of cute little ladybirds."

"Why don't you join us?"

"Sure. Why not. Hey Franco—bring my two ladyfriends over here."

More chairs were squeezed round the table, and Butch's two girlfriends appeared. They were a pop singer's wife, and a freaky black lady with dyed

225

blond hair. They seemed more interested in each other than anything else.

"How's the movie shaping?" asked Jackson.

"Slow. I've been over here three months now, and I'm getting beachsick. Man, I really miss my little um er shack at Malibu. Up in the morning, straight in the ocean for a swim, jog along the beach, barbecued bacon for breakfast. Can't beat it."

"Sure," agreed Jackson. "Do you know everyone here, Butch? Laurie, Jon, Muffin, Erica, and you know Mike James of Hampton Records, don't you?"

Butch shook hands with Mike earnestly, "Never had the pleasure, but I know B. B. and Mary Ellen. What a couple!"

Laurie licked her lips. "I saw *Romantic* five times," she announced. "It made me cry."

"I saw it twice," joined in Muffin. She squeezed Marty's thigh under the table to let him know her thoughts were still with him.

"How about that!" exclaimed Butch, flashing his famous smile. "I got paid peanuts for that goddamn picture, and it's one of the biggest grossers of all time. I bumped into the producer the other day—how about giving me some of your action I asked him—I got paid gurnshit. Tough shit—the guy said —tough shit! That guy has made millions from that film—millions!"

"It was so sad when you died at the end," confided Laurie. "You know it was so real."

Butch beamed. "That's why the film was a success, sweetheart."

"Hey," said Jackson enthusiastically, "you thought any more about making a record?"

"I can't sing . . ." protested Butch.

"Can Lee Marvin? Rex Harrison? Telly Savalas? What ya think, Mike? Great idea huh? Butch Kaufman on the Hampton label. Wanna offer him a contract now?"

"You were with my wife last night," Mike stated coldly.

"Pardon?" asked Butch, not sure if he had heard correctly.

"You were with my wife," repeated Mike.

A lull of silence had fallen over the table. Butch tried desperately to remember the names of the two girls he had ended up in bed with the previous evening. It was a lost cause, because he had never got as far as finding out their names.

"I was?" Butch said at last, his smile cracking at the edges.

"Cleo is my wife," Mike said icily.

"Oh, Cleo!" exclaimed Butch. "Yeah. Great lady. She's writing a piece on me for *Image*."

"I know," said Mike shortly. "She told me all about it."

"That's nice," mumbled Butch nervously. How much had Cleo told the husband? "She's a fantastic person. Have you um er been married long?"

"Four years," Mike stated shortly, "didn't she tell you?"

"Nope. Well you know how it is with us actors, always talking about ourselves. I never did get into any *personal* conversations with Cleo. Hey, Jackson, can I borrow your girlfriend for a dance?"

"Sure," agreed Jackson. Laurie jumped eagerly up from the table, and she and Butch went off together.

"What's with the jealous husband bit?" inquired Erica with an amused smile.

"I'm not jealous," stated Mike. "I just wanted to let that beach boy prick know where it's at."

"Where is it at?"

"Never mind. Drop it."

"Are you and your wife separated?"

"No, we're not."

"You just go your own ways."

"No we don't. Cleo is tired, she's sleeping, that's why I'm out without her tonight."

"What does that make me?"

Mike shrugged. He was still burning with anger at Butch Kaufman's sneering grinning face. Of course Cleo would never have done anything with him—he knew that for sure. But the bastard had probably tried. Any man would want to try with Cleo.

"If you make love to me," said Erica, "what would be wrong about your wife making love with another man? Fair's fair, isn't it?"

Mike treated her to a scathing look. "Whatever I do is my own thing. Cleo's different. She wouldn't be interested in making out with transient studs. She has me."

"What utter conceit!"

Mike scowled. "Call it conceit if you want. Cleo wouldn't cheapen herself, she has too much style."

"Jesus!" exclaimed Erica. "What a sweet old-fashioned boy you are at heart."

"You know something?"

"What?"

"On a dressing-room floor you're a lot of fun, but sitting at a table spouting dumb opinions on subjects you know nothing about, you're a pain in the ass."

Now that Butch had taken Laurie off to dance, Jon launched into a heavy conversation with Jackson. Muffin took the opportunity to whisper in Marty's ear, "It's all fixed."

"Wow!" he declared. "It's certainly gonna blow everyone's mind."

"I know," giggled Muffin. She squeezed his knee, and let her fingers slowly creep up.

"Watch it," warned Marty, "you know what that's gonna make me do."

"Put your napkin on your lap," whispered Muffin.

He did as she requested, and Muffin slid her hand underneath and got a grip on his satin encased hard-on. He had changed from his stage suit into blue satin trousers and a matching shirt.

Muffin was fumbling around. "Can't find the zipper," she muttered.

"Isn't one," groaned Marty.

Muffin giggled. "How do you pee?"

Marty's voice was muffled. "I take them off."

"That's rude!" exclaimed Muffin.

"What's rude?" inquired Jon, suddenly tuning in.

"Oh nothing." Slowly, Muffin slid her hand out from under the napkin.

"I think we may go straight to New York after shooting the calendar stuff in Barbados," Jon said. "Jackson's got some ideas for you that could really work out."

"Smashing!" replied Muffin. "Doesn't that sound smashing, Marty?" And they both burst out laughing.

Jon scowled. He could not stand Muffin when she got in one of her silly childish moods.

Chapter 36

Cleo woke early. She felt fresher, more alert, and more able to cope with everything. She ordered coffee, juice, scrambled eggs, and after gorging herself on that she sat down and wrote her piece on Daniel Onel.

Four down, only one to go, then her assignment would be finished and she would be free to do as she pleased.

She called the desk and told them it was O.K. to put through calls now. Then she phoned and requested a temporary secretary to do her typing.

The phone rang as soon as she put it down. Surprise, it was her mother, the impeccable Stella.

"We haven't seen you, darling," announced Stella. "Nikai is back from Athens so we thought a little dinner party would be nice."

"That would be lovely," lied Cleo. "When did you have in mind?"

"Tonight, dear. About eight. Wear something pretty."

The phone rang again. This time it was Mike. He was contrite. "I'm phoning for that appointment you promised me."

"That was *before* I had a heart to heart with *your* friend Ginny."

"Oh come on, Cleo, we have to talk."

"Why?"

"Well ..." Mike stumbled for words, "I want to explain ..."

Cleo laughed flatly. "Explain? Explain what?"

"You know what I mean, the things you've heard."

"And what about the things I've seen?"

"Nobody's perfect."

"I'm not looking for perfection, I'm looking for truth, and frankly, Mike, I don't think that you're the man who can give it to me."

"I can give it to you, baby, you *know* I can give it to you."

"Oh, Mike. It's very sad. With you everything always comes down to sex and smutty little innuendoes."

There was a long silence, then Mike said, "I need you, Cleo. I can't make it without you."

"You managed before I came along."

"You can be a hard bitch."

"So I've been told."

There was another silence. Finally Mike broke it with—"I've been thinking about things, Cleo. I've been thinking that maybe we should go back to the beginning."

232

"The beginning, Mike?"

"Start again. Right back to square one."

"It's a little too late for that."

"It's never too late," he pleaded desperately. "We could do all the things you always wanted. Like maybe a family."

"I'm sorry, things just aren't the same any more."

"We could make them the same."

"Not me, Mike, not me."

He hung up then, and Cleo sighed. It was going to end with bitterness. What was the point of letting him trot out all his lies and excuses? It would be a painful experience for both of them. It was better that he should think of her as a bitch, that way she could assume the burden of his guilt, and he would feel better.

The phone rang yet again.

"Cleo. This is Shep Stone. You'd better get that friend of yours off my back. She's causing me a lot of problems, she's nutty as a fruitcake, a real ding-a-ling."

"What are you talking about?"

"Your friend, Dominique, She is some mad broad. She is accusing *me*, Shep Stone, of stealing her diamond ring."

"Stealing?"

"You heard it right the first time. Look, I want to tell you the whole story, maybe you can clear it up. It's urgent. Can you have lunch?"

"I suppose so," agreed Cleo reluctantly.

"I'll pick you up in twenty minutes."

"O.K." Jesus! Yet another problem to be faced. What *was* going on? Before she could get as far as the bathroom to comb her hair, and touch up her make-up, the phone rang again. After this call she must tell the desk no more. It was getting ridiculous.

"Yes?" she inquired.

"It's Butch. I'm at the studio. Why didn't you tell me you had a jealous husband."

"You didn't ask."

"*Funny*. I met him last night, and like he was um er very uptight. You tell him anything?"

"Not yet."

"What do you mean *not yet?* He's the kind of guy goes right for the balls, and I still need mine."

"Where did you meet him?"

"*Tramp*. He had a blond draped across him, but he sure didn't like the fact that you've spent time with me."

"I'm sorry if it made you nervous."

"Aw shit, I'm not nervous. Just thought I'd let you know. By the way, what *is* the scene with you two?"

"I'm getting a divorce." It was the first time she had said it and it felt good. Her feelings toward Mike were becoming numb. He was so upset about their marital break-up that he already had a blond in tow.

"That's cool. Want to have some chow tonight?"

"Sorry, tonight is family night."

"Only *you* would turn me down for your family. Tomorrow? Or are you babysitting for a friend?"

"Tomorrow would be great if I don't have to fly to Rome. I'm doing Paulo Masserini."

"Rephrase that please."

"I am interviewing Signor Masserini."

"That's better. I have feelings too you know."

"Oh shut up."

"Hey—I hear you turned Ramo down. He's destroyed. It's the first time a lady has gotten a look at supercock in the buff and said no thanks."

"There's always a first time. By the way, wasn't I supposed to be out with *you* that night?"

"Yeah. Don't know what happened, we were all so stoned. Anyway thanks . . ."

"For what?"

"For not digging the Arab. I love him like a brother, but I don't want you to."

"I don't get it. It's O.K. for you to lurch off in the bedroom with two scrubbers, but it's good that *I* didn't indulge with Ramo. Why?"

"Because I'm a rat and you are a beautiful lady. And I believe in bullshit double standards which I really should shit on. Talk to you tomorrow. Ciao."

Cleo rang the reception to tell them no more calls. Her temporary secretary arrived to type up the Onel interview.

"Three copies," Cleo instructed. One for New York. One for herself. And maybe one for Daniel, she would have to think about that.

In the lobby Shep Stone waited. "I'm flying tomorrow so I am *very* nervous," he confided, "and your girlfriend is not making life easy." He took her by the arm. "I've got a car and driver. I thought we'd go to *Terrazza*."

"I can't stay long," warned Cleo.

Just as they were leaving Mike pulled up in a cab.

Cleo pretended not to see him, but he pounced over and grabbed her by the other arm.

"Shep," Cleo said wearily, "I'd like you to meet my husband, Mike James."

"Mike!" greeted Shep. "Haven't seen you in years. Cleo is *your* wife."

"*My* wife. Where are you taking her?"

"We're going to lunch, got a little problem Cleo's helping me with."

"Oh, really. Perhaps I'll join you."

"Perhaps you won't," interrupted Cleo sharply.

"I didn't know you were married to Mike," Shep said accusingly. "Mike and I go back quite a few years together." He slapped Mike on the shoulder. "How's it going, old pal? I didn't even know you were married."

Cleo wondered blankly if it would have made any difference at all to Shep if he had known. Maybe she would have been spared the flash of that red and angry cock, and the voice pleading, "Just a little head!"

"Are you writing a piece on Shep?" Mike asked sarcastically. "Are we on to singers now?"

"No," replied Cleo sweetly, "we're eloping to the nearest office couch we can find."

"Cleo and I met on the plane over," Shep confided. "She helped me through the journey, you know how I am about flying."

Mike ignored him. "I want to talk, Cleo."

"Then she introduced me to her girlfriend, pretty girl, but nuts!" continued Shep, oblivious to the taut atmosphere.

"If we don't talk I'm not going to leave you alone. I'm going to follow you everywhere, and cramp every horny little bastard's style." He glared at Shep.

"O.K.," said Cleo, "we'll talk."

"Now?"

"Tonight. Only I want you to promise me that if we talk, that's it—no more phone calls, visits, or contacts."

"You'll change your mind after we talk."

236

"Just promise me, Mike."

"All right, I promise. What time?"

"Seven-thirty, eight."

"I'll see you then."

"You going to have lunch with us?" Shep inquired of Mike in a falsely jovial voice.

"No, he's not," responded Cleo firmly. "Come along, Shep, if you have problems you'd better tell them to me, otherwise it will be time for me to go."

"Later then," said Mike warmly. "Take care of my old lady, Shep, she's very very special."

In the car Shep repeated accusingly, "You didn't tell me you were married to Mike James."

"You didn't ask. If I remember correctly on our initial meeting you were rigid with fear, and after that all our conversations were about you."

"You should have told me," insisted Shep.

Cleo frowned. What a boorish man Shep Stone was. She tuned out as he launched into a running commentary of the first time he and Mike had met.

Of course it was inevitable that she would have to sit down and talk it out with Mike. You couldn't just brush four years with someone aside without an exchange of words. There were things to be settled. Possessions to be divided. A divorce to be arranged. She did not want a penny from him. He could have their apartment, their furniture. Most of it was his anyway. She wasn't even sure if she wanted to go through the trauma of dividing up possessions. These three Diana Ross albums are mine—you can have the Marvin Gaye. In her mind she had a plan. A plan of freedom.

Wouldn't it be great to have one suitcase that contained everything you needed. You could just wander around the world. Take yourself wherever you fancied. Interview anyone that struck you as interesting. She had enough money to get by. She could sell the interviews. Russell would probably want to buy them for *Image*, and if not there were plenty of other magazines. After her interview with the Senator she had had plenty of offers. It was an idea that appealed to her immensely.

At the restaurant Shep made a lot of noise greeting the waiters, and generally revelling in the fact that everyone recognized him.

They both ordered spaghetti and white wine, and finally Shep confided, "I balled your friend you know."

Cleo nodded.

"She's very pretty. Like it was her suggestion, and I'm a red-blooded American male so I wasn't about to say no. We went back to my hotel and made love, and that was that. You see I'm a married man, and I can't afford to get involved."

"Of course," agreed Cleo sarcastically.

"Well, after that, she started to bug me with phone calls, and I tried to put her off nicely, but she wasn't having it, and the next day she burst in on me while I was in the middle of talking to my wife on the phone, and shit—I had to fight her off. She wanted to grab the phone and tell my wife everything. I had to get off the phone quick, and in the scuffle your friend got herself a black eye. It was an accident, but goddamn it she was like a wild cat." Shep paused to gulp down some wine. "Anyway," he continued, "she got excited and started ripping off her clothes, and by this time I knew she was bad news so I didn't want to do anything. Well this made her even more angry, and she started screaming about a diamond ring and accused me of *stealing* it. I'd never even *seen* any goddamn ring. Any-

238

way I finally got her calmed down, and the only way I could do it was by making love to her. I didn't want to, but there was *no other way*—she was screaming about getting the police and phoning all the papers. I *had* to do it. I can't afford that kind of publicity. I have a family image."

"You should have thought about your family in the first place," Cleo pointed out.

"I know that now. I made a mistake."

"Yes, your mistake was that you went to bed with someone who wanted more than just a quick fuck."

"I don't need a lesson in morals," Shep snapped. "I have learnt my lesson. I finally got her out of there, and I left word at the desk *no more* calls from her, *no more* visits." He fished in his pocket and pulled out a telegram. "This morning I got this." He handed the telegram to Cleo, and she read it slowly.

PHONE BY SIX OR I WILL CONTACT THE POLICE AND YOUR WIFE AND THE NEWSPAPERS. DOMINIQUE.

"My wife is in bed expecting a baby next month," Shep mumbled. "She's had two miscarriages, so this time they've kept her in bed. No excitement. No worries. If this gets to her . . ." he trailed off miserably.

Cleo shook her head sadly. "Why didn't you think of your wife earlier?"

"I wasn't doing anything to hurt her."

Is that what Mike was going to say?

"You must help me, Cleo."

"Yes, I suppose I must. Only I'm not helping *you*—I'm helping your wife. *You* make me sick."

Shep averted his eyes.

"I'm not promising that I'll be able to do anything," Cleo added. "Dominique has seemed a bit strange lately, but I'll go over and try and talk to her. Can you lend me your car and driver?"

Shep cheered up. "Of course. Anything."

Chapter 37

"I think," Jon announced, when they arrived home from *Tramp*, "that we are well in there, Muff."

"Pardon?" yawned Muffin.

"With Jackson. The Americans. It will be red carpet for you all the way when we get there."

"Oh."

"Is that all you've got to say—oh? You should be dancing around with excitement. This is just the connection I've been looking for. Come here little girl, I want to feel your connections!" She was bending to pet Scruff, and Jon sneaked up behind and goosed her.

"Stop it!" said Muffin crossly.

Jon laughed, and started to pull down her polka dot bikini panties.

Muffin stood up quickly. "I said *stop it.*"

"You're not still mad about that article? *I* didn't write it."

"I'm not mad about anything. I'm just tired."

"After your night of screwing," Jon snapped.

"I wasn't screwing. I was with a girlfriend."

"Oh, don't play that record again." Jon felt surprisingly high. Everything was slotting nicely into place. His divorce. The Schumann Calendar. Jackson.

"Let's take some pictures," he suggested.

"What pictures?"

"Personal pictures, for fun."

"I don't feel like it."

"Come on, you'll enjoy it."

"I won't."

"Where are the last Polaroids we took?"

"I threw them away."

"You what?"

"I cut them up in tiny pieces and got rid of them."

"Why?"

" 'Cos they were dirty."

"Dirty!" Jon snorted. "They were fun. After all they were only for us to see."

"I don't want close-ups of your great big thing!",

"You wanted them when you were taking them."

"That was different."

"Let's take some more."

"No."

"Why not?"

"I told you, I don't want to."

Jon shrugged. "What did Laurie tell you about Jackson?"

"Nothing."

"What do you mean—nothing. You and Erica

were in the ladies' loo with her for twenty minutes."

"Erica was telling us about Mike James."

"What about him?"

"He did it to her on the dressing-room floor while we were all watching the concert."

Jon grinned. "Good old Erica, true to form."

Muffin had started to undress. She was down to her sweater and panties.

Jon was sitting on the bed. "Come and sit on my knee," he instructed.

"Why?"

"I want to give you one."

"I don't feel like it," Muffin retorted primly. She pulled her sweater over her head. Jon made a quick move; imprisoning her head in her sweater, and caressing her bosom with his free hand. Muffin squealed with anger. Jon laughed, and maneuvered her on to the bed.

"I can't breathe!" Muffin pleaded.

"You are my prisoner, little girl," declared Jon, pulling down her panties.

"You're a bloody swine!" mumbled Muffin.

"So I am," he agreed, undoing the zip on his jeans and shaking himself free.

"Let me go," demanded Muffin.

"Not until I have had my way with you, woman." He entered her, and she wriggled about vigorously. "Ten strokes of the whip," laughed Jon, "or shall we make it twenty?"

There was no response. Muffin enjoyed games. In fact it was *she* that usually instigated them.

"How's it feel getting raped?" Jon joked.

Muffin remained silent, but he could feel her approaching a climax, and he joined her in her efforts.

"You really are a swine," Muffin complained after.

"What's up with you then? You loved it."

"I didn't want it."

"Yes, but you got it and you loved it."

"Well, don't tell anyone then."

"Who am I going to tell? The Queen?"

"I want to go to sleep now."

"I'm not stopping you." Jon shook his head.

Sometimes Muffin could be such a funny little thing.

Jackson, Laurie, and Little Marty rode back to the hotel together. When they arrived Jackson confided to Marty, "I gotta surprise for you."

"Gee, thanks. What is it?"

"Go to your room and wait, when I knock three times let me in." Jackson wheezed with laughter, and nudged Laurie conspiratorially. "I'm a telling you, boy, it's something gonna blow your little old mind. Take it from your old Uncle Jackson."

"I like surprises," remarked Marty, "when I was a little boy my daddy once surprised me with a piano—that was before he died of course."

Jackson laughed drunkenly. "This ain't no piano, but I'm here to tell you it's got legs—yeah baby! Legs! You like chocolate ice-cream, son?"

"You know I do, Jackson. Only I'm not supposed to order it on account of my spots."

Jackson doubled up with laughter. "This dish will knock your spots right out." He hugged Laurie. "Right, baby? Am I right?"

"You sure are!" giggled Laurie.

Marty went up to his suite, took off his satin outfit, and put on his towelling bathrobe. He hoped that Jackson's suprise was something to eat. He would give anything for a cream-topped banana split, or a double chocolate sundae. He wondered if Muffin liked things like that. He hoped she did, because when they were married instead of proper meals they could have ice cream feasts. There would be no one to stop them. Jackson couldn't go around telling him what to do when he was married.

There were three distinct knocks at the door, and Marty went to answer it.

Laurie stood in the corridor stark naked apart from "Present from Jackson" daubed across her breasts in bright red lipstick.

"Jesus Christ!" exclaimed Marty in a cracked and startled voice.

"No. Just Laurie baby," and she giggled, and sauntered into the room. "Come over here, sugar, and I'll teach you how to be a *star!*"

Chapter 38

Cleo had never visited the house in Hampstead where Dominique lived, but Shep's driver seemed to know the street so it didn't take them too long to reach it.

It was a nice looking house with a short drive-in and flower beds neatly kept. Two cars were parked in the driveway, and a baby's pram stood empty outside the front door.

"Will you wait please," Cleo instructed the driver. "I shouldn't be too long."

She hadn't yet decided what she should say to Dominique. Perhaps if she explained about Shep's wife, or maybe if she could just make Dominique see what a worthless animal Shep really was. If Dominique started to insult her again she would just ignore it. Their friendship went back a long way,

247

and Dominique was obviously going through a difficult time. Deep in thought she rang the bell.

Dayan answered the door. It hadn't occurred to
her that he would be home. He looked upset. He
looked like he had been crying. He stared at Cleo
without a flicker of recognition.

"I'm Cleo. Cleo James, Dominique's friend. We
met the other night, remember?"

"Yes," he said at last. "I remember."

Cleo stood uncomfortably on the doorstep waiting for him to invite her in, but he didn't move or
make a welcoming gesture, he just stood there with
a dour air of finality.

"Can I come in?" asked Cleo.

"How did you know?" questioned Dayan, "did
she tell you?" He suddenly started to sob, burying
his face in his hands.

"I'm sorry," stammered Cleo, "I don't know
what's going on. Has something happened? Is Dominique here?"

At that moment Isaac appeared. He looked
gaunt and worried. He took his friend by the arm
and gently guided him inside the house. To Cleo he
made a gesture of silence, and she waited with a
sudden horrible sense of foreboding while Isaac
took Dayan off.

He returned in a minute. "Dayan is very
shocked," he explained. "We all are."

"What has happened?" asked Cleo urgently.

"I'm sorry. I thought you knew. I thought that
was why you came."

"Knew what?"

"Dominique killed herself this morning."

"Oh my God! I don't believe it . . ." Cleo felt
her knees start to buckle and the blood rush from
her head.

248

Isaac held her and helped her inside. "Sit down," he said softly, "I'll get you some brandy."

She sat on a chair in the hall, and buried her head on her knees. It was unbelievable. Someone like Dominique wouldn't kill herself.

Isaac returned with a brandy, and she gulped it down.

"Why?" she questioned.

Isaac shrugged. "Nobody knows. She went through depressions, she had tried it before."

"But she was so young," sighed Cleo, "and she had—everything."

"Everything," agreed Isaac.

"How did she do it?"

"It's best that I don't tell you. It wasn't very—nice."

"Who found her?"

"Dayan. He phoned me and I arrived at the same time as the police. He has no one here you know. All his family are in Israel. I don't know what he will do."

"Where is the baby?"

"The nanny took her out."

"Did she leave any notes? Any explanation?"

Isaac shook his head. "Nothing. She was on tranquillizers, sleeping pills. Any little thing could set her off into one of her black moods."

"I wish I had known. I don't think I was very sympathetic towards her. If I had known she was ill . . ."

"How do you think I feel?" interrupted Isaac. "I could have helped her more than anyone, but instead I just complicated matters. We were lovers you know."

"Yes, I knew. She told me."

"A few days ago I told her we must quit. I

loved her, but Dayan is my best and dearest friend and I couldn't do it to him any longer. She was furious, she couldn't accept any kind of rejection."

Cleo nodded. "I know."

"She told me all about the American. I think she thought it would make me jealous—it did. Last time I spoke to her she told me she was going to the States with him. Was she?"

"He was married. More rejection. I guess it all added up."

"I suppose so. God, I feel I should have done *something*. But what?"

"I don't know. I feel the same way. But I didn't know she was depressed, I thought she had just changed." Cleo stood up. "Shall I go and see Dayan?"

"I think it is best if he's just left alone."

"I would like to come to the funeral. If there is anything I can do . . ."

"I'll tell Dayan."

Almost in a daze Cleo made her way back to the car. She wanted to cry. She wanted to sob the way Dayan had done. But she couldn't, no tears would come. Just blankness, and a numb feeling of disbelief.

Back at the hotel she telephoned Shep. "Your problems are over," she told him.

"Great!" he exclaimed. "I knew you could do it. What happened? What did she say?"

"She didn't say anything. She killed herself this morning." Quietly Cleo replaced the receiver. Yes, you bastard, she killed herself, and you gave her more than a little help. I hope you choke on the next woman you pull in for an afternoon hump.

Stella was immaculate in a black Yves St. Laurent dress, her short ash-blond hair newly styled by Ricci Burns.

"You look like sisters," enthused Nikai as he greeted Cleo. "Nobody would believe Stella is your mother."

"Don't be ridiculous, darling," admonished Stella chidingly. "Everyone knows I'm an old bag!" She slipped a thin arm through Mike's and flirtingly trilled, "And how's the second most attractive man I know?"

"Who's the first? I'll kill him," mocked Mike.

"My husband of course," laughed Stella. "Cleo darling, Mike is looking absolutely marvelous, what have you been doing to him?"

Cleo wanted to say—he's been fucking a lot of blonds, mummy. That always brings out the best in him.

Instead she smiled vaguely and admired a new star ruby and diamond ring that her mother was featuring.

"A present from Nikai," confessed Stella. "He spoils me, don't you, darling?"

Nikai agreed happily. "If I didn't spoil you, somebody else would."

Oh, what a mistake to have come, thought Cleo. What a boring egotistical woman her mother was. All she craved out of life were presents and compliments and a certain amount of adoration. Fuck her; and fuck Nikai; and fuck Mike too.

"You look tired, darling," observed Stella.

"I am tired. I had a lousy day. Do you remember my friend Dominique?"

"The pretty girl with the lovely red hair?"

"That's right. She killed herself today."

251

"Oh dear, how awful. Mike darling, would you pour me out a teensy weensy martini, it's all mixed in the jug on the table."

Was that it, Cleo wondered. Oh dear, how awful. Was that going to be Stella's only comment on Dominique? She had *known* her, *remembered* her. Even Mike, when she had told him earlier, had shown more concern than that, and he hadn't even *known* Dominique.

"I think," said Stella, "that after dinner we should be really naughty and pop along to *Annabels* for some of their delicious bitter chocolate ice cream."

"Unbelievable!" muttered Cleo.

"What, darling?" questioned Stella.

"Nothing. You wouldn't understand."

"How about a game of backgammon, Mike?" inquired Nikai. "You do play, don't you?"

"Sure." Mike glanced over at Cleo to see if she minded.

"Go ahead." After leaving the house in Hampstead the rest of the day was a blur. She had phoned Shep. Checked through her article on Daniel Onel which had been typed out. Made a couple of business calls. Then she had gone out and wandered around Hyde Park.

She had quite forgotten about Stella's dinner, and also her arrangement to meet and talk to Mike. When he had turned up at her hotel there had been only one answer. Take him along to Stella's. After all he was still her husband, it would not look odd as Stella knew nothing about their problems.

So here they were; and she felt trapped. Her only family; and it didn't matter one little bit if she never set eyes on any one of them again. Why should you have to like someone just because they were your mother?

Ever since she could remember, Stella had made her feel ugly and inferior and stupid. Isn't your mother young! Friends from school would exclaim in envy and surprise. Isn't she beautiful! And so she bloody well should be. She spent every waking hour at the masseur or the hairdresser or the beauty salon or the dressmaker or the health farm.

When other kids' mothers were tramping round the zoo with them, or struggling to maneuver a small boat round the pond in Regents Park, Cleo's mother would be getting her winter suntan in Jamaica. "Don't bring your friends home," Stella was apt to complain. "They're so noisy, I can't have my rest."

Somehow Cleo struggled through the dinner. She had to admit that she was glad Mike was there. He turned on his full wattage charm and saved the evening. Stella loved him. He told her how young and desirable and gorgeous she was all through dinner.

When the suggestion of *Annabels* came up again Cleo declined. "It's been a lovely evening," she lied, "but I'm so tired I just wouldn't be able to stay awake."

"You should take a daily dose of wheat germ and honey," Stella admonished. "It gives you lots of energy and does wonders for your skin." She peered closely at Cleo. "You are getting to an age, dear, when you should be looking after your skin."

What was it Ginny used to say—a mouthful of sperm a day keeps the doctor away—and beats the shit out of face creams!

"Goodnight, Stella." Cleo kissed her on the cheek.

"Goodnight, darling, and do write when you get back."

"You never reply."

"I just never find the time, darling. But write anyway, I like to hear from you."

In the car Mike said, "My hotel or yours?"

"I don't suppose you would understand if I said I just wasn't up to talking tonight."

"I don't suppose I would."

"O.K.," Cleo shrugged helplessly. "Your hotel."

Mike instructed the driver and they rode in silence, both immersed in their own private thoughts.

Mike was gaining his confidence back. His hotel, that was a good sign. Once he got her upstairs, once they got to talking, once they got their clothes off . . .

He certainly couldn't take much more of being without her. The previous long night spent at Erica's apartment had begun to pall. Erica, it turned out, was very kinky indeed. Almost too kinky for Mike's rich and varied tastes.

He had sneaked out early in the morning while she still slept.

They rode up in the elevator in continued silence until Cleo said, "This isn't a good idea, Mike, it's only going to end in a screaming match."

"You're wrong," he shook his head, "we can work it out, we always have before."

"We always worked things out that involved the two of us."

"All I ask is a chance to explain."

He opened the door of his hotel room and ushered Cleo in. Sitting on the sofa reading a magazine and wrapped in a bath towel was Erica.

Chapter 39

Muffin feigned sleep until Jon had left their flat. Rotten bastard, making her do it with him the previous evening. She hadn't wanted to—he had *forced* her. It could almost be called rape.

She had arranged with Little Marty to meet him at his hotel at seven.

"It will be cool by then," Marty had instructed. "I'm recording all day, and I'll tell Jackson I'm tired if he wants me to do anything in the evening."

Muffin packed a few things. She wanted to get out of the flat long before Jon came home. She planned to buy an outfit to get married in. White would be nice, something frilly and virginal.

When she was made up, dressed, packed and ready, she scrawled a short note for Jon. "Gone to a friend's. Will phone you tomorrow." That would stop him from worrying. It was a shame really that she couldn't invite him to her wedding, but of course that was out of the question.

The phone rang as she was leaving the flat. It was Laurie. "Come to lunch," she insisted. "I've got mind-blowing news!"

"What?" questioned Muffin.

"Too good to tell you over the phone," boasted Laurie. "You just won't believe it! I want to see your face. Two o'clock at the *Carousel*—O.K.?"

"O.K."

Lunch with the girls would be fun. But it would also be tempting. She was bursting to tell *someone* about herself and Little Marty Pearl, but to tell the girls would only mean trouble. They couldn't be trusted. They would *race* to tell Jon, and then Jon would try and stop her, and it would all become boring. Who could she tell?

Her mother. She could tell her mother. She could swear her to secrecy. Bubbling with excitement Muffin took a cab out to Wimbledon.

"Two visits in so many days," remarked her mother, "it's not my birthday."

"I know, mum. Have you ever heard of Little Marty Pearl?"

Her mother wiped workworn hands on a dish cloth. "Take a look in the twins' room. Little Marty Pearl's picture is all over the walls."

"Really? How terrific. Mum, don't faint, but I'm going to marry him."

"So is Josie, but I've told her she's got to wait until she's sixteen."

"Mum, I'm *serious*. I'm going to marry him, and we're getting married secretly tomorrow morning. We met at a photo session and he's lovely and we fell in love."

Muffin's mother sat down heavily. "What about Jon?" she asked at last. "You're engaged to Jon."

"He doesn't mind," lied Muffin airily. "He quite understands. He never wanted to get married anyway."

"Well . . . it all seems so sudden. Why tomorrow? You're not in trouble are you?"

Muffin giggled. "Of course not, mum. Don't be so silly."

"I always thought you'd have a white wedding, flowers, and Josie and Penny as bridesmaids. A nice reception at the townhall, all our relatives. Auntie Annie, Uncle Dick . . ."

"Mum! Is that all you've got to say?"

"It's a shock, dear. A disappointment almost. I was so looking forward to a nice ceremony, a *church* ceremony."

"Oh, mum!"

"I can't help how I feel, dear. I can't hide my feelings. Your father will be disappointed too. We're both so proud of you, and it would have been . . ."

"All right, mum," Muffin interrupted, "no need to go on. Perhaps you'll change your mind when you come and visit me in Marty's house—*our* house—in Hollywood."

"Has he got a house in Hollywood?"

"I expect so. Anyway if he hasn't we'll *get* one. A big house with a swimming pool. And we'll have two cars and lots of cute little dogs. And I won't have to take my clothes off in photos anymore. Imagine that!"

"There's a lovely photo of you in the *Sun* this morning. Your hair looks lovely. Do you want to see it?"

Muffin never turned up at the *Carousel* for

lunch. She was deflated by her mother's lack of enthusiasm, and after leaving there she went shopping for a wedding outfit. She found what she wanted, a tiered and frilled white calico ankle length dress. It had a chemise top which plunged alarmingly, and a matching shawl.

"Aren't you Muffin?" the girl in the shop asked.

"Yes," agreed Muffin.

"I would have thought you would have got all your clothes for free, someone famous like you."

Muffin's mood improved. It was nice to be regarded as someone famous.

"Well?" inquired Jackson, digging Marty in the ribs. "Was that a present or was that a present?"

"Thanks, Jackson," said Marty lamely.

"I told you I'd take care of things in future," he winked. "I tested out the goods myself first. Hot stuff. A little soul food is good for you. You want her again tonight?"

"No!" said Marty hastily. "I want to get some sleep tonight. Let me sleep late tomorrow too. I think I've got jet lag, I really feel flaked."

"Not used to it, huh?" Jackson laughed. "Not used to hot nookie as your bedtime snack."

"Guess not."

"I understand. I'll book you a call for twelve tomorrow. We're visiting the factory that makes your records—then we've got a photo session and we tape a kid's TV show. Nothing heavy."

"I'll see you in the morning then," said Marty. He glanced at his watch, it was six-thirty.

"If that's the way you want it, kid. By the way, that was a good session today."

"Mike didn't seem to think so."

"Mike's having personal problems. Take it from

me, it was good. Things are moving just the way we want them to."

I hope so, thought Marty. I hope Muffin turns up. I hope we make it tomorrow without getting found out. I hope by tomorrow night I'll be a married man.

"Goodnight, kid," said Jackson.

"Goodnight, Jackson," said Marty. When I am a married man I do not want you to call me kid anymore. I am going to drink and swear and whore around just like all the other married men I have seen.

"Sure there's nothing you want?" inquired Jackson.

"Nothing," replied Marty.

"See you in the morning, then."

Chapter 40

The shock of finding Erica sitting calmly in his hotel room was too much for Mike to take.

Cleo took off immediately. "Some other time," she threw at him when he attempted to follow her. "Like in a year or two."

He tried to argue but it was no use, so he let her go and went back to his room where Erica still sat. "What the fuck do you think you're doing here," he exploded. "Get up! Get out! Piss off!"

Erica put down the magazine and shrugged. "I thought you would be *pleased*. I thought I would *surprise* you."

"You surprised me all right. And you've fucked me up with my wife. Just get dressed and *out*."

"Suppose I don't want to go?"

"Suppose I said I could make you go?"

"Make me."

"Don't fuck around. Don't you know when you're not wanted? Just move it out of here—and fast."

"You wanted me last night."

"And I had you. And I don't want more, so just get it together and *out*." His anger was like a tired throb. It seemed whatever happened was wrong. Since Cleo had caught him with Susan there had been a trail of disasters. Now this. Cleo would never forgive this. It was the final straw.

Erica stood up and undid the tie on the bath towel she was draped in. It fell around her ankles. Slowly she brought her hands up and started to massage her nipples until they stood out erect.

Mike watched.

"Want to join me?" breathed Erica.

"No," he snapped, but he couldn't help watching.

Her hands moved down to her stomach, caressing herself lovingly. Then she parted her legs. "Come on," she pleaded.

Mike stood unmoving.

She knelt down on the floor and parted her legs further. She started to groan and her movements grew more frantic. "Please!" she begged him.

He didn't move.

She was nearly there, and suddenly Mike could stand it no more. The hell with it all. He unzipped his trousers and walked over to her. Roughly he thrust himself into her mouth, and as he did so she shuddered to a climax.

He gripped the back of her head, and rocked himself quickly back and forth. Three or four strokes and he was there. He held her head tightly, nearly choking her.

"Is that what you wanted?" he growled when he was finished.

"Oh yes!" she sighed.

"Good. Now you can get your clothes on and get out."

He was aghast. What came over him? Did he have no control? What if Cleo had relented and come back? Christ! He really was a shit. Maybe Cleo was right to want to leave him. Maybe it wasn't in him to change. Maybe he didn't really want to change.

He turned his back while Erica dressed.

"Are you sure you want me to go?" she whispered.

He ignored her. He didn't turn around until he heard the door close.

Cleo wondered if Mike had done it purposely. My hotel or yours? That had been *his* question. He must have known that there would be a girl waiting at his, so why had he taken her there? It was almost as if he *wanted* her to catch him.

She didn't understand him. It was just another shitty move in a week of shitty moves.

Anyway it had saved a long and painful conversation. There would be no conversations now, there would just be polite legal communications, and then a nice quick divorce. She would even be prepared to fly to Reno if that would make things quicker.

It all hit her at once. Dominique's death. The final realization that things with her and Mike really were over.

She got into bed and found that she couldn't sleep at all. Her mind was racing in a hundred different directions. The more she tried to sleep the more impossible it became.

In the morning she got a call to confirm her interview with Paulo Masserini, so she phoned the airline and booked herself on the next flight to Rome. She felt terrible, but she didn't want to cancel the interview, she just wanted to get it over with.

Mike phoned, but when she heard his voice she just quietly replaced the receiver without saying anything. She wasn't even upset, just disappointed. Once she had loved him. Now she just felt sorry for him.

On an impulse she telephoned Daniel Onel before leaving. "I finished the piece," she told him.

"Did you?" he questioned vaguely.

"Yes. I think you'll like it. Look, if you like I'll drop it off to you on my way to the airport."

"Are you going back to America?"

"No, I have to go to Rome to interview Paulo Masserini."

"You have my sympathies."

"Do you want to read the piece or not?"

"Certainly. Can I change it?"

"No changes. The original has already been sent to New York."

"I don't think I'll bother then. It will only frustrate me."

"Oh." Cleo was deflated. "So I won't bother to drop it off then?"

"Thanks for the offer, love, but there is really no point to it. If I hate it I'm powerless—I couldn't stand that."

"I don't think you'll hate it."

"*You* wouldn't—*you* wrote it."

266

"All right then," she paused. "I guess I'll send you a copy of the magazine when it appears."

"You're very sweet."

Very sweet indeed. Why hadn't he wanted to see her? Why had she wanted to see him?

It was much too soon to be thinking of getting involved with another man. Anyway Daniel Onel was very much involved already, she knew that; and anyway she had only ever met him once.

However there was something about him... just something....

Chapter 41

Muffin never had been able to write properly. She had a large childish scrawl which actually aggravated Jon as much as the contents of the note. Sometimes he felt that he was living with a six-year-old. She couldn't even spell friend.

He read her note through twice, and then crumpled it into an angry ball and threw it down the toilet.

He had planned a special evening. Champagne, a bottle of which he had brought home with him. Flowers, a big bunch of pink roses—her favorite. And two airline tickets for Barbados booked for three days later.

Now she had ruined it all. Staying with a friend indeed! Did she take him for a fool? She was shacking up with some guy, and while one night was just about acceptable—two nights certainly wasn't.

He racked his brain to think who it could be.

She had recently worked with Dave Ryle, and he was a bastard with the ladies. If Dave Ryle was moving in on Muffin . . .

Who would know?

Erica knew most things that were going on. He phoned her, but there was no reply. So then he phoned Dave Ryle, and made some vague inquiries about a new camera on the market. Casually he finished up with—"Oh by the way, is Muff there?"

Dave gave a dirty laugh. "La Crumpet doesn't put it about over here—more's the pity. You lost her then?"

"No," assured Jon, "she's just late home. I thought she might have dropped by your studio to see the contacts of the session you two had last week. She mentioned that she might."

"If she appears, me old son, I'll tell her you're waiting."

"Thanks, Dave." And he imagined them in a naked clinch laughing at the fact that he had phoned.

He tried Erica again. Still out.

He was more than slightly put out. He was furious. When Muffin came giggling home tomorrow he was going to give it to her straight. No more other guys—agreement or no agreement. And if she didn't like it . . . Oh God, what if she didn't like it?

Early in the morning when they were deciding that perhaps a couple of hours' sleep would be a good idea, Muffin snuggled up to Marty and said, "I shouldn't have spent the night with you."

"Why?"

" 'Cos I'm going to be a bride today, and we should have spent the night apart."

"Wow!" sighed Marty. "Look what we would have missed!"

"Wow!" agreed Muffin. "You're right!"

Neither of them could sleep, and eventually Muffin got up and started the long and elaborate ritual of getting herself together for an occasion.

She bathed, and shampooed her hair. Then while it was drying she started on her make-up—which on days when she wanted to look really special took at least an hour. When every false eyelash, and freckle, and glosser was in place, she put up her hair in heated rollers.

Marty, meanwhile, was peering at a new and angry crop of red spots on his forehead. He decided that the best form of coverage was to put a light make-up base over his entire face. He wondered if Muffin's heated rollers would do anything for his hair. Sexual activity seemed to equal limp and lifeless hair. He asked her, and with enthusiasm she carefully put rollers around the front part of his hair.

"Do you know," announced Muffin, "I once tried to dye Jon's eyelashes—they're so pale. Anyway he was furious—absolutely mad with rage. I think men should be into beauty stuff—it's fun. Shall I dye *your* eyelashes?"

"Not this morning," Marty replied quickly.

"Oh no, not this morning, silly. I thought maybe on our honeymoon. Where shall we go for our honeymoon?"

Marty had actually thought no further than the marriage ceremony. A honeymoon hadn't occurred to him. They would get married, come back to the hotel, tell Jackson, and then Jackson would take over. Jackson made all his arrangements, and when he was a married man Jackson would have to treat

271

him with a little more respect. Of course Jackson wouldn't be thrilled—but it would be too late for him to do anything about it.

"I don't know," said Marty vaguely. "I've gotta finish this tour thing."

"O.K.," agreed Muffin brightly, "we'll have a delayed honeymoon. How about Hawaii?"

"Yeah."

"It looks so super on TV. You know—Hawaii Five O—and Steve Mcgarret, and all those fellas in a boat. Come here, I'll take your rollers out."

When they were both finally ready they left the hotel by the back entrance. They were hardly an inconspicuous pair. Marty in his white buckskin suit with a magnificent quiff of hair—the rollers had worked beautifully. Muffin, like a pretty painted doll in her long frilled calico dress. They held hands and giggled nervously.

It was a short taxi ride to the register office, and it wasn't until they arrived that Muffin realized they had forgotten to acquire two witnesses.

"We could ask two people from off the street," Marty suggested.

Muffin grimaced, "I wouldn't like *that*."

"What then?" snapped Marty. He could feel a nervous rash breaking out all over his body. Oh god—what would Jackson say? He just wanted to get it over and done with.

"I know. I'll phone a couple of girlfriends."

"Can they get here *quickly?*"

"I'll tell them it's a matter of urgency."

A tall thin lady had appeared, and she ushered them into a small ante-room and offered Muffin the use of a phone.

Muffin phoned Kamika first. For a model Kamika was most dependable, and trustworthy. She

272

promised to be there in fifteen minutes. Muffin then tried to decide whether to contact Erica or Laurie, theirs were the only other phone numbers she knew off by heart. Of course they were both bitches, but how much harm could they do at this late hour?

She finally decided on Laurie. She didn't tell her anything, she just requested that she get there immediately without a word to anyone.

Marty had started to chainsmoke.

"I didn't know you smoked," stated Muffin in surprise.

"Jackson doesn't let me. Bad for the vocal cords. Did you get two friends?"

"They're on their way."

The tall, thin lady had been staring at them in silence for some time. She suddenly said, "The photographers will be here soon, do you want us to allow any of them in?"

"What photographers?" asked Marty in alarm.

"The newspapers."

"Oh shit! How do they know?"

The tall, thin lady lowered her eyes in embarrassment. "I'm sure *I* don't know."

Marty jumped up. "We can't wait for your friends, Muffin. If somebody has told the press, Jackson will be down here like a flash."

"But we have to have two witnesses."

"*She* could be one." He indicated the tall, thin lady. "Couldn't you?"

"No. I have to be able to receive people, answer the telephone. I work here. The registrar wouldn't allow it."

"Does he allow you to tip off the papers?"

"*I* didn't tell them."

"Oh, sure . . ."

At that moment Kamika arrived. "What urgency?" she inquired. "I have no breakfast, no time for make-up."

"Kam!" Muffin fell upon her with relief. "I'm getting married."

"Where is Jon?"

"Not to Jon, to Marty. I want you to meet Little Marty Pearl."

Kamika shook her head in amazement. "I don't understand . . . Yesterday, at lunch Laurie said that she and . . ."

"Laurie will be here in a minute," interrupted Muffin.

"Laurie?" questioned Marty, a confused blush spreading under his make-up.

"You English girls are so—liberal," said Kamika. "In Japan . . ."

"Why ask Laurie?" snapped Marty.

"Why not?" snapped back Muffin.

"Well, she's er—well she's Jackson's friend."

"I didn't tell her anything."

"It was stupid to ask her."

"*So sorry*. I didn't exactly have a huge bloody choice."

Laurie burst in then, clad in a button through jeans dress which concealed little. "Hey. The streets are alive with photographers." She raised her shades. "Marty! What are *you* doing here. Jesus! I must take a pee. Muffin baby, what *is* going on?"

"We're getting married!" Muffin declared triumphantly, "Marty and me."

"Whaaaaaat?"

"Let's go," said Marty quickly. "Let's do it and get out of here."

"I'll show you through," said the tall, thin lady primly.

"I'm *nervous!*" exclaimed Muffin.

Laurie shook her head. "I guess I'm just dreaming. This is unreal."

"Laurie," asked Kamika, "did you not say at lunch yesterday that you and . . ."

"Shush! We're at a wedding, Kam. Let's just cool it with the gossip."

They all trooped into the room where the marriage was to take place. The registrar appeared, and without further ceremony he proceeded with the legalities of getting married.

Fifteen minutes later it was all over. Marty had forgotten to purchase a wedding ring, so Kamika slipped hers off and lent it to him to put on Muffin's finger.

"I just don't believe this whole thing!" whispered Laurie. "If I had known what was happening I'd have dressed for the occasion."

"We're married!" Muffin exclaimed, as they left the room. "I'm Mrs. Marty Pearl." She hugged Marty who appeared to be in somewhat of a daze. "Let's go back to the flat and celebrate!"

"What flat?" asked Laurie.

"My flat?"

"What about Jon? Doesn't he mind?"

"Oh creeps! I forgot about Jon. He doesn't know."

"Doesn't know! Oh baby, I want to go home."

"I think I go home too," joined in Kamika.

"O.K.," pouted Muffin. "Let's go to the Dorchester, Marty, that would be fun. I've always wanted to go there for breakfast."

Outside they were besieged by photographers.

"Wow!" exclaimed Muffin. "Now I *really* feel famous!"

Chapter 42

"Do you mind if I smoke?" asked the fat man on her left.

Cleo smiled. Right on cue—she had known exactly when he would deem it the right moment to strike up a conversation.

The fat man took her smile as encouragement. "I'm not the world's best flyer," he confessed.

"I bet you're not the world's best anything!" replied Cleo.

"Pardon?" He was not sure that he had heard her correctly.

"You should really go on a diet," observed Cleo. "Too much cholesterol. A middle-aged man like you is asking for a heart attack."

The fat man reddened. "Excuse me." He headed for the back of the plane where he could chat up the hostess without fear of being insulted.

Cleo yawned. In the morning she had felt terrible, now she felt good for the first time in days. She felt free. She felt exultant. Was this the way you were supposed to feel when you decided to get a divorce? Probably not—but the hell with it. She felt great! Perhaps going without sleep was good for you.

A British pop group was aboard the plane, and they were reeling up and down the aisles, generally annoying everyone. There was one, about nineteen, with long black freaky curls and horny green eyes. Cleo smiled at him. He smiled back.

Oh how sweet to be a baby-snatcher!

If she was Ginny she would chat him up without further ado. He must be at least ten years younger than her.

He kept on passing by in his too tight jeans and sequinned jacket.

The fat man returned and squeezed back into his seat without a word.

Cleo got up and went to the back of the plane where she leafed through the magazine rack. Long black freaky curls appeared and studied her through cynical nineteen-year-old eyes.

"Wanna joint?" he finally inquired in American cockney tones.

"Here?"

"Naw. We can squeeze in the john together. I can give ya more than a joint." He winked hopefully.

An airborne fuck! A fantasy that Mike had always wanted to play out. But going with strangers had never been her style, tempting as the offer was. "No, thanks." She smiled to show that there was no animosity.

"O.K.," freaky curls shrugged. "Just thought it might be a groove."

And well it might have been. Perhaps with Daniel Onel it might have been more than a groove —but then again screwing in aeroplanes was probably not Daniel's scene. There she went again— thinking about Daniel.

There was a car at Rome airport to meet her and take her to her hotel. The publicist for Paulo Masserini met her in the lobby and confirmed her appointment with the star at four o'clock.

Reports were that Paulo Masserini was a conceited egomaniac, but at least he seemed to be an organized one.

She was getting bored with interviewing actors. There was not enough meat on the bones to make a meal, and she was hungry for a politician. Ramo, Butch, Sami, Daniel, now Paulo. Some women would give anything just to meet those men, but they were only ordinary people, who by their looks and talent and charisma had been propelled into positions of great fame. A man who had achieved things with his brain was a far more interesting proposition.

Still, she could not complain. Butch Kaufman had helped her make up her mind about her future. Daniel Onel had made her realize that Mike was no longer the most interesting and attractive man around. In retrospect Mike had stopped being that a long time ago.

Paulo Masserini was all that everyone had said he would be. Tall, blondish, fortyish. With blue eyes that pierced right through you, and an Italian flavored accent that smoothed over you like milk chocolate.

He kissed Cleo's hand, ordered her a Pernod

and milk—because that was what he was drinking—and launched into a thousand and one stories about how witty, handsome, and sexy he was.

God, but he was boring! For once in her career Cleo was unable to summon up that fixed look of interest that convinced the person who was being interviewed that they were indeed irresistibly interesting.

Openly she yawned, and her cassette tape came to the end and she couldn't be bothered to turn it over.

What a way to make a living. She needed a holiday. Interviewing actors was enough to make anyone need a holiday.

After two hours his wife arrived to collect him. She was a large lady of mammoth dimensions. She looked more like his mother than his wife. He did not seem anxious to go, and there followed a short, loud argument in Italian.

Cleo sat blankly through it. She didn't have an interview, there was nothing he had said that was remotely interesting enough to repeat.

Or maybe it was her. Maybe she was losing her touch.

At last his wife led him away into the protective custody of his white Rolls Royce.

"He is a marvelous man!" the publicist said loyally.

"Quite a talker," observed Cleo.

"But interesting."

"Of course."

"You have a good interview?"

"I'm sure I have more than enough."

"Oh. There is a message for you. Signor Kaufman will be arriving at the hotel by six. He is expecting you to dine with him."

They sat in a pavement restaurant.

"I er um didn't think that a lady who was just about to get a divorce should spend the night alone in Rome."

"That's very thoughtful of you."

"Not so thoughtful. I've been dying for a plate of decent spaghetti for weeks."

"How did you know where I was?"

"A little detective work."

"Was it difficult to get away? What about the movie?"

"I had two days off. I didn't tell them—there would only have been a hassle. Anyway we'll be back in the morning. Jeeze, but this wine is *good!* So tell me about pain in the ass Masserini? Still as full of bullshit as ever?"

"I guess so. Let's face it—an actor is an actor. I think I have a lousy interview."

"Don't insult the profession by calling Masserini an actor. He's a lump of Italian pigshit."

"You really like him, don't you?"

"I really like you." Butch stared at her searchingly. "What do you say?"

"About what?"

"About us? Like er um how about giving things a try?"

"What things?"

"Like Malibu—the house. Living together. Moving in. Having a few laughs."

"We hardly know each other."

"Don't give me that sweet old-fashioned girl crap. I think we could make things happen together. What's to lose?"

"I thought you had a girl living with you."

"She's just a friend—nothing heavy. I would like to play at being heavy with you."

"I'm just climbing out of a marriage."

"Climb in with me. I finish the movie in a week—we could fly back to L.A. together. No hassles, just fun."

Cleo laughed. "This is so sudden..."

Butch laughed. "Whoever is writing your dialogue must be fired immediately! Finish your spaghetti and we'll go to a disco and get chased by the papperazzi."

Being with Butch made her feel safe. He was the sort of man you could be involved with without being involved with. And most important—he was totally honest.

Later, in bed, Cleo considered his proposition. A few weeks—maybe even months—lying around at Malibu could be just what she needed. She could see lawyers in California to arrange her divorce. She could stop work for a while and just relax. Butch was nice, easy to be with, they got along. What was there to lose? He was also a stud in bed, and maybe that's what she could do with right now. A little ego boosting in that direction after Mike was just what she needed.

In the morning she said, "O.K. Let's give it a try, Mister Kaufman."

He grinned. "Good decision. We can have some laughs, see what happens..."

"Yes," she agreed, "we'll see what happens."

Chapter 43

The jostling crowds terrified Marty. People pushing and shoving, and photographers yelling for him to look their way.

Where had all these people come from? They were running in all directions, joining the back of the crowd, craning to see what was happening. A girl clung on to Marty's sleeve, he brushed her off. Where was his car? Where was Jackson?

Realization dawned. There was no car. There was no Jackson.

Muffin was unconcernedly posing for the photographers; she didn't seem to mind the crush, she didn't even appear to be aware of it.

Marty pulled her back inside the register office and slammed the door shut. He was perspiring and out of breath.

"What's the matter?" asked Muffin, slightly annoyed at being yanked out of the spotlight.

"Those crowds, they're dangerous."

"Don't be so silly!"

"Call us a taxi," Marty informed the tall, thin lady. "Is there a back way out?"

"I like having photos taken," pouted Muffin.

Marty didn't reply. His stomach hurt. He had a mild ulcer that played up under strain. His mother usually carried his pills for him. Now Jackson probably had them.

The taxi arrived, and they were ushered out the back way, but photographers had gathered there also, and there was more shoving and pushing.

"This is fun!" exclaimed Muffin, eyes sparkling.

"I've got a belly ache," complained Marty.

Their taxi was followed, and more pictures were taken outside the Dorchester.

"I'm going to eat a huge breakfast," announced Muffin, "eggs, bacon, sausages, and champagne!"

"I feel sick," declared Marty.

Waking up was never the best time of the day for Jackson. He usually had a hangover, and a million and one minor problems to deal with.

His immediate problem on this particular morning was how to get rid of Erica. He had encountered her leaving Mike James' room the previous evening, and since he was alone, he had automatically invited her to his room for a drink. One of Jackson's mottoes was never pass up a going opportunity. Of course, after polishing off a very fine bottle of brandy, they had ended up in bed. She was a maniac! Dangerous. Even Jackson wasn't ready for a repeat performance. He just wanted to get her awake and out.

He slid quietly out of bed, and grabbing some clothes locked himself in the bathroom.

Ruefully he examined his body. He was a mass of bites and scratches. He ached all over. Talk about a hungry woman! She acted like there hadn't been a man in years. Perhaps Mike James wasn't all he was cracked up to be. He had been dying to ask her, but talking was not part of her curriculum.

Quickly he dressed. Would Erica be wanting money like Laurie? *She* should be paying *him*.

The phone beside the bed began to ring, and before Jackson could reach it, Erica stretched out a long naked arm and picked it up. "Yes?" she breathed.

Jackson removed it from her. "Hello," he snapped, "Jackson here." And then he wished he hadn't. He wished he had stayed in bed asleep.

Jon didn't sleep at all. He was so annoyed at Muffin's behavior that he stayed up all night brooding about it. By morning he had bloodshot eyes, and he didn't feel at all like getting it together and photographing a fashion session.

He was just about to pick up the phone and cancel, when it rang.

It was Laurie. "I think I should tell you," she said.

"What?" questioned Jon.

"After all I'm just as much your friend as Muffin's."

"What?"

"And I really don't think she's being very fair."

"Is it Dave Ryle?"

"Huh?"

"Nothing. What do you want to tell me?"

Laurie took a deep breath, "Muffin and Little Marty Pearl just got married."

"Don't be stupid," responded Jon in disgust. "Is she there with you? Is this her idea of a joke?"

"It's a fact, Jon. I was *there*. They just got married."

"Are you serious?"

"'Course I am. I wouldn't joke about something like this. I think it's . . ."

"Where are they?" asked Jon urgently.

"I think they said they were going to the Dorchester for a wedding breakfast. I didn't go. I . . ."

"Is Jackson with them?"

"He doesn't know. That's the whole point—no one knows. They . . ."

Jon hung up. That bitch! That dirty little bitch. How could she do this to him?

He phoned Jackson and a girl answered. It was Erica.

"He just rushed out of here," she drawled. "What *is* going on?"

Jon was already dashing out of the flat.

Marty's stomach pains were getting worse, and when he saw Jackson come striding into the restaurant his only thought was that he would be carrying his stomach pills.

"You little cocksucker!" smiled Jackson, pulling up a chair, and waving amicably at a couple of reporters who had taken up residence at a nearby table. "I told you, you get a hot nut it's *me* you run to. *Me*—not little Miss Golden Tits."

"I've got my ulcer pains," complained Marty. "Can I have my pills?"

"I'll stuff your goddamn pills up your goddamn ass. What the fuck game do you call this? Because I

286

call it marrying yourself right out of a job."

"Morning," chipped in Muffin brightly. "Some-one got out of bed the wrong side today."

"Shut up, you little cunt. Do you *know* what you've done?"

"I want my pills," whined Marty. He was thoroughly fed up with the whole thing, and he was glad that Jackson had arrived to take care of everything.

"Don't you call *me* names," asserted Muffin. "Marty, did you hear what he called me?"

"Where's your boyfriend?" demanded Jackson. "Does *he* know about this?"

Muffin scowled.

"Jesus! You are two stupid kids! Whatever got into you both? Jesus!"

"We love each other," declared Muffin.

"I am gonna get the check, and the three of us are gonna walk nicely out of here, and when I get you back to the hotel, Marty, I am personally gonna break your scruffy little neck."

Marty hung his head. Where was all the respect he was supposed to get now that he was a married man?

Languidly Erica reached for the phone and asked for Mike James' room. "I'm in the hotel," she informed him.

"So?"

"So I thought you might like me to pay you a visit."

"Don't push it."

"Yes or no?"

He was silent. Cleo had just hung up on him. He sighed. "Please yourself."

"I always do."

287

Jon caught them just as they were about to get into the car.

"Do join us," intoned Jackson, "you can beat the shit out of her, while I strangle this cute little prick."

"I wish you would stop being rude!" complained Muffin.

Jon climbed into the car.

"My stomach hurts!" moaned Marty.

"Make the most of it, son," said Jackson, "right now that's the *least* of your problems."

Muffin attempted a smile at Jon. "Don't be mad," she said sweetly. "*You* never really wanted to marry me anyway."

It was true. He couldn't deny it. But he *would* have married her. To protect his investment he *should* have married her.

Jackson said, "I gotta plan."

"What?" asked Jon. He was deflated.

"Annulment," announced Jackson triumphantly, "we got them early. Annulment—the only answer."

"But . . ." began Muffin.

"No buts," insisted Jackson, "annulment. O.K., Marty?"

"Yeah," agreed Marty miserably, "can I have my pills now?"

Chapter 44

Mike James checked in at the Pan American desk and handed the counter clerk two tickets for New York. He was glad to be going home. Christ! He hoped they had taken good care of his Ferrari.

Erica stood behind him. She looked cool and classy in a pale green midi suit, her blond hair smooth and shining. She had been booked to do a TV commercial in America; they needed a long cool English blond and she had been picked immediately. Mike had suggested they travel together. In fact he had suggested that she could stay in his apartment. Erica had not objected. In fact she had been delighted.

What the hell—Mike had thought—Cleo wasn't coming back—so he might as well enjoy himself. Erica would be fun to take around New York. A new face. What the hell . . .

A day earlier he had seen Little Marty Pearl and Jackson safely off on their European tour. Oh, and Mrs. Emma Pearl had been recalled from America and was with them also. When last seen she had been stuffing Marty with stomach pills, and complaining about dirty foreign foods. Mike laughed at the thought.

Cleo was a bitch. He should have realized it long ago. Selfish, conniving, cold, hard. Good riddance.

Erica had more style in her little finger.

Fuck you, Cleo James—running off with a superstud like Butch Kaufman. Fuck you—bitch.

Later in the day there was a flight leaving for Los Angeles.

Muffin arrived at the airport wearing a seethrough peasant blouse, and faded jeans tucked into outrageous wedge-heeled boots that appeared to be made out of the American flag.

"Hey—Muffin!" the photographers called— "over here. Turn sideways. Beautiful! This direction, darlin'!"

Jon organized the luggage and sorted out the travel documents—visas, passports, tickets, etc. It had been a tough week—but thank Christ for Jackson. After his initial fury he had calmed down and taken complete control of the situation. Quietly he had taken Jon to one side. "You don't want these two babies shitting on you do you?" he had inquired. "No way," Jon had stated. "Then no sweat," Jackson had replied, "I'll deal with it." And he had.

Muffin had been a bundle of scorned girlhood. Marty had been relieved. Jackson had pulled all the right strings.

"What was the *real* story with you and Little Marty Pearl?" a photographer was asking.

Muffin dimpled cheekily. "Like I've said a million and one times, it was just a joke—a silly joke that misfired."

She turned to hug on to Jon. "This is my man, always has been, always will be. We're going to marry soon, aren't we, sweetie?"

Jon disentangled himself. "Sure," he agreed, "we'll be shooting pictures for a calendar spread that Muffin is doing, then who knows . . ."

"Is the marriage with Little Marty legally off?" asked a reporter.

"It was never legally on," replied Jon. "It was declared null within a couple of hours. Look, fellas —we've been through this all week. You know the facts. Can we drop it now?" He took Muffin firmly by the arm and led her away.

"*You are hurting my arm*," complained Muffin, "you don't own me."

"I own your contract for the calendar deal, so just shut up and come on."

"Pig!" muttered Muffin.

"Can it, Muff. Don't vent your childish little temper on me. *I* didn't marry you one minute and wriggle out of it the next. You're lucky you were saved from that teeny bopper wonder so quickly."

"Shitty socks!"

"Listen. We're going to Hollywood. We're going to stay in a beautiful house all arranged for and paid for by Jackson. We're going to shoot some incredible pictures. *Then* we go to Barbados. What more could you want? Relax. Enjoy it. We're going to have an incredible time."

"Pooh!" said Muffin, and stuck out her tongue.

Once Muffin had passed through, the photographers turned their attention to Butch Kaufman, who had just arrived.

Cleo left him to be photographed, and perused the magazine stand. She saw a newspaper with a picture of Shep Stone hugging a pretty woman on the front page. The copy read "Shep Stone 39 greets his wife dancer Mary Lou 22 who arrived from Florida today."

Mary Lou looked in the pink of health. Certainly not eight months pregnant. Certainly not just recovering from a miscarriage.

So much for Shep Stone and his lies. He had fooled her. And what had he done to Dominique? Cleo sighed, most people thought only of themselves. She had attended Dominique's funeral. Shep Stone had not even sent flowers . . .

The latest edition of *Image* was on the magazine stand, and Cleo bought two copies. "Who's Afraid Of the Big Bad Wolf" was advertised on the cover, and Russell had opened the series up with her piece on Butch. "If you are after American prime stud . . ." her article began. Is that what she had been after? Is that what she had got?

"Hey, baby," Butch came rushing over, "don't want to have your er um photo with me—huh? All those guys are asking me who's the mystery lady, who's the pretty girl with the long sexy legs. Then Daniel Onel arrived and they turned their lenses on him. You had a lucky escape."

"Daniel Onel—here?"

"Yeah. He's on the same plané—staying at the Beverly Hills for a couple of weeks. I told him to come by the house. You don't mind do you?"

"No, I don't mind." She turned to look, and sure enough there was Daniel trying to brush his way

292

past the photographers, and there was his Danish au pair princess posing happily.

Cleo smiled. Perhaps Los Angeles would turn out to mean more than she had hoped.

Daniel suddenly saw her, and for a moment he stared, and that stare meant everything.

"Come on, baby," drawled Butch, "we've got an um er plane to catch."

Los Angeles
Six Months Later

Chapter 45

Life with Butch had its advantages.

Like—an easy time lying in the sun with nothing much to do except concentrate on getting an incredible suntan.

Like—no taxing conversations. He and his friends drifted easily through life discussing nothing more serious than surfing and health foods.

Like—Butch did all the cooking on his trusty Hitachi barbecue. And all the shopping. He actually *liked* being recognized at the supermarket.

Like—sex.

Life with Butch also had its disadvantages.

Like—wondering if seeing that your inner thigh tanned exactly the same color as the rest of you was really that important.

Like—being bored to death with his bunch of brainless friends.

Like—endless barbecued steaks, chicken and salad. And never any cookies or candies in the house as Butch refused to buy them on the grounds that they were poison.

Like—sex.

And then there was the Beverly Hills social scene. Occasional little sorties into town to attend parties that Butch thought he should be seen at. After all he was an actor—and actors had to put themselves about—flash the profile and remind everyone that they still existed and had not vanished in a puff of celluloid.

Cleo had never looked so good in her life. She hardly recognized herself. Was this finely muscled suntanned creature really her? This lady full of boundless energy stuffed full of barbecued steaks and health food. This woman who jogged patiently along the beach next to Butch. Who did push ups and leg bends and yoga. This woman who had not written one solitary word since arriving in California.

Her body was active. Her mind was lying dormant. She didn't care. She needed this break in her life. A period of limbo where she could try and decide what she *really* wanted to do.

Mike was but a distant memory—a *divorced* distant memory. No longer a part of her. And now that he was permanently gone she didn't even miss him. Perhaps she had never really loved him in the first place. Perhaps it had been his cock she had loved—his long thin weapon of pleasure and his tight hard balls. When she had heard how indiscriminate he had been with his equipment... well ...

Butch was no husband substitute. He was some-

298

one to coast along with. Nothing heavy or binding. Although lately he had taken to calling her "my old lady"—and that irritated her. She didn't belong to him just because she had chosen to share his house. She was nobody's old anything.

Every month she received a six-page letter from Russell Hayes. Gossip about mutual acquaintances, a few funny comments on his latest statuesque girlfriends, and always, at the end of the letter, a request to know when she was going to start work again. She sent him a postcard in return. A view of the beach with a few scrawled lines of greeting. It was good to know that Russell had returned to the "good friend" category, and was no longer lusting after her body. She giggled when she considered Russell lusting after anyone, and Butch, ensconced beneath a giant sun reflector—all the better to capture the best of the March rays—said, "What was that babe?"

"Nothing," replied Cleo lazily, turning her body on the slatted wooden boards of the front deck of Butch's house.

She wondered why they were still together. She was hardly his type. Before her they had all been seventeen with enormous boobs. Once she had questioned him about this.

"You got class and intelligence," he had replied. "Can't beat *that*, babe."

As far as she knew he didn't screw around. And if he did—well she didn't much care. It wasn't that sort of relationship.

She was quite prepared to sleep with another man if she could only come across one that she fancied. The only vague contender was a friend of Butch's who lived up the beach. Another movie star with shifty eyes and a sly grin. A good actor with an Oscar in his kitchen to prove it. But he was a bastard with a capital B. And so stoned most of the time that he didn't realize he was a bastard. Cleo steered warily clear of him.

Occasionally her thoughts turned to Daniel Onel. She had seen him twice, nothing to get excited about. Once, while shopping on Rodeo Drive, she had recognized him strolling toward her. Quickly she had crossed the street, she didn't know why.

The second time they had attended the same party and exchanged a brief hello. To Cleo's annoyance he didn't seem to *remember* her, his greeting was very vague. Then it occurred to her that maybe he hadn't liked the article she had written on him. Actors were funny about seeing the truth about themselves in print. The hell with him anyway—he was just another aging egotistical movie star— probably as boring as all the rest if you got to know him. She hadn't got to know him. She had wanted to at the time, but she hadn't. Conveniently he faded gradually from her thoughts—although she couldn't help reading about him.

Butch had a passion for movie magazines, and they littered the house, full of juicy gossip about which superstar was doing what to whom. Photos of himself he cut out, and a secretary pasted them into a series of giant scrapbooks. He had tried to persuade Cleo to appear in a photo spread with him, but she had steadfastly refused. She had looked through his scrapbooks, she had seen the endless layouts of Butch partaking in a variety of activities with numerous busty females.

"I don't want to join the photographic tits and

ass club," she had joked when he sulked about her refusal.

"You'll change your mind." he had said confidently.

Oh no I won't—she had replied silently.

So what did she read about Daniel? Items of great interest. The fact that he was into yoga—who wasn't? The fact that he was a vegetarian—nothing new about *that*. The fact that his favorite color was green. His hobby was reading. He was most comfortable in casual clothes. Hated cats. Loved cars. And his favorite pastime appeared to be women.

After the Princess got dumped there was a never-ending supply of different females in his life. From fifteen to fifty they were photographed with him everywhere he went. You certainly could never accuse him of having a type. All shapes, sizes and color hues seemed to suit him just fine. He was hardly the womanizing type—but he certainly seemed to be enjoying a riotous success.

"Hey, babe," drawled Butch, interrupting her lazy thoughts.

"Yes?" she questioned shortly. Butch's "hey babes" always heralded a request, and she didn't feel like getting up and making him a tuna fish sandwich or whatever it was he was going to ask.

"I guess we're makin' out pretty good," Butch stated, throwing an arm across her stomach and stroking her finely muscled flesh the way he knew she enjoyed.

"I guess," she agreed. "Why? What's on your mind?"

"I like you—you like me. We're a couple—a real couple. You understand what I'm saying?"

She knew what was coming. Every so often he

mentioned marriage. She wasn't interested in marriage. Why was it when you told a guy you were in no way anxious to get married, *that* was the time it became his strongest desire in life.

She had explained to Butch how she felt. Two marriages behind her. Who needed it? She was surprised he kept on pushing—after all he had two ex-wives—hadn't he learned his lesson?

Butch removed the sun reflector from around his face and placed it on the ground—a sure sign that he wanted a *serious* conversation.

Cleo sighed. She liked him—he was undemanding, easy to be with, a sexual athlete, and fun. She did not love him. She had no wish to become any further involved than she already was. In fact she knew the time had come to be moving on—all this sun and health was stupefying her brain. She needed to be stimulated mentally for a change.

"What's on your mind, Butch?" she asked again.

He laughed. He had a boyish laugh—one of his most endearing qualities on the screen. "You always know when I got somethin' to say," he chortled, "like I could never *lie* to you—you'd pick up on it in a minute."

The sun disappeared behind a cloud and she shivered, sat up, hugged her knees to her and gazed at Butch expectantly.

"I never lied to you, babe," he said sheepishly. "There's just somethin' I never got around to tellin' you."

"What something?"

"Like I gotta daughter," he said quickly.

"A daughter! Why didn't you tell me? How old is she?"

"*That's* why I never told you . . . she's er um . . . thirteen."

"Thirteen! But Butch—you're only twenty-eight yourself."

"Yeah, I was a child father."

Cleo shook her head in amazement. "So where is she?"

"S'why I'm tellin' you, babe. She's gonna be here—tomorrow. Her mommy is sendin' her out from New York—figures I should take a little er um responsibility."

"And who is mommy? Your first wife?"

"Hell no. Had the kid five years 'fore I got married the first time."

"This is some bombshell. You with a thirteen-year-old daughter. I just can't believe it!"

"You'll believe it all right—she looks just like me."

"When do you see her? And how come you've never mentioned her before?"

"I always visit them when I make New York. Shelley and me—that's the kid's mother—always got along good. I lay a lot of bread on her—see that everything's nice and tight."

"Does the kid have a name?"

"Vinnie. She's a little tomboy—cute as hell—wants to get into movies. Course I gotta tell everyone she's my *sister*—can't blow the image. Hey Cleo —you'll love her, I just know it."

They talked long into the night. Cleo was fascinated that Butch had managed to keep it a secret so long. He told her everything. How Shelly had been a rich girl of thirteen living in a high class apartment building with her family. He had delivered the groceries once a week—and finally he had been delivering more than groceries when Shelley's mother was out. Hot sticky afternoons of passion atop the best living-room couch. Fast but fun. Fumbling with

French letters, disposing of them down the waste disposal unit after the deed was done. Then the weeks of agonizing while Shelley waited to get her period—and waited and waited. . . .

Her elder sister took her to a doctor and the dreaded pregnancy was confirmed. Butch threw away his stock of rubbers in disgust. Shelley wanted the kid. She actually wanted it—and nobody could talk her into an abortion although they all tried.

Butch was summoned by her father. "You're too young to get married," he snorted in disgust, "but you get the hell out of my little girl's life or I'll have the police after you."

Terrified, Butch had hitched across country to California, and there he had stayed—drifting into acting, two marriages, and stardom. He and Shelley had always kept in touch. They were real good friends. After his first marriage broke up they had even talked about marrying each other—but it had seemed too much like incest. They were brother and sister now—why spoil it?

Shelley was into ballet dancing. At twenty-six she suddenly wanted a career, she had been through three marriages and wanted something lasting. She had called Butch and said, "I'm sending Vinnie out to you, it's about time *you* had your turn at playing daddy."

He hadn't argued. It was the first time in thirteen years Shelley had asked anything of him.

Cleo was quite excited at the prospect of a child arriving. She hoped that they would get along —it certainly wouldn't be *her* fault if they didn't. Already she was making plans. Disneyland, and Magic Mountain. A trip around Universal studios, maybe a drive up to San Diego to visit Sea World. These were all things that Cleo had promised herself to do, but somehow—alone—it didn't seem like fun.

In bed Butch stroked her body in his usual expert way. His tongue, starting on her mouth, drifted down to her breasts, her stomach, her thighs.

She moaned softly. It wasn't time to move on—not yet anyway.

Mike James swore quietly to himself. How did you get rid of them? Moving in seemed to be an easy enough process. One day it was a hairbrush and a few jars of make-up—the next—all of their life's possessions. Clothes, magazines, hair dryers, photographs. Jesus! When would he learn?

Since Erica, three girls had taken up what they obviously intended to be permanent residence—and each time it seemed to get more difficult to persuade them to pack up their things and go.

Erica had been the easiest. Six weeks of gradual boredom on both sides and then Erica had announced she was moving in with Jackson.

Mike had not been sorry. He had even helped her pack, and when she begged to come back, two weeks later, Samantha was already in residence. Samantha of the slidey green eyes and strange exotic body odor. She had lasted a month. Then Tulea, a sweet, docile, very pretty Philippine girl. Three months—perhaps a record. She had cried when he asked *her* to go. Cried for a week. All very upsetting, so Annie Gamble, raunchy independent model girl, had seemed like a good thing at the time.

Annie was no longer a good thing. Talk about demanding! Equal orgasm wasn't in it. She wanted equal everything, including a drive of his Ferrari. *Never.* He asked her to go.

"When I find another apartment," she replied

dismissively, studying her beautiful face in the mirror, and applying silver eyeshadow. "Let's trip out and boogie, baby."

He had no desire to do anything with Annie any longer.

It didn't seem to bother her. She eased herself into a silver cat suit, thigh-length boots, and went out to boogie without him.

He sulked around the apartment, taking stock of her numerous possessions, and finally went to bed with a plan forming in his mind. The plan was to buy a large trunk, wait until Annie was out, pack all her things, change the locks, and hey presto—he would be a free man again. And this time he really had learned his lesson. No more moving in. Fuck and out. Better still—go to *their* apartment—don't even let them through the door of his.

Satisfied with his solution he finally fell asleep, only to be woken by Annie at four o'clock in the morning. She was attempting to get some action out of his fast asleep penis. "Come on, baby," she crooned, "mama is feelin' mighty horny."

Mike drew away angrily. She reeked of booze and sweat, and the hell with her. He wasn't some sex object to be used at her convenience.

"You're all fuckin' faggots at heart," Annie mumbled in disgust, and reeled off into the bathroom, where the sound of her plastic vibrator filled the air.

Annie was the worst of them all. Very beautiful —but so what? *She* acted like the man with her independence, sexual demands, and total dedication to her own pleasure.

Mike thought of Cleo—he often did. And he had a horrible feeling that he would never find another woman like her.

The next morning he bought a trunk—a large one. And as soon as Annie left the apartment he started to pack it.

This one would never be allowed back.

Chapter 46

"Open your legs," requested the photographer in a matter-of-fact fashion.

Muffin pretended she hadn't heard. She smiled in her cute girlsy fashion, and thrust her pretty little tits out even further.

"Hey," said the photographer, "these pix are for *Hard* magazine. *You* know what they want. Be a good girl—after all you're getting paid a lot of bread for a few shots of pussy. Bring your knees up—let them fall open—come on sweetpuss."

The sun was blazing down on the gleaming luxurious swimming pool. Muffin, lying naked on a sunbed beside it, reluctantly obeyed. Legs up, slightly open. She knew what he wanted. Christ—she had been doing it for the last five weeks. She had *had* to do it. Who wanted straight nude stuff any more? Who wanted a pretty face and a beautiful body?

Forget that scene—it was over. If a girl didn't open her legs for a camera it was forget-it time. No work. No bread. And Jon leeching off her like a fucking ponce. There was no money left. Everything had gone sour. The great American dream had turned into this.

"Wider," said the photographer. "Come on—you've got a beautiful snatch—what are you trying to hide it for?"

Wider. Sure. He wasn't a photographer. He was a fucking gynecologist.

Muffin wished she had smoked a joint or sniffed some coke before the session. Jon had promised to get her some. Big promise. Nothing. Some husband.

Why don't you throw your hand across your thigh," suggested the photographer. "Let it trail—yeah—let fingers loose—yeah—that's it—great!"

Click. Click. Click. He stopped to change his film.

Muffin stared up at the cloudless blue sky. Everyone complained about the smog in Los Angeles. What smog? Sweat was forming on her body. She felt sticky and dirty. Very dirty.

Oh Christ! At first it had all been so great. Jackson—true to his word—had set them up in a magnificent house on Summit Drive—five minutes from the very center of Beverly Hills. For six weeks they had languished in the sun, swimming in their own pool, playing tennis on their own court, entertaining a variety of Jackson's friends. Jon had started the calendar pictures—incredibly innocent shots to what she was doing now. Then Barbados. Three weeks of pleasurable work—and glowing with success they had returned to L.A., where Jackson had said he would set about getting Muffin work. He was happy to let them move back into the same house—but this time at an enormous rental.

Jon had agreed. Jon had dollar signs weaving in front of his eyes. Jon was convinced she was going to be the biggest thing since sliced bread. Jon had swept her off to Mexico with a pile of friends and finally married her. Only by now she knew it wasn't love. It was called protecting your investment.

Oh yes—in Los Angeles she had grown up. She had changed from a dizzy little dummy into a disillusioned resilient hard nut.

Los Angeles was full. Pretty. Beautiful. Exotic. Erotic. Legs. Tits. Ass. You name it—you could get it.

Muffin was no big deal in America. Couldn't sing. Couldn't act. Couldn't dance. A lot of their money went on lessons. She still couldn't sing, act or dance.

When the money started to run out she suggested that they go back to London.

"Are you kidding?" Jon had said in total amazement. "How can we go back as failures? *You* might be able to do it—but *I* certainly couldn't. We'll make it here if we just hang on."

Hanging on, to Jon, meant staying in the house. And somehow the rent had to be paid. Eventually he had suggested she do some layouts for the girlie magazines. "Just once or twice—the money will keep us going."

She hadn't really realized what she was letting herself in for. The first session Jon photographed her himself. He got her very stoned, and it was all sort of hazy fun. When she opened her legs it was for him not the camera—and in the middle he had made love to her—and she hadn't realized how she had been conned until she saw the photos . . . There was no going home to Wimbledon now. She blushed with shame that her father might see them. Oh God! Jon was a bastard. She finally understood why his first wife had always said that he was.

The American dream. Open your legs and I'll show it to you.

The photographer had reloaded and was ready to start again. "Let's go sweetpuss," he said briskly, glancing at his watch. "I've got two more sessions to shoot today. Open up those pearly gates!"

"Move your arm," the girl giggled in clipped British tones. "You're hurting me!"

Jon obliged, extracting his arm from around her thigh.

"My leg's gone to sleep," she complained, lifting it up and shaking it. "Ouch! Pins and bloody needles."

They were entwined naked on the floor of her mobile dressing-room. Jon and Diana Beeson— English movie actress—two films to her credit and all the producers clamoring for more.

She was twenty-eight. A ladylike sex symbol. Long dark curls, cat eyes, a luscious mouth. She had been in Hollywood for eight months and had a reputation for being hard to get into bed. Many had tried. Most had failed.

It had taken Jon with his baby-faced charm seven days.

Diana caressed his flaccid penis affectionately. "We have another ten minutes before they come knocking on my door," she suggested.

Ten minutes. Get it up you fool. Don't blow it.

He rolled on top of Diana and started to nibble at her erect nipples.

She sighed happily. She was a very beautiful girl. He thought of Muffin. Thought of the photos he had taken of her. Miraculously he was hard, and mounted Miss Beeson and gave her what she required.

She laughed. She moaned. She came.

She got up off the floor and checked her appearance in the mirror. She brushed her luxurious dark hair and slipped a bathrobe over her nude body. She blew him a kiss.

"When they knock tell them I've popped along to make up, all right luv?"

She didn't wait for an answer. She was gone. Very independent lady, Miss Beeson. Very successful. With the right man behind her . . .

Jon got up and stared at his skinny body in the mirror. No muscles. Bones sticking out here and there. He could still pull whenever he wanted to.

Diana had left her mark. Two deep scratches across his rib cage. It didn't matter. Muffin wouldn't notice. She didn't notice anything anymore, she was always too stoned. Oh Christ! He remembered with a flash of guilt that he had promised to get her a joint before her photographic session. Shit. She would be really pissed off and more whiney than ever. Whatever happened to the Muff he used to know? Whatever happened to his sweet little girl?

Hollywood. That's what happened. And all the accompanying bullshit that went to her dumb little head.

He scowled at himself in the mirror. If only she had listened to him. He *could* have made her a star.

Too late now. Posing for snatch shots. Christ! She had *really* blown it. Conveniently he forgot that it had been *his idea* in the first place. Anything to pay the rent on the fucking palace Jackson had saddled him with. Fuck Jackson. And fuck his drugged out friends.

Slowly Jon pulled on his clothes. He knew he had to dump Muffin before she dragged him down with her. If only he hadn't married her . . . how easy it would be . . . when was he going to *learn?*

Now if he could only move in with Diana. Get a quickie divorce. She had a nice beach house, simple but comfortable. Not the kind of house a future star should be living in. He would soon change that.

It had been a clever stroke on his part to get in touch with some of his contacts in England. Middle-aged lady photo editors were only too pleased to commission some work from him. And one of them had wanted a cover story on Diana Beeson.

A phone call. Diana had agreed. Now all week he had been on the set photographing her.

As soon as he had set eyes on her he had known that she could be his new passport to the big time. Carefully, subtly, he had planned to have her.

Seven days wasn't bad for a girl who was supposed to be very hard to get. Not bad at all. Now if he could only figure out what to do with Muffin. . . .

Chapter 47

Cleo was excited. For the first time in months she had something to look forward to. Butch's revelation about having a thirteen-year-old daughter had startled her at first, but now suddenly, inexplicably, she was delighted.

When Butch drove off to the airport she cleaned the house. The place was filthy—housecleaning had never figured high on either of their lists. The room that Vinnie was to have had no more than a bed and bureau. It was not too late to pretty it up a little. On impulse Cleo dashed out to her car and drove into Beverly Hills. She went straight to Robinsons where she perused the linen department and chose candy striped sheets and a matching frilled coverlet. Then on her way out she passed the toy department and spotted a large

Snoopy dog. Little girls were *never* too big for Snoopy.

Pleased with her purchases, Cleo piled them in the boot of her car, and headed back to the beach.

On the way she stopped at the supermarket. Why not get some cookies for a change? And candy, and ice-cream and fudge nut brownies. Butch called them all "poison foods"—but Cleo was sure that Vinnie wouldn't feel the same way. Vinnie. Funny name for a girl. Short for—what? She had forgotten to ask Butch. She put her foot down on the gas hard—maybe she would just make it home before them. Time to set the room up, get it looking pretty.

Butch's car was not out front. Good. She had made it first. Quickly she parked, staggered from the car, and piled high with packages, let herself in.

Rock music assailed her senses. The loudest hardest rock she had ever heard. Jesus, where was it coming from? It was impossible.

"Hey—" she called out, but her voice was drowned in the sound.

She dumped the packages on the kitchen table, explored further, the noise drumming into her head like a hammer. The living-room was empty.

"Butch?" she called weakly. Where the hell *was* he.

She walked into Vinnie's room. Empty. Only one place left. Their bedroom, and yes—that *was* where the ear shattering music seemed to be coming from. She threw open the door. A blonder version of Butch sat in the middle of the bed. A female blond version, with flowing silky hair and firm jutting breasts, barely concealed by the mini-kini she was wearing. Bright tough little blue eyes stared in an unfriendly fashion. A tape recorder propped between her legs issued forth the awful noise, and she was engaged in painting her toenails a glittering shade of gold. A cigarette—grass?—dangled from full jammy lips. *This* was Vinnie? *This* was his *child?*

"Who're you?" the girl asked in a gravelly voice.

Cleo couldn't actually hear the words, she lip-read them.

Vinnie, having asked the question, apparently lost interest in the answer, and returned to painting her toenails, cigarette ash scattering over the bed.

For a moment Cleo was speechless—then anger took over at the blatent *rudeness* of this grotesque child person. She stepped briskly forward and slammed the Off button on the nerve-racking sound.

"Whassamatter?" drawled Vinnie. "Dontcha like to get it on?"

"I guess you're Vinnie," Cleo stated, hoping that maybe—please God maybe—she might be wrong.

"I guess I am," replied the girl, studying Cleo through narrowed eyes, "so—I'll try again—who're you?"

Hadn't Butch told her? Surely he couldn't be *that* dumb. With a sinking feeling Cleo realized that he could.

"My name's Cleo," she said tightly, attempting a smile, "and I live here. Actually that's my bed you're spread out on."

The girl made a clicking sound through her teeth—a sound that indicated amusement. "So you're the latest huh? You sure don't look like the others. Aintcha kinda skinny for Butch?"

Cleo swallowed anger and attempted to remain cool. "Where is your father?" she asked politely.

"He hadda go inta town."

Yes—thought Cleo grimly—I bet he did. What a goddamn coward. "Well," she said brightly, "I guess we'll start by getting you settled in your own room. Come along—bring all your things."

"I'm jake here. Butch said I could go where I wanted."

"I don't think Butch had it planned we would sleep three to a bed."

"I'm not gonna *sleep* here," Vinnie said scornfully. "I'll move offa here in time for you to screw."

"You'll move off now!" snapped Cleo.

"Jeezel Are you uptight!" Vinnie dragged deep on her cigarette and stubbed it out in an ashtray. Then she picked up her tape recorder and nail polish, and slid off the bed. Without another word she exited through to the living-room, and from there through the screen doors to the wooden deck. The tape recorder was clicked on and the heavy rock blasted out.

Cleo sat on the side of the bed. She couldn't believe it—just couldn't believe it. Was this what thirteen-year-old girls were like today? Was this *monster* the sweet little daughter she had been expecting? God! How wrong could you be?

Somehow she had a strong feeling that it wouldn't be long before she was moving on.

Butch did not return until after six. He breezed into the house like nothing could possibly be amiss. Kissed Cleo casually on the cheek, and swept Vinnie up in an affectionate bear hug. "How's my little beauty?" he crowed proudly.

Vinnie struggled free. "For crissakes don't hand me the shit you hand out to all your girls."

Butch laughed. "Watch your mouth, shortstuff."

"Aw—shove it." Vinnie retreated to the beach.

"Great kid," Butch enthused. "Spunky—just like her um—er good old dad."

"And where has her good old dad been?" Cleo asked coldly.

"Didn't I tell you? Had a meeting with Lew Margolis over at Paradox. You know something—the new rewrite on *Surf Stud* is not that bad. If they up the bread I just might be tempted."

"Butch—why didn't you tell me Vinnie was so—well—so precocious?"

He opened up a can of beer, swigged from it, wiped his mouth with the back of his hand. "She is?" His surprise was genuine.

"Don't tell me you haven't noticed. Lolita isn't in it. And why didn't you tell her about me?"

He smiled boyishly. "I knew the two of you would get along just fine."

Cleo raised her eyebrows. "You know something, Butch? You're more stupid than even the newspapers give you credit for."

"Hey . . . come on babe . . ."

"I mean it. If you think for one sweet minute I'm going to have little Lolita running wild all over *this* house—Well—*babe*—just think again."

Butch went over to her, enclosed her with his arms. "Hey . . . easy. Give the kid a break. She's disorientated. A coupla days and we'll all be one big happy family!"

Two days later Cleo was packing her suitcases. Enough was enough. Vinnie was impossible to live with—no wonder her mother had wanted to get rid of her. She smoked, drank, swore. She was untidy, dirty, inquisitive to the degree of searching every closet and drawer in the house. She was rude, insulting and surly. And Cleo had considered it the final straw when she came across 'sweet little Vinnie'

319

screwing the attendant from a nearby gas station on *her* bed. "Out!" she screamed.

"*You* get out," Vinnie had retorted. "This is my dad's home and I'm a minor. *I'm* the one that stays —so screw you, lady."

There was a certain logic in what she had to say. Butch was out. Cleo decided waiting to discuss it with him was a waste of time—as far as he was concerned Vinnie was Little Miss Cute Ass. So she began to pack.

Moving on was no great wrench. Six months of baked brains was enough for anyone.

Chapter 48

Karmen Rush was one of the new style movie stars. Exotic, rich, talented and ugly. She compensated by surrounding herself with beautiful men, and throwing the best, most bizarre parties in Hollywood. If you weren't invited to Karmen's you just didn't exist.

Jon maneuvered an invitation to the latest bash. A latenight party to welcome superstar Al King to Hollywood.

"I don't want to go, I'm beat," Muffin had complained. Several Quaaludes later she had changed her mind.

It upset Jon to see her so dependent on pills and drugs, but then again if that's what kept her going ... besides a little grass or coke never hurt anyone. Half of Hollywood was stoned out of their heads most of the time—and they still managed to take care of business. Jon did not indulge. He wanted to keep his head crystal clear at all times. He had noticed that Diana wasn't averse to a little snort of coke occasionally. He would soon get her off *that* kick.

"Are we nearly there?" Muffin questioned. "I'm famished."

Jon was driving their rented Cadillac, Muffin's photographic fee for her day's work would have to go on the latest payment. The car was the last thing Jon wanted to lose. "Five minutes," he said, "don't worry, it will probably be the best meal we've had all week."

Karmen Rush lived in a huge glass house on the Malibu Colony. Guards saw them through on to the private estate, and then Jon surrendered the car to a muscle-bound parking attendant.

The magnificent house was already teeming with guests. Loud rock music issued forth from every corner. A Charlie Chaplin movie played soundlessly on a plain white wall. Perspex tables, supported by sculptures of naked men, groaned under the abundance of food.

Muffin headed in that direction first. She stuffed her mouth with egg roll and chunks of crabmeat, spare ribs and giant prawns. The food was delicious. Satisfied, she turned and looked around for Jon. He had vanished into the crowd. It was not unusual, he always seemed to leave her alone at parties. The thing she hated about Hollywood was the fact that she didn't seem to know anyone. In London, at any party, she had known *everyone*. And she had always been the center of attention. Here she was just another pretty girl in a city brimming over with pretty girls. She grabbed a glass of champagne off a passing tray and looked around.

322

One side of the house was totally open to the beach, and she noticed that here and there parts of the ceiling rolled back to reveal the sky. Some house.

She gulped her champagne down and wandered out onto the sand.

Jon surveyed the scene quickly. Who would it do him the most good to talk to? He spotted Butch Kaufman, a face he hadn't seen since London. He went straight over.

Butch was friendly, introduced him to his sister, Vinnie, and then said, "Look after her for me, will ya? I gotta take a piss."

Vinnie glared at him. "Look after me." she sneered. "Who are you anyway?"

"Name's Jon."

"Got any grass?"

"You don't look old enough to be . . ."

"Aw—cut out the lecture. You got any or not?"

The girl didn't look any older than fifteen, in spite of the skin-tight black satin outfit. "Not," said Jon. He had heard of young but this was ridiculous.

"So screw you then," replied Vinnie. "Guess I'll just have to find someone that has—and that ain't gonna be difficult with all these freaks around." She teetered off on extremely high heels.

Jon looked around again. Thought he spotted Warren Beatty. Wasn't sure. Then he saw Diana, and headed straight in her direction.

Muffin seemed to have got herself involved with a spikey-haired rock star and his entourage. The fact was he knew who she was—coming from England and all. He also knew all about her brief

323

marriage to Little Marty Pearl. "The guy's a cunt," he announced dismissively. "Right fellas?" His entire entourage nodded. "What you doin' here anyway?"

"I got married. I'm doing photographs."

"Naughty naked ones, eh? I always did think you had the best tits in the business!"

"It's not her tits they're photographing any more," interrupted one of the entourage. "Didn't you see this month's *Core?*"

"Missed that," the rock star said. "Maybe I can get me a personal view. What you say, Muff?"

She felt mortified. Now everyone would know. It was one thing doing the photos—that was bad enough. But to actually meet people who had *seen* them. "'Scuse me." She pushed her way out of the group. Tears were stinging her eyes, the effect of the Quaaludes was wearing off. She just wanted to get out of there.

So where the hell was Jon? Where the hell was her wonderful husband?

"What's your star sign, lover?" A stoned redhead had accosted Jon—squeezing between him and Diana.

"Do go away, darling," said Diana coolly.

"You a Scorpio?" slurred the redhead. "Gotta find me a Scorpio."

"Well run along and find him somewhere else," snapped Diana. "This one's taken."

The redhead swayed away.

"I do believe you could have had her," Diana smiled. "What do *you* think?"

Jon grinned, "I think it's about time I moved in with you."

"Oh yes? And what about your wife?"

"I married her in Mexico—a quick divorce—no problem."

Diana surveyed him quizzically, "I'm not going to marry you," she said, an amused smile hovering on her extremely sensuous lips.

"I wasn't asking you to," Jon replied, "but I'd be good for you—you know that."

"Hmmm . . . maybe."

Jon put on his best young and innocent face. "Don't take too long to make up your mind—somebody else might snap me up . . . a nice young English lad like me . . ."

Diana laughed. "Knock it off, Jon, I am not impressed by the baby-faced looks."

Jon dropped the expression at once. Wouldn't do to push it. One thing about Diana—she wasn't dumb.

Muffin was in the line of fire when several people got pushed in the swimming pool that snaked sinuously through the center of the house. She couldn't swim, and was dragged out spluttering and choking by Keeley Nova, Karmen's dress designer boy friend. He took her to a bedroom, waited while she stripped off her soaking wet clothes, and then leapt at her.

"Stop it!" she objected, struggling. "I thought you said you were going to get me some dry clothes."

"Don't you want to fuck?" he asked in surprise. "I'm not with Karmen for the length of my nose you know."

"Honestly!" snapped Muffin, wrapping herself in a handy bedspread. "If Karmen Rush is your girlfriend—this little scene wouldn't exactly thrill her."

"Where do you think she is, chicken? She's

fucking her brains out with Al King right this very moment."

Muffin widened her eyes. "Don't you mind?"

Keeley shrugged, "Why should I? She does her thing—I do mine. It's a mellow situation. Hey—who are you anyway?"

"Muffin."

"That's a name?"

"Have you got some clothes for me or not?"

He stood back and surveyed her, squinting through stoned eyes. "You'll never get into any of Karmen's things. She's like a stick and three feet taller than you."

"Thanks a lot."

"You'll have to make do with one of my sweaters and a pair of shorts. What do you do?"

"I'm a model."

Keeley fell about laughing, "*You're* a model. Jesus! I'd never put you into any of *my* clothes."

"In England I was *the* top nude photographic model."

Keeley was busy rummaging through a closet—finding her some things to put on. "No kidding? You interested in movie work?"

"What kind?" Muffin asked suspiciously.

"Beautiful stuff, sweets, I gotta friend could make you a star and multo bread. If you're interested give me a call and I'll arrange a meet. She'd like you, oh yeah, she'd freak out over a baby like you . . ."

Diana said, "I am going to go home. I have an early call, and this party is getting distinctly rowdy."

Jon grinned. He loved her clipped English accent and prep school words. Very classy. And contrasted beautifully with her sensuous looks. "I'll walk you out to your car," he offered.

"Don't bother darling. I think I see a certain short person reeling out of a bedroom—dressed in a most *peculiar* outfit. Isn't it your child bride?"

Jon followed Diana's gaze. It was indeed Muffin. Christ—what was she dressed up in? He scowled.

"See you tomorrow, sweetie." Diana edged her way out through the crowds.

Jon pushed his way over to Muffin and grabbed her roughly by the arm, "What the hell are you wearing?"

"I fell in the pool."

"Christ! Can't you do anything right. Come on, we're getting out of here—I've had enough."

Chapter 49

Cleo took a room at the Beverly Wilshire hotel. A temporary move, far too expensive to make it permanent Not that she would even want to. It was decision time. Time to decide what she wanted to do with her life. Bumming around for six months had not produced any answers.

She telephoned Russell in New York. He couldn't have been more thrilled. "I'm flying out," he informed her. "Richard West has written a new book and I want to tie up the rights. I'll be there tomorrow and we can discuss your future."

She hung up the phone thoughtfully. Yes, she did have a future, and it was about time she started looking after it.

She surveyed her clothes: two suitcases full of bikinis, shirts, jeans. She needed to go shopping. She looked like a beach bum herself—what with the tan and the tangled mass of jet curls. A manicure wouldn't be a bad idea either, and maybe a haircut —get rid of all the frizz and look like a person again.

She couldn't help giggling quietly to herself. If her mother could see her now—the ever-elegant Stella. "What have you done to yourself?" Stella would exclaim in horror. "You look like a gypsy. And your skin—don't you know what the sun *does* to your skin!"

Russell arrived accompanied by five Gucci suitcases.

"How long are you here for?" Cleo asked in surprise.

"As long as it takes to bring you back to New York," he replied smugly.

"I didn't say I was coming back."

"You will when you hear what I have to offer you."

Oh God! She hoped to Christ it wasn't his body.

They went to dinner at Matteos, and Russell regaled her with stories of mutual friends. Tactfully he waited until the coffee to mention Mike. At the same time Cleo observed a group of five come in and settle at the next table. Three women. Two men. One of the men was Daniel Onel.

She could hardly concentrate on what Russell was saying. For some stupid insane reason her stomach was doing flips and her mouth was dry.

". . . so the dumb bastard drinks too much, screws around too much—and frankly—looks dreadful." Russell paused for breath. "I don't think he'll ever get over you, and who can blame him. Would you care for a brandy?"

She jumped. "What?"

330

Russell pursed his lips. "Weren't you listening to me?"

"My mind was just wandering."

He nodded knowingly. "Yes. Divorce is upsetting, I'll never forget *my* first one . . ."

Once again her thoughts drifted as Russell launched into the long and boring saga of his first divorce. She had heard the story of all three of his divorces. So had everyone else in the office.

What was it about Daniel Onel that made her into a nervous wreck? He was certainly no matinee idol. Not even a Jack Nicholson. He was hovering on the brink of fifty, really quite ordinary looking. But, oh God, something about him . . . He turned her on with a vengeance. And she wasn't the only one who felt like that if the newspapers and magazines were anything to go by. Reports of Daniel and his women abounded. Only recently he had been splashed all over the front pages announcing an engagement to a dark-haired neurotic superstar. That had lasted exactly five minutes.

Cleo moved surreptitiously to see who he was with. At that precise moment he left the table and they came eyeball to eyeball. "He-llo," he greeted her, smiling warmly. A slight difference to their last meeting. "How are *you?*"

Suddenly she was glad she'd had her hair cut, bought a new dress, bothered about her appearance for a change. "I'm fine." She couldn't think of anything else to say. Oh God—if she couldn't think of something he would be gone.

"I was just thinking . . ."

"Er, do you know . . ."

They both started to speak at the same time. "You first," said Daniel, laughing.

Cleo smiled, took a deep breath, "I was only

going to ask you if you knew Russell Hayes—my editor. Russell owns *Image* magazine."

"I don't think we've met," Daniel shook him warmly by the hand. "What are you two doing now? I was just going to phone my housekeeper and warn her that I'm coming back to run a movie. The new Woody Allen. Why don't you join us?"

Daniel lived in a rented house on Benedict Canyon. By Hollywood movie star standards it was simple—but comfortable and nice—and as soon as Cleo walked in she knew that she was going to stay the night.

The other two couples were business. A major director and his girlfriend, and Lew Margolis— chairman of Paradox Television studios, and his wife Doris Andrews—a movie star famed for her "nice girl" roles.

Russell was very impressed. "I spot at least three exclusive interviews here," he hissed at Cleo. "See what you can tie up."

She had no intention of tying anything up. She wasn't working for Russell again—not yet anyway.

The Woody Allen movie was another gem. Cleo laughed and tried to relax, but she was only too aware that Daniel was within touching distance, and she wanted to touch him desperately. Angrily she brushed Russell's hand off her leg when he attempted to place it there. He didn't try to put it back.

At the end of the movie Daniel offered Irish Coffees. Cleo sipped hers slowly, trying to keep her eyes off Daniel, but not succeeding. Somehow their eyes kept on meeting and conducting a silent conversation of their own. Then Doris Andrews said she was tired, and the director said he was off early on a location scout, and everyone started to make a move.

Daniel glanced at Cleo. "Why don't you stay on," he suggested quietly. "I'd like to talk to you."

"O.K." she agreed.

"What about your friend. Shall I see if Lew can give him a lift?"

"Either that or he can take my car."

"Good idea. Shall I tell him or will you?"

Russell was not at all pleased. "I can stay with you," he insisted.

"No," Cleo was firm. "I have to talk to Daniel alone. I promised."

"Talk?" sneered Russell.

"Or fuck," replied Cleo, suddenly angry. What business was it of his?

Russell departed, angry and affronted.

"Did he think he was going to end up in your bed?" Daniel asked.

"I don't know and I don't care." She stared at him, willing him over to her.

They stood very close together, not touching, just having an eye to eye confrontation.

"Did you want to stay?" Daniel asked.

"What do you think?"

His lips were like fire, burning down on hers, and creating a sensation of excitement and abandon that seemed to have been buried for quite some time.

She wasn't aware of the clothes slipping from her body. But she was aware of the way his fingers traced every outline of her form, creating exquisite electric shocks of ecstasy.

She struggled to get his clothes off. Tore at his

shirt, ripped the zipper on his trousers. "I want you so, so badly," she murmured. "I've wanted you for months and months. It seems like forever."

He touched her breasts, played with them gently, fingered her nipples until she wanted to scream. She wanted to beg him to make love to her.

She reached for his balls. It was always exciting feeling the body of a new man. The surprise of each penis. Whoever said they were all the same in the dark was lying. Every one was a revelation. Size, texture, smell, taste. Daniel's was small, but beautifully formed. No Butch Kaufman—somehow she knew it wouldn't matter.

She knelt in front of him and took him in her mouth. He groaned his pleasure, then drew her head away, and knelt on the floor with her. Together they fell on the carpet, rolling over and over, laughing, enjoying every beautiful minute. Then he mounted her, thrusting himself in. She rose to meet him, clinging her legs tightly around his back. Immediately she started to come. He wouldn't let her go. It was agony and ecstasy. Usually she needed time between orgasms, she couldn't bear to be touched. Daniel clung on to her, and then suddenly it was all right again—in fact it was more than all right—it was goddamn *marvellous*. A heightened sensation of sexual energy and power.

Daniel felt the change in her, and rolled over so that she was on top of him. Now her mind, brain, and body concentrated on only one thing. He was guiding her buttocks, slow . . . slow . . . then faster . . . faster . . . His cock was the greatest organ of pleasure she had ever known. Then suddenly she was coming again. An uncontrollable come that swept over her in exhausting waves of intense delight. And she was screaming as loud as she could. She, who had always made love soundlessly before.

Then Daniel was joining her. Squeezing her ass. And she could feel his glorious juices pumping into her.

This wasn't screwing. This was nirvana.

"Oh my God!" At last he had let her go. "Oh my good God!" She lay on the floor inert and motionless.

"Enjoyable?" Daniel asked quietly.

"Absolutely unbelievably!"

He started to touch her again.

"Enough!" she protested.

"When you're having fun it's never enough."

"Please . . ."

He didn't listen to her objections. He brushed over her nipples lightly, then his fingers were between her legs, opening her up, making way for his tongue which was an object of great delicacy.

"No more . . . please . . . no more . . ." But even as she said it she surrendered herself to his delicious probings, and when she reached orgasm for the third time it was incredibly gentle and beautiful and totally draining.

She couldn't help herself, she drifted into sleep, and when she awoke an hour or so later she found that Daniel had put a cover over her and a pillow under her head.

She sat up, alone and suddenly embarrassed. She had wanted to talk to Daniel, communicate—not fall into his arms like every one of his highly publicized romances probably did. And it wasn't even a first date—truth was it wasn't a date at all.

Now she knew the secret of his magnetism. He was a wonderful lover—certainly the best *she* had ever experienced. He was a sensualist, a man who actually liked a woman's body and didn't make certain plays and moves because that is what *Playboy* and *Penthouse* magazines *told* him to do.

It was dark in the living-room, and the floor was getting to be an uncomfortable resting place. She got up and gathered her clothes together. Daniel was asleep in the bedroom. It niggled her slightly that he could just fling a cover over her and leave her out in the livingroom.

She stared at him. He slept soundly, snoring very softly.

She was at a loss. What to do? Crawl into bed with him? Or go back to her hotel?

What would he expect her to do? Was this just one night of good sex, or was it the beginning of a relationship?

Cleo had never felt so out of control in her life. Usually *she* called the shots. Damn Daniel. He was making her feel like a teenager, for crissakes!

She decided to dress and go home. It seemed to be the safest bet. And yet ... she had a passionate longing to pull all the covers off him and have *her* feast. She wanted him in her mouth, enclosed and warm ... she wanted to suck the juices out of him as he had done to her.

She dragged the covers down. He was wearing pajamas. It made him seem somehow vulnerable. She eased her hand into the bottoms—feeling for him—playing with him until he started to come to life in her hand.

She slid her head down, took him half in her mouth teasingly—licking and caressing with her tongue.

"You're beautiful," she murmured.

"I'm awake," he mumbled.

"Good." She drew him over with her until she was lying on the bed and his penis was in her mouth.

Now it was his turn to try and protest. But she had him, her hands on his ass to prevent his escape. He began to pump into her mouth, but every time he got near the peak she forced him to withdraw and wait.

"What are you doing to me!" he protested.

She laughed softly. "Beautiful suffering. Remember? You taught me, now I'll play too."

When she did let him reach his climax it was an explosion. "Oh Jesus Christ! That was the *best!*" he exclaimed. "The absolute *best*." He slid down next to her and she fitted into his arms.

"I'd like you to stay the night," he said, "think you could manage that?"

"Yeah. I guess so. Nobody at the Beverly Wilshire is going to miss me."

"Except maybe your friend."

"Russell? I told you—he's business not pleasure."

He hugged her. "And me?"

"Pleasure of course. What do you think—I'm going to write a story about our night together?"

"I *am* slightly paranoid about reporters. That's why I fought getting involved with *you*."

"We're involved?"

His hands were exploring her body again. "What do *you* think?"

She laughed softly, suddenly very secure and warm in his arms. "I think I wanted you that first day I came to interview you."

"Mutual."

She was delighted. "Really? But you were so offhand when I called to show you the article . . ."

"Which I quite liked," he interrupted.

"Why only quite?"

"Because I just don't like reading about myself period. But to get back to you . . . well, the timing was off . . . I had Heidi to get rid of . . ."

"And a million others since."

"Don't believe everything you read."

"Would half be a fair estimate?"

"Are you jealous?"

"*Of course* I'm jealous."

"Don't be. Anyone to while away a lonely night."

"Oh thanks . . ."

He kissed her. "Not you, idiot. I've been saving you since the day you crossed the street to avoid me. That's when I knew you were the girl for me."

"I never even thought you saw me."

"I saw you—like I saw you at that abysmal party with Butch Kaufman. What the hell were you spending your time with a dumbhead like him for?"

"Waiting for you." And as she said it she knew that it was true.

Mike James found that having no live-in playmate was almost as bad as having one.

Living alone was a drag. It was peaceful, quiet, and very, very lonely.

He employed a maid to come in and do the work. She was a tight lipped Irish lady who appeared at nine o'clock, cooked him a solitary breakfast, and then cleaned the apartment to horrible perfection. When he returned from the office in the evening the place smelt of disinfectant and leather polish. The toilet was always filled with a white foam cleanser. Everything in the fridge was hygienically sealed beneath virgin tin foil.

He hated it. He yearned for the smell of woman. Something was missing in his life, and he wasn't sure what. Since getting rid of Annie—a nasty scene, she had scrawled obscenities all over his front door—he had dated girls carefully, and kept to his new rule of not bringing them home.

This meant evenings in their apartments if he wished to get laid. This meant sitting through tasty gourmet dinners for two recommended by *Cosmopolitan* or *Glamour* magazine. This meant instant indigestion and stomach ache. This meant his sexual performance wasn't up to his usual standard. This meant shrill girlish voices complaining. This meant —shit.

Mike was not leading the perfect life.

Russell had called to tell him he was flying to the coast to see Cleo.

"So?" Mike had replied shortly. "She's nothing in my life any more. We're divorced."

"Then you won't mind if I try my luck?" Russell had replied.

Bastard. Cleo would never look at you. Bastard. Mike had forced himself to remain non-committal. "Do what you like."

Russell had flown off in high spirits, and Mike had sulked.

If it wasn't for Cleo maybe he could have settled down with one of his live-in playmates. But he had Cleo to compare them with, and, much as he hated to admit it, there was no comparison.

Chapter 50

At first Muffin could not believe that Jon would do such a thing to her. But as the days passed it became increasingly obvious that the short terse note he had left her was true.

She sat in their luxurious mansion and waited for him to come back. Oh she knew Jon had changed in Hollywood—they both had—but to have changed to such a degree that he could just dump her. Leave her alone to face all their debts and bills—it was downright cruel.

She had exactly twenty-six dollars and fifty cents, and that was it. Not even enough to pay her fare back to England—hardly enough to keep her in food for more than a few days. And the bastard had even taken their car—the rented Cadillac that *she* had been posing for porno pictures to keep up the payments on.

She had never been alone in her life. Never had to fend for herself and make decisions. From the day she had moved away from her family Jon had always been there. Jon, who had always professed to love her so much. Yeah—he had loved her—just so long as she was making good bread. Muffin realized for the first time that Jon had been *using* her, promoting and pushing her in every direction. And *that* was why he had been so angry when she had married Little Marty Pearl. Losing a good investment— only in Hollywood the investment turned out to be a dud. In Hollywood she just couldn't cut it. Too many pretty girls, and sexy bodies, and what made her special?

Jon had left her in the same way a racing driver would abandon a defunct car—a tennis player a broken racket. God! But she should have realized what a bastard he was. Hadn't his first wife, Jane, said so a million and one times—and when he left Jane it had been with two little kids, If he didn't care about his *children* what chance did she have?

Jon bloody Clapton—with his blond innocent good looks, and his scrawny body. Honestly! How could she have fallen for such a bastard! Three and a half years of her life she had wasted with him, and where had it gotten her? Exactly nowhere. Exhibiting her snatch in a bunch of filthy magazines. Charming!

Thinking about Jon was not going to pay the bills, and she didn't even have enough money to do a moonlight skip. Where exactly could she skip to on twenty-six dollars?

She didn't know who to turn to. Somehow all the friends they had made had been Jon's. She didn't even have a girlfriend to help her out.

She sat and thought. There was Little Marty Pearl—now a big television star on a weekly spectacular with his sister—the two of them all teeth and smiles, they looked like a very glossy toothpaste commercial. He probably wouldn't appreciate getting a call from her. They hadn't even spoken to each other since the fateful day of their short marriage.

Then there was his manager, Jackson. But he gave her the creeps, and if she asked him for help he would want *plenty* in return. She may flash for pictures, but she certainly wasn't ready to fuck for anything. Some of her Wimbledon background stayed firmly with her. You had to draw the line *somewhere*.

She couldn't think of anyone else who might help her, and she realized the only thing she could do was pose for some more of those photographs. The open your legs and smile variety.

The thought depressed her. No Jon to get her stoned and in the mood. No Jon to sweet talk her through the session.

Rummaging through her clothes she came across the shorts and shirt Keeley Nova had lent her. She tried to remember what he had said to her. Something about . . . make you a star . . . plenty of money . . .

He seemed like an O.K. guy. Maybe it was worth a phone call. After all—they hadn't cut off the phone—not yet anyway.

"You are a sonofabitch," drawled Diana. "Haven't you even phoned?"

Jon was busy massaging her back. She had a lovely back. "Nope," he replied patiently. "If I call

343

she'll cry and whine and beg me to come back. Believe me, it's better this way. She's got a lot of friends, she'll manage."

Diana sighed. "You know best, darling. And God knows you've put up with so much. I think you've been a positive martyr—no other man could have stood it."

Sadly Jon said, "Yes, it was tough." And he was glad he'd laid it on as thickly as he had. Diana had been more than sympathetic to his tales of Muffin's other men, drunken orgies and pornographic exhibitions. He had even shown her a picture of Muffin au naturel—au very naturel indeed. "I begged her not to pose for photos like these," he told Diana, "but she just does what she wants."

Diana had held his hand and consoled him. "Move in with me, darling. No man should have to stand for that sort of behavior."

Now she was worried that maybe it had been a hasty move. She wanted to be certain that Muffin wouldn't publicly complain. After all . . . that sort of publicity . . . who needed it?

"Turn over," Jon said.

"You have incredible fingers," Diana murmured, doing as he asked.

"All the better to touch you with." Jon shook a few drops of baby oil on to her stomach and started to massage it in.

"Delicious!" Diana sighed luxuriously. "Who knew that when I got you I got the best masseur in town too! My God! Just think of the money I'll save!"

The Rush mansion was a magnificent sight in the daytime, sprawling along the ocean front like a series of white bizarre monuments. Karmen had started off owning one house, and during the course of her fame had purchased the neighboring six, and joined them all together making one wide strange incredible mansion. Karmen's house was almost as famous as she was.

Nervously Muffin paid the cab off with the last of her money. She certainly hoped the trip was worth it. Keeley Nova had been very friendly on the phone. He remembered her, and when she had asked him if he had been serious about introducing her to someone who could "make her a star" he had laughed and said, "Sure—if you got what it takes you got it made. Come on by the house around four o'clock."

So here she was, pretty and pert in satin jeans and an off-the-shoulder frilled blouse. Her hair was freshly washed, and cascaded in tangly orange-tipped curls. Her make-up emphasized her wide China blue eyes, and pouting full lips.

Under her arm she carried a large portfolio of her photographs. Glamour nude stuff, none of the open leg variety.

There was a long cord by the massive double front doors. She pulled it, and loud chimes rang out, and a lot of dogs started to bark.

After a while Keeley appeared. "Had to chain the monsters up," he explained. "If they don't like you . . ." He shrugged explicitly, and pantomimed a slit throat.

Muffin shivered as she followed Keeley into the house. He was wearing white jeans, that was all, and his back was covered in fresh talon-like scratches.

She felt uneasy. There was a strange atmosphere in the house.

"How you 'bin?" Keeley asked.

"Fine."

"I'm glad you called, took me up on what I said. Sit down—you wanna snort some coke? The lady ain't ready for you yet."

Muffin collapsed onto a cushion; there was no normal furniture as such.

Keeley squatted down beside her and produced a small phial of cocaine. He tipped some carefully into a miniature spoon and handed it to Muffin. She pinched a little between her fingers and snorted it up her nose. It was a tickly sensation, but she had tried it several times before and the effect was wonderful.

Keeley did the same, sighing with pleasure.

"I brought some pictures with me..." Muffin ventured, handing the portfolio to Keeley.

He leafed quickly through the book. "You photograph good," he commented, "but this job is more than tits 'n' ass." She was silent. How much more? He had mentioned making her a star, and a lot of money. But how?

Suddenly a voice screamed throughout the house. A perfectly pitched—"Keeeeeellleeyyy!"

He jumped to attention. "The lady is ready," he said, facial muscles taking off in a nervous spasm. "Come with me little girl. Money, fame, everything I said. Let's go audition; babe. Let's see if you got what the lady has been looking for."

It pained Jon to discover that not only did Diana have an agent, to whom she was paying ten percent of her earnings, but she also had a business manager who peeled off a further fifteen per cent!

"Ridiculous!" Jon exclaimed. "The guy's a rip off merchant."

"Nonsense," replied Diana. "He's a perfectly

legitimate, highly recommended, *very good* busi-nessman."

"Who recommended him?" scowled Jon.

"Daniel Onel, and *he* hasn't done too badly."

Jon couldn't argue with that. Everyone knew that Daniel Onel, Diana's current co-star, was now one of the richest actors in Hollywood since moving his base from England—land of crippling taxes.

"I still say," grumbled Jon, "that paying out twenty-five per cent of your income is a load of bollocks. *I* could handle your career, and it wouldn't cost us a penny."

Diana burst out laughing. "Jon darling—as a lover I adore you, but if you think I am foolish enough to put my financial affairs in your hands—just forget it."

"I did all right for Muffin," argued Jon.

"Oh yeah?" replied Diana, "and what do you both have to show for it?"

He shut up. Couldn't argue with the truth. It would take time to soften Diana up. At least he had a roof over his head, and all the bills were paid. But what to do when the next payment on the Cadillac became due? And how about when Diana finished the movie she was working on and wanted to go out at night? Somehow he did not think that Diana was the sort of lady who would take kindly to picking up the check.

Karmen Rush lolled in the center of a huge triangular bed. The room was entirely black—walls, cushions, thick fur rugs. Daylight zoomed in through the top—there was no ceiling, just a vast expanse of sky. Indian sitar music drifted into the room from various hidden speakers.

"Hello," husked Karmen, in a deep, almost masculine, voice. She held up her hand to indicate silence. "Don't speak until I switch on the recorder —I want to catch every word. Who knows . . . One day our first conversation might be worth a fortune."

Muffin gulped. She was stunned and speechless anyway. She hadn't expected to meet Karmen Rush. Wow—what would they make of *this* whole scene back in Wimbledon!

Keeley said, "Shall I stay or go?"

Karmen crushed him with a look. "Get out. I don't want *you* on tape. Go make a jug of black currant juice." She fixed Muffin with a moody look. "Come and sit on the bed, let me get to know you. Let me see if our vibes are in tune."

Keeley gave her a little shove, and gingerly Muffin approached the bed and balanced on a corner.

She couldn't help staring at Karmen. The woman was—well—weird looking, with her whiter than white face, dramatic Egyptian eye make-up, and slashed blood-red lips. She was wearing some sort of caftan—black naturally. And her jet hair hung in multiple braids around her head.

Muffin had always been a fan of hers. Karmen Rush had the most beautiful incredible singing voice. She was also one of the few bankable female stars in the world.

"How old are you?" Karmen asked.

"Twenty," mumbled Muffin.

"Fortunately you look younger," observed Karmen, studying her through slitted eyes.

"Oh yes," agreed Muffin quickly, "people are always telling me I look *much* younger."

"Did Keeley tell you anything?"

"Not really . . . I brought some pictures." She handed the book to Karmen, who took her time studying each photograph intently. Suddenly Muffin wished that Jon was with her. She felt out of her depth and very much alone.

"I like your body," Karmen stated matter of factly, "slightly plump, but I like that. The audience will like that. Little Miss Ordinary—a girl they can identify with. Take your clothes off dear, and walk around the room for me."

The request was unexpected. Muffin hesitated.

"You're not shy, are you?" Karmen questioned coldly.

"No, of course not. I just sort of wondered . . . well, what kind of a job am I auditioning for?"

"A lot of money, a lot of fame. Are you interested in those two things?"

"Yes . . . but . . ."

"We are two women here together." Karmen's voice was more gentle. "I am not regarding you as a piece of meat, but I must see your body."

"Sure." Muffin's voice sang with false bravado. She stood up and unzipped her satin trousers, wriggling out of them in what she hoped was an unconcerned fashion. Then the blouse, peeling it down, until she was totally exposed.

Karmen stared at her. "Walk around," she commanded.

Muffin followed her bidding, wondering why she felt more naked than she ever had in her entire life.

"Perfect breasts," Karmen observed, "short legs. I like the combination. I like your face."

"Can I dress?"

"Not yet. I need to see more."

"More?"

"Muffin dear," Karmen spoke deliberately, slowly, "I think you are the girl I have been looking for."

"Yes?" Muffin didn't know if she should be pleased or not. This whole scene was weird. Parading around starkers in front of a movie star. Maybe it was all a put on. What job could Karmen Rush possibly have for her?

"Yes," agreed Karmen, "I am directing a film—a marvellous story about an ordinary little girl who comes to Hollywood—and the things she has to go through to achieve fame."

This was more like it. Muffin could see herself in a part like that.

"Of course it's going to be a very honest film," Karmen continued, "the *real* story of what it's all about. And I should know—I've been there and back twenty times before I finally made it." She sat up; her eyes gleaming. "I wrote the script myself. I have one of the best lighting cameramen and a small tight crew. We are ready to begin—but we have not found the right girl. You could be that girl. You could be as big a star as me in your own way."

Muffin had caught some of Karmen's enthusiasm. But still . . . what was the snag? There must be one, there always was.

"Do you want the part?" Karmen asked.

"Yes, of course. But . . ."

"If every detail is perfect the job is yours. Our camera will be very . . . probing. You saw *Deep Throat?*"

"No."

"You missed nothing. Ugly bodies, ugly women. Whoever auditioned them did not do a thorough job."

"It was a pornographic movie, wasn't it?" Muffin asked. Jon had seen it and come home laughing.

"What is pornography? Life is pornography. Our movie will be *beautiful* pornography. *You* will be beautiful." Karmen stood up. "Muffin, dear, you will make a lot of money, I promise you that. You will live here in your own section of the house —the movie will all be shot here. Six weeks of your time and instant fame. Trust me. Believe me I know. I *will* make you a star. But first. . ."

"What?" Excitement was flooding through Muffin. She *could* be a star. Karmen Rush was saying so, and somehow she *trusted* her.

"I must look between your legs. I must see if you are as perfect there as everywhere else. After all—my movie is called *The Girl With the Golden Snatch*, and it wouldn't do to disappoint, would it now?" Karmen reached toward her, lightly touching her breasts. "Lie down, sweet little girl. Let the audition begin."

Chapter 51

At Daniel's invitation Cleo moved in with him. She debated for some while as to whether she was doing the right thing or not. Straight from one actor to another. Surely that wasn't a wise move?

But no way could anyone possibly compare Daniel and Butch. They were so utterly different. Butch had been a resting space while she recovered her strength. Daniel was a whole new life. Besides which, she loved Daniel, a fact which was painfully nice. Since Mike there had been no one that she had contemplated sharing her life with—on a permanent basis that is. Now there was Daniel.

She felt reborn. Happy, enthusiastic, and ready to work again. Only after a six month lay off she was not exactly in demand. Of course there was always Russell. She hadn't seen him since her first night with

Daniel—he had checked out of the hotel, flown back to New York, and left her an uptight note.

Image magazine could no doubt hand her some interesting assignments in Los Angeles, and she was *so* ready to work. Daniel was out all day on the movie he was shooting—and three weeks of wandering around Beverly Hills alone, and catching afternoon movies, was almost as stupefying as the beach.

The evenings and weekends compensated. Daniel was an exciting companion. Witty, informative, inquisitive, and charming. Never boring, always alert and interesting and amusing.

And of course there was the love-making. Long drawn out evenings of discovering each other's bodies all over again. Passionate hours of sheer sensual delight. Daniel was a master—*the* master.

Cleo phoned Russell early on a Monday morning. She timed the call to catch him as he entered the office—New York time being five hours later.

He tried to be cool, but she knew he was secretly pleased.

"I'd like to do some exclusives," she suggested. "Any ideas?"

"Had your fling with that senile actor?" Russell had to be snide.

"He's only eleven years older than you."

"And twenty years older than you," Russell retorted quickly.

"Let's drop the subject, Russ. I'm in no mood for an argument."

"No argument—just advice."

"No thanks."

"He's a three-time-married loser neurotic bum."

"So are you, but we're still friends—right? Now —what do you have for me?"

Russell sighed, and promised to phone her back with some suggestions.

She knew that he would, and sure enough he was on the phone again within an hour.

"Richard West," he suggested. "They're making a film of *Sex—an Explanation*. I'd like to have his thoughts on the way they are going about it. You know the sort of stuff I want—is the writer getting screwed as usual etc. Sort of a sex expert Joseph Wambaugh."

"Did Richard West do his own screenplay?"

"I think he worked on a couple of drafts."

Cleo laughed dryly. "I thought *Sex—an Explanation*, was a sort of sexual textbook. Do tell—what's the plot?"

"That's for you to find out. You want the assignment?"

"Sure. Anything else?"

"Your old boyfriend—Butch Kaufman. That should be an easy one for you."

"I interviewed Butch already—in the *Big Bad Wolf* series. Remember?"

Russell indulged in a short coughing fit, then, "Of course I remember—that series pulled in more readers' letters than the office could cope with."

"So? Why Butch?"

"Because if you read your morning papers out there, you would see that Butch Kaufman has signed for a movie called *Surf Stud*, and that his co-star is his thirteen-year-old sister, Vinnie. Good stuff, Cleo, and you *do* have an inside track."

Oh boy—if he only knew *what* an inside track!

"I'd like fifteen hundred words on Dr. West, and around an eight hundred-word piece each on Butch and his sister."

"And you want it by tomorrow, right?" Cleo intercepted.

"The weekend will do."

"Oh—great. That gives me a full four days."

"I can remember the time you interviewed in the morning, wrote in the afternoon and had it in by the next morning."

Cleo sighed. "That's when I was young and in action."

Russell gave a nasty laugh. "I didn't notice any changes."

By the time Daniel arrived home from the studio Cleo had all the interviews arranged. Dr. Richard West would see her at his house in Beverly Hills the following morning. A publicist for the film company had been the intermediary. "Dr. West doesn't give interviews, but because of his relationship with the editor of *Image* he will be glad to oblige," the publicist said.

Cleo wondered how Dr. West's relationship with Ginny Sandler was progressing.

Butch, she called directly.

He was distinctly off. She couldn't blame him, maybe she *should* have left a note. Once she mentioned "interview" and *Image* though, his voice perked up considerably, and he agreed to see her at two o'clock the following day.

The thought of interviewing sweet little Vinnie filled Cleo with mirth. Now it was *her* turn—and the pen was mightier than that Lolita brat's tiny little voice any day.

It occurred to Cleo that she did have a pretty good exclusive story. The fact that Vinnie was daughter not sister—headline making stuff. Should she use it? Yes—the reporter side of her said. No—

the personal side insisted. It was a confidence between lovers. But still . . . it *was* tempting. . . .

Daniel was exhausted but loving. "Only two more days on the movie," he said, "then I thought a short vacation before the next. How about the Bahamas? Ever been there?"

It hadn't occurred to Cleo that once she started working again Daniel might not be working himself. Actors, between movies, were what is politely known as a pain in the ass. Worried about the film they had just completed. Worried about the one they were about to do.

Daniel, of course, would be different.

"That would be lovely," Cleo said. "How long for?"

"Ten days, a couple of weeks." He was peering in the mirror studying his face.

"Guess what I did today?" Cleo asked brightly.

"Got any tweezers, luv?"

"Er . . . yes." She found him the tweezers and began again. "Daniel? Do you know what I did today?"

Industriously he started to pluck away at some hairs on the bridge of his nose. "What?"

"I . . . I went back to work."

Somehow Daniel tweezering at his face, irritated her. "I called Russell, told him I was ready, and . . ."

"Did you ever make love to him?"

"What? *No*—of course not. I *told* you that."

"Why call him? There are plenty of other magazines—*Los Angeles*—*People*—*Newsweek* . . ."

"I know. But well . . . I have a special connection with *Image*."

Daniel laughed sarcastically. "Yes. I realize

that." Stoically he continued to pluck at his eyebrows.

"For crissakes," Cleo snapped, "can't you do that in the bathroom?"

He stopped abruptly, threw the tweezers at her, and walked out of the room.

She was stunned. Followed him through to the living-room. "What's the matter with *you?*"

"*Me?*" he shouted in reply. "More like *you*."

"I don't shave my *legs* in front of you. I can't help it if I think some things should be private."

"Christ almighty! What kind of a sanctimonious statement is that!"

"I believe in being honest."

"Yes? So why don't you admit you made it with Russell Hayes?"

"Oh Daniel! How many times do you want me to tell you? I didn't. You *know* I didn't."

"Sure."

Suddenly they were embroiled in a screaming row. Their first argument, and so ridiculous that after they had screamed themselves out they couldn't help laughing, and then they were touching, and peeling each other's clothes off. Suddenly they were both caught up in the intensity of their love-making.

"We have something special together," Daniel whispered softly, when they lay moist and warm in each other's arms.

"Yeah, a passion for the floor!" giggled Cleo. "Can't we try a bed for a change?"

"Let's get married," Daniel suggested quietly. "We could do it in the Bahamas next week. I promise you we'll spend our honeymoon in a bed!"

Cleo was more than surprised. She hadn't considered marriage with Daniel. She hadn't considered marriage with anyone. Butch had mentioned it on occasion, but it had been a jokey thing—a proposition she had never taken seriously.

Extracting herself from Mike had set up one giant barrier against marriage. Who needed that little bit of paper that led to lies and deceit? Who needed "belonging" legally—when not to be tied by law seemed to lead to a much more honest relationship?

If she and Butch had married they would be embroiled in a big hassle now. Who owned what. How to split the money. As it was she had just been able to pack up and go. And Butch had not been able to feel it was his right to come running after her.

She would never forget Mike's face as he chased her around London. "You're mine—you bitch!" his expression had said. "So get right back into this marriage where you belong."

Oh no. She didn't want to go through *that* again. Not with anyone. Not even with Daniel.

And yet—in two months time she would be thirty years of age. And she wanted a child. And she wouldn't mind at all it being Daniel's child. In fact. . . .

"I don't think we should spoil everything by getting married," she murmured, snuggling close to his body, and running her fingers through his furry chest. "We've both been through it enough times to know better. We love each other. I don't think we need a piece of paper to prove it." She moved her hands down to where she knew he would be ready for her. "But I would love to have your baby—our child. Daniel? Can we?" She didn't wait for his answer. She slid on top of him and guided him inside her.

The next morning she threw away her supply of birth control pills. In the heat of the moment, the night before, Daniel never *had* answered her, but she was sure it was the right thing to do. A baby was a far more personal bond than a marriage contract.

Dr. Richard West did not resemble the ordinary-looking, unassuming, middle-aged man that Cleo had met in Russell's office nearly a year previously. He had changed considerably. Gone was the short sandy hair. Gone was the heavy body. Gone were the unstylish clothes. The only thing that seemed to have remained were the Mick Jagger lips. Somehow they looked more at home in a deeply tanned face, the eyes obscured by tinted shades. A heavy beard covered his chin, and his hair—now incongruously blond streaked—grew thick and long. He was wearing white tennis shorts and a Tee shirt, all the better to show off long tanned legs, and nicely muscled arms.

"Hi there," he greeted, "good to see you again. Come on in and pop a few vitamin pills."

Gone was the charming reticence. California and the whole success trip could claim yet another victim.

"I hardly recognized you," Cleo confessed, over a breakfast of prunes, yoghurt, wheat germ, and rose hip tea. "You must have lost at least twenty pounds."

"I got my body together along with my head," Richard confessed. "I shed thirty-two pounds of unnecessary body weight and forty-two years of unmitigated garbage from my mind. I am a new man. In tune with my real needs for the first time in my life."

Cleo sipped at the rose hip tea; it didn't taste

bad at all. "Do you still see Ginny Sandler?" she inquired.

Richard frowned. "Ginny was not a woman who knew what she wanted in life. To her, sex was the ultimate. She never considered her mind, just her genitals."

"But you write about sex . . ."

"Not any more. My new book is called *A Trip Around The Inner Brain*. Tell me Cleo, have you ever taken acid?"

She staggered out of his house two hours later bogged down with his pontificating. Boring. But she did have a wonderful interview, and she couldn't wait to write it. What a number she could do on him—a real tongue in cheek piece.

She wished that Butch wasn't on the agenda next, because her mind was alive with ideas. But still, it was all on tape—and later she could let it all pour out. Russell was right. He knew her. He knew that once she got excited about something there was no stopping her.

She felt exhilarated as she drove toward the beach. Suddenly her life seemed to be fitting into place. Daniel. Work. A baby. She felt alive again, no longer a stupified beach bum.

Butch regarded her through slitted blue eyes, his little boy hurt expression prominent. "You let me down," he whined, "takin' off without so much as a fast goodbye."

Funny, when they had lived together she had never actually noticed the whine in his voice. But it was there, coming through loud and clear.

"I did plenty for you," Butch continued. "I took real good care of you. Got you away from that schmuck you were married to. Gave you a home and plenty of fantastic lovin'. Jeeze, Cleo, look in the mirror. You never looked so good in your life. And you can thank *me* for that—I relaxed you—made you a real beautiful woman."

Cleo sighed. "Butch," she interrupted, "let us not forget you *wanted* me to come and live with you. I was not some charity case you took pity on. You came to Rome and asked me to move in with you. No ties on either side. Plenty of laughs. Remember?"

"Aw ... shit ... Cleo. Whyn't you move back? We were doin' O.K. together. Vinnie will be workin', so she won't be around to bug you. What d'ya say? Shall we give it another crack?"

Cleo shook her head. "It wasn't Vinnie, she was maybe the catalyst—but I was ready to move on. Let's face it Butch—we gave each other everything we had to give—and I'm sorry—for me it wasn't enough."

Butch made a face. "First time a woman walked out on me in my *life*."

Cleo touched him lightly on the arm. "There's always a first time. You *know* we would never have made it as a permanent fixture. Can we be good friends?"

His face cracked into a grin. "Occasional lovers?"

She grinned back. "I don't think so. I had in mind more of a brother-sister deal. Wouldn't it be nice for you to have *one* female you didn't feel obliged to screw?"

"Hey, that's not such an um er bad idea."

"You could tell me all your problems."

"Yeah, can I start now?"

Cleo indicated her tape machine. "Tell you

362

what, give me an interview first, then I'll give you an hour problem time. Deal?"

"You always were a classy lady. I gotta say this, when you dump a guy at least you do it with style!"

Butch loved talking about himself. It was, without a doubt, his favorite pastime. He had a carefully worked out interview persona, but with Cleo he was more natural and genuinely at ease. After six months of living with him she knew most of his views on everything from the Pope to Carter. What she wanted from him were some provocative quotes.

Halfway through the interview he grabbed her in that old familiar way. "Let's screw," he suggested, "for old times' sake."

"Let's not. I'm working."

"I just cancelled the interview."

"Cancel your hard-on instead. We're at the good friends stage. Remember?"

"If I don't, I know you'll er um remind me. Hey—what's with the rumor about you and Onel?"

She clicked off the recorder. "Where did you hear that?"

Butch laughed. "Can't keep secrets in this town. I hear you moved in with him."

"So?"

"Don't get defensive with me, lady. I just wouldn't have thought he was your bag...I mean..."

"You mean after a big horny stud like you— why the hell would I look at a guy like Daniel Onel?"

"Somethin' like that."

She smiled, a special smile. "That's one secret you can't find out."

"Yeah." Butch made a face. "So he's a good

actor—that don't make for the perfect relationship. Now you and I, we had somethin' different. Like really mellow and steady. I . . ."

Vinnie interrupted them. She appeared on the slatted deck and planted herself firmly between them. She was wearing sawed-off jeans that clung like second skin, and a skimpy halter top barely concealing her pubescent breasts.

"You gonna interview me or not?" she demanded. "I gotta date. I can give you fifteen minutes then I gotta split."

Butch chuckled proudly, "She's a star already." He tapped her on the bottom. "Watch the way you talk to this lady."

Vinnie threw him a scathing look. "He tell you about the new girl living here now? Outasite! Biggest tits I ever saw, and she's only nineteen. Must make you feel kinda ancient."

"Will you shut up," Butch interrupted. "You need your ass spanked."

Vinnie gave him a challenging look. "You gonna do it, daddy dear?"

Butch stood up. "She's all yours," he said to Cleo. "Try to get some sense out of her—you know she's not as smart as she makes out. She's really just a sweet—um—er—misunderstood little girl."

Vinnie rolled her eyes heavenward. "What garbage!"

Butch winked at Cleo and headed for the house. "See you later."

Vinnie slouched into his chair. "Didn't he tell you?" she pursued.

"Tell me what?" asked Cleo, inserting a fresh tape into her portable machine.

" 'Bout his new piece of gash."

"I love your vocabulary."

"She's *gorgeous*."

"Good."

"Aren't you mad?"

"Why should I be?"

Vinnie shrugged. "*I* don't know. Don't you love him?"

Cleo burst out laughing. "Vinnie! Where on earth did you learn great big sentimental words like love?"

Vinnie scowled. "Don't make fun of me."

For the first time Cleo felt a sense of compassion for the objectionable child woman. The girl actually had feelings. "I'm not making fun of you. Just relax, Vinnie. Let's talk. Let's see if we can get some communication going here."

Two hours later Vinnie was still talking. It appeared that nobody had ever listened to her before. Mommy was pretty, rich, and spoiled, and into men and group sex. Daddy was the big movie star who patted her on the head and thought she was cute as hell but for crissakes don't tell anyone she was his daughter.

Vinnie was the classic case of too much too soon. Now she was to become a movie star herself, and Cleo had no doubt that the child would create a very successful world out of celluloid fantasy.

"Sure, I'll be a star," Vinnie said. "I got the looks. I got the talent. Tatum and Jodie can go suck. I'm gonna be the biggest."

"Yes," Cleo agreed. "I think you will be."

"Hey." Vinnie's usually sullen expression brightened. "You ain't half bad, you know that? This bimbo he's moved in is dense, but a real nothing. She'll last five minutes. You gonna move back?"

Slowly Cleo shook her head. If she had learned one thing in life it was that there was no going back.

She leaned forward and touched Vinnie lightly on the hand. "I wish I had bothered to get to know you when I was here. You're not nearly as bad as you'd have everyone believe."

Vinnie actually blushed. "Oh yes I am," she replied defiantly. "You bet your ass I am."

When Daniel arrived back from the studio, Cleo was right in the middle of her piece on Vinnie and Butch.

She looked up from her typewriter and blew him a kiss.

"I'm beat," he announced. "If Diana Beeson could act it would make everyone's day a hell of a lot easier." He sat down in a leather chair and proceeded to remove his shoes. "Any tea?"

"Mrs. K.'s in the kitchen," Cleo replied absently.

"That sonofabitch, Mark Hughes, can't direct himself out of a paperbag," Daniel complained. "I'm practically directing the goddamn picture."

"Sweetheart," Cleo said softly, "do you mind if we talk later? I must finish this, and I'm losing the thread."

"What are you doing?" Daniel asked, getting up, coming over, and peering over her shoulder.

Instinctively Cleo covered the paper. She *hated* anyone reading her work when it was in progress.

"So *sorry*," said Daniel sarcastically, "I didn't realize Ms. Rex Reed needed total privacy. Do let me know when you're finished. I wouldn't *dream* of disturbing you further." He stamped out of the room.

"Daniel," Cleo called after him. "Daniel? Come back, don't be so silly . . ."

She heard the kitchen door slam, and the sound

of him talking to his housekeeper. He was being petty. He would just have to understand about her work. After all, when he was reading a script, silence had to prevail. That he had made very clear right from the beginning. And if one of his old movies was on television the only time you could breathe was in the commercial.

She contemplated following him to the kitchen and making peace. But then she would *never* get back to the typewriter, and it would only take her another hour or so—and goddamn it—working again was such a *kick.*

Chapter 52

It was not the ordeal Muffin expected it to be. She had left the rented house, packed up her two suitcases and just moved out. Straight in with Karmen, Keeley, and the monster dogs. Straight into the title role of *The Girl with the Golden Snatch*.

Karmen said her qualifications were the most perfect she had ever seen. "She should know," Keeley said. "She's bin auditioning for six months."

Muffin had thought the matter out as best she could. She was alone in Hollywood. Jon had abandoned her. She had no money. What choice was there really?

Karmen offered her a place to live. A starring role in a movie. Money. Friendship.

Of course it was a porno movie. But if she showed everything in photographs for a little bit of money—then why not show it in movies for a lot?

She had made her decision, and within a day of auditioning had moved into the Malibu mansion.

She was given her own room, the run of the house, and a script to study.

When she read the script she almost changed her mind. The storyline was familiar. Girl meets boy. Loses boy. Gets boy in the end. In between girl goes to Hollywood to make her fortune and gets propositioned by everyone and everything from a midget stuntman to a Great Dane dog. The point of the story was the girl maintains her sweet innocence throughout every one of her ordeals.

The other point was every ordeal would be shot in detail. Every detail. Close up detail.

"Don't worry 'bout a thing," Keely assured her. "I'll set you up so good you won't care *what* you're doing. In fact you'll get a kick out of it."

True to his word on the first day of shooting he greeted her with a combination of pills that made her feel absolutely incredible.

Karmen had a studio built on to the side of her house, and most of the film was to be shot there. She had assembled a small crew of professionals—and Muffin established immediate rapport with them. In two days of shooting she didn't have to remove one item of clothing, and by the time she *did* have to she felt she was among old friends.

Karmen was so encouraging and supportive. Always praising her, making her want to do better. "I love your accent," she would say. "Just a little more emphasis when you say no in that scene. That's it sweetheart—that's exactly what I want. Clever girl."

Somehow Muffin slipped naturally into the role.

And when the time came to indulge in things she had only ever indulged in in private—well strangely enough it was enjoyable. It was a turn-on. It was exciting.

"You're beautiful," Karmen never tired of telling her, "a little golden puppy dog. Do you *realize* how many guys are going to fall insanely in love with you?"

Muffin hadn't thought about *that*.

Revealing herself to so many men . . . and all of them horny . . . and wanting her . . . her . . . *her*.

She giggled at the thought.

Halfway through the movie Karmen summoned her to her bedroom one night. She lay back in the big bed thoughtfully pulling on a joint. "Keeley and I thought you deserved some fun. You've been working so very hard little one, we thought you should relax."

Muffin shivered. She had been expecting them to approach her, but it was still a surprise.

"Come here," said Karmen lazily. "That's if you want to. No one around here is going to force you to do anything you don't want to."

Muffin did want to. Very much.

Keeley walked out of the bathroom. True to his original boast Karmen was not with him for the size of his nose.

Muffin glanced at him and quickly looked away.

Karmen smiled, a very knowing smile.

"Shall I tell Keeley to go?" she asked softly.

Muffin nodded.

Diana Beeson was a bitch. Jon found that out in no uncertain terms. And what was worse was the fact that she was an intelligent bitch. He couldn't talk her round, string her along, or get her to do anything she didn't want to.

He had moved in with her, and she expected service with a smile. "Go to the supermarket, Jon." "Fill the car up." "Go buy the trades." "Fetch my cleaning." "Walk the dog." Instead of moving in as her manager and taking over, he was chief gofer. *And he didn't like it. It was not what he had had in mind.* Apart from which he had no money and she was as tight as the proverbial drum.

It occurred to him that he had better move on. But where to? It was no good going until he had something better lined up. The way things were, staying with Muffin would have been better than this. He wondered briefly how Muffin was making out. His guilt was minimal at abandoning her. She would be alright. All she had to do was call up Jackson and he would come running—he had always had a hot nut for Muffin. And she could do worse than Jackson.

"Jon!" The sound of Diana's impatient call from the bedroom. "Come and zip me up, sweetie, will you. And do hurry, otherwise we'll be late, and you know how I hate being the last to arrive."

Another boring party. Now that Diana's movie was finished she wanted to go out every night. She loved the parties, the attention she always received, the propositions from the local stud talent. And Jon trailed behind her, the unknown idiot, boyfriend of the star. It was not a role he was happy in. But until something better came along it would have to do.

Muffin had never imagined herself involved in a sexual relationship with a woman. Oh sure—she knew all about it. You were not a model in London

372

without finding out a thing or two about life. Some of the girls had been very dykey—fed up with randy, grabbing men. Extolling the virtues of how different a female liaison could be had been one of their main topics of conversation.

Muffin remembered a certain location trip to Spain where Erica and Kamika had indulged right in the same room as her! "Come and join in," Erica had urged. But Muffin knew that if Jon ever found out he would kill her. Anyway—the idea just did not appeal.

With Karmen it was a whole different trip. Karmen, with her broody Egyptian eyes, and thin erotic body.

Karmen, with her low enticing voice and scented black bedsheets.

Karmen excited Muffin as much as any man ever had. And the things she did in bed surpassed anything any man had done to her.

Muffin felt more protected and loved than she had felt in her entire life.

When the movie was finished Karmen threw a big party to celebrate. First she took Muffin on a shopping trip to celebrate, and they glided through Beverly Hills, along the Strip, and to several obscure exciting clothes boutiques, in Karmen's all-black Mercedes. Karmen was treated like a Queen by all and sundry, and she played the part to the hilt.

Keeley travelled with them, dancing attendance, jumping at Karmen's every wish.

Muffin enjoyed every second of it. Because she was with *the* Karmen Rush, she too was treated with reverence and respect. Suddenly she *was* somebody again. It was great and she loved it.

"Just wait," Karmen husked. "Within months

they'll all know who you are. They'll be asking for *your* autograph. Just you wait, little sweet thing, and you'll see how right I am."

Jon was surprised to see Muffin at the Karmen Rush party. She looked good too, prettier and bouncier than he had seen her in ages.

He hoped she wouldn't spot him, didn't want a whole big scene. Diana would not appreciate that. Diana liked to keep a low profile as far as her personal life was concerned. So low in fact that in a recent cover story in *People* she hadn't even mentioned his existence. Bloody marvellous. What was he—the invisible man? After all he *was* living with the bitch.

"Is that wifey pie I spot hovering around the great Karmen?" Diana questioned.

"Where?" asked Jon insincerely.

Diana raised an eyebrow. "Right in your line of vision, darling. The one with the boobs."

"Oh yeah," Jon agreed, with a suitable note of surprise in his voice.

"Are you going to talk to her?"

"Why should I? I'm divorcing her, aren't I?"

Diana shrugged. "Do what you like, it makes no difference in *my* life."

It bloody wouldn't. Why couldn't she be jealous like normal people? He looked around the room searching for Jackson. Better make peace with him about running out on the rent for the house. He couldn't see him. Oh well. . . .

Diana had drifted independently off as usual. Jon turned sharply and collided with a woman. The drink she was carrying spilled down her ample cleavage. "Oh shit!" she said sharply.

Jon recognized her at once. She was April

Crawford, a fiftyish movie star of past glory—recently and very publicly divorced from her fifth husband.

"Why don't you goddamn look where you're going?" April snapped.

"Sorry," said Jon quickly, turning on the boyish look and English accent full wattage. "Can I get you another drink?"

April looked him over—a sharp head to toe scrutiny. Her face relaxed into a smile. "Why not? Double scotch on the rocks. Light on the rocks—and why don't you join me?"

"I'd like that," Jon replied quickly. At the very least he could get a cover picture out of it. April Crawford always had been, and always would be, news. He smiled. "Why don't you sit down and I'll fetch it to you."

"Yeah," replied April, winking, "why don't I."

Muffin saw Jon at the party and she couldn't even be bothered to go over and tell him what a bastard she thought he was. He didn't matter in her life any more. He was past news, over and finished.

Keeley had told her that Jon would be the one that got chased for all their unpaid debts. That would teach him a lesson.

After half an hour of partying, Karmen got bored. She never did stay at her own parties. A brief appearance was all that was necessary.

She took Muffin by the hand and led her into the famous black bedroom. They locked the door, settled on the vast bed, and switched on the room to room television system. Scenes of the party filtered onto the screen. "The only way to attend," Karmen murmured. "Pour the brandy, pass the cocaine. You and I will have our own kind of party."

Chapter 53

Daniel suffered from depressions. In the Bahamas Cleo got her first taste of his illness. He took to his bed for almost the entire trip, just lying there and gazing into space.

At first Cleo tried to joke him out of it. "Come on, get up. If you don't get a suntan people will think we spent our entire time here screwing!"

No response. Daniel was totally uncommunicative.

She tried sympathy. He responded to that alright. He burst into racking sobs and didn't stop for an hour.

She tried anger. "For crissakes get up. What *is* this crap?"

In the end she just left him alone. As soon as she stopped taking any notice of him he got up.

"I get these black attacks," he told her solemnly. "I just can't do anything. Can't function at all."

"What about when you're working?" Cleo asked crisply.

"Funny, it doesn't seem to happen then."

"Hmmmn . . ." She was sceptical.

Once up again, Daniel was his usual charming self—and they were out and about playing golf, swimming, snorkling, eating delicious dinners under the stars, and gambling.

His good humor lasted exactly two days, and then a new problem arrived. He became impotent. After two nights of incredible lovemaking he suddenly couldn't get it up.

"Don't worry," Cleo soothed, "it's nothing. Happens to everyone some time or other."

"Yes—you *would* know that," Daniel raged. "How many lovers have you had? Fifty? A hundred? Two hundred?"

"Including you, five actually," Cleo replied calmly. "And how about you? How many Princesses, movie stars, and other transient ladies have passed through *your* talented hands?"

In no time at all they were in the middle of an insult-throwing row. They seemed to be getting rather adept at arguments.

By the next day Daniel's good humor had returned along with his hard-on. They made long leisurely love in the morning, and then sat out by the pool. Everything was fine until Daniel accused Cleo of flirting with the pool boy—a finely muscled lad and all of eighteen. Cleo, of course, denied it. But they were soon embroiled in another fight, and right in the middle of it all Cleo found herself thinking—What the hell do I need this for? This guy is nuts. Jealous. Insecure. Petty. She left him alone in the hotel for the afternoon and went off on her own. When she returned he was full of apologies.

They dined in the hotel restaurant, and in the middle of their dinner a vacuous pretty blond came and sat herself down. She was Swedish, introduced herself as Ingmar, smiled patronizingly at Cleo, and proceeded to hold a lengthy and intimate conversation with Daniel.

Suddenly Cleo realized what was going on. Shades of darling ex-Mike. Ingmar featured the same self-satisfied smile as Susan big tits used to wear. Ingmar had recently been laid, and with a burning anger Cleo realized that it was by Daniel, that very afternoon. "You sonofabitch!" she hissed, pushing her chair away from the table and getting up. "You *bastard!*"

"What's the matter, darling?" Daniel asked innocently.

"Don't give me that *shit!*" She stalked back to their suite. Daniel soon followed.

Cleo was packing. Throwing her things into a suitcase with venom.

"I don't understand . . ." Daniel began.

"I thought you at least were different . . . but you're all the same, the whole bloody lot of you."

"Cleo. What am I supposed to have done?" Daniel stood there misunderstood and confused.

"You know what. That . . . that . . . person. You gave her one didn't you? This afternoon, right in this very room."

Daniel started to laugh. "Of course not. How could you possibily think that?"

Angrily Cleo glared at him. "Sixth sense. I'm not an idiot you know."

"Baby, baby, baby." He put his arms around

her. "Sixth sense indeed! What kind of an opinion do you have of me anyway? Do you honestly think I would do a thing like that to you?" He was still laughing, and kissing her, and pushing her hand toward his crotch. "Here, feel this. It's yours—all yours. If it goes anywhere else you'll be the first to know!"

"Oh Daniel!" She could feel her anger collapsing. She touched his face softly. It had been a ridiculous thought.

His hands were sliding inside her dress, and within moments she had forgotten all about Ingmar and thoughts of leaving.

It was a sexual thing. But it was also more. She loved Daniel. Depression, moodiness, jealousy, and all. She really loved him.

"Dynamite!" Russell shouted down the phone. "The piece on Butch and Vinnie is a gem. We're running it as the cover story next issue. Where have you been? I've been trying to contact you for weeks."

"The Bahamas. Daniel wanted a rest."

"You might let me know when you just take off. In-house reaction on your two stories is so strong that everyone in the goddamn place is coming to me with ideas on who you should do next. What we want to do is make your piece a regular spot—you know what I mean, a two or three page in-depth interview. I think . . ."

"Hang on Russ, I don't want to be tied to a weekly thing."

"You will, when I tell you the fee involved. Now, can you fly here and discuss everything?"

She was tempted. "When?"

"Soon as possible."

"I'll call you back on it."

"Don't vanish again."

"Wouldn't dream of it." Thoughtfully she hung up. Even more thoughtfully she ran her hands down her body. Her breasts felt swollen. Was that good or bad? She grinned to herself. She would have to find out. Being pregnant was a whole new experience.

Daniel lay out by the tennis court reading scripts. Now she had things to tell him. But telling him about the baby had to be a very special moment. She would savor the news to herself until the time was right.

"Hey—guess what?" she said, squatting on the grass beside him.

"What?" mumbled Daniel, immersed in a script.

"*Image* loves the stuff I did—they want to offer me all sorts of money to write a weekly interview piece."

"That's nice."

"It's more than nice. They want me to fly to New York to discuss terms and things."

Daniel placed the script carefully on the grass. "Who is they? That pimped-up editor or whatever he is?"

"Well Russell runs the show . . ."

"Why don't you tell me the truth about Russell? I know you've slept with him."

"I haven't. I keep on telling you that," she sighed, "And anyway, even if I *had*, what difference would it make?"

Daniel got up. "So you have?"

"No I haven't."

"Go to New York," Daniel snapped, "if that's what you want to do."

"I would like to . . ."

"So go. I won't stop you."

"But I don't want you to mind. Why don't you come too?"

"I hate New York. How long will you be gone?"

"Two days."

Daniel picked up the pile of scripts and headed for the house.

Cleo followed him in. "You do understand don't you? I *have* to work, it's important to me—and Daniel, if it's important to you about us getting married—well, I was thinking . . . Why don't we?"

"What happened to your 'I don't think we should spoil everything by getting married' speech?"

"I changed my mind. I love you. I have my reasons which you will be the *first* to know about."

"Tell me."

"When I get back."

"When are you going?"

"I thought the sooner the better. Tomorrow morning, and I'll be back before you know it."

Russell said, "Cleo's coming into town."

Mike concentrated on the ball. They were playing squash—a weekly game they had together.

"What happened to the old actor?" he replied casually.

"I don't know, maybe he's still around. But Cleo is definitely into working again."

"For you?"

"For the magazine. Did you read her cover story on the Kaufmans?"

"No," lied Mike. He had devoured every word of it. She was writing well. He wished she wasn't. He wished that she had faded into obscurity. He didn't want to be reminded of the beautiful intelligent woman who had once been his wife.

"Great stuff," said Russell, slamming a shot against the wall. "She seems to have acquired a sharp edge she never had before."

"She always had a sharp edge," said Mike bitterly, "only she kept it well hidden."

"Don't be bitter," chided Russell. "It's about time the two of you were friends."

"Let's quit." Mike threw his racket down none too gently. "I need a drink."

"We have the court for another fifteen minutes," protested Russell.

"So play with yourself, I've had it."

Mike left Russell at the sports club and went to a bar where a lot of the models and photographers hung out. He was too early, the place was nearly empty.

He needed a little company. He needed a little fucking.

He moved on to another bar used by the show business group. And who should he run into but Ginny Sandler, all girlish blond curls and plumpness.

"Mike!" she squealed, as if London had never happened. "One day in this town and I bump into *you!*"

Ginny had moved to Los Angeles, and was an extremely powerful and important agent. Mike had read about her success in the trades.

"You look wonderful, Ginny," he said, eyeing her opulent boobs escaping from the confines of a hardly buttoned silk shirt.

She introduced him to the group she was with and ordered him a drink.

383

"Mikey," she whispered, a hand straying to his thigh, "you are looking vereee tasty." She giggled, "But then you always did."

Ginny he could take home. Ginny would no more think of moving in than taking up knitting. She took her fucking like a man—straight.

"Are we going to . . ." he began.

"Of course!" giggled Ginny, "don't we always?"

Cleo had missed New York. She didn't realize it until she was riding in the cab from Kennedy airport, and then, suddenly, she knew how much she had missed the hustle and grind of the city.

It occurred to her that she hadn't even bothered to book a hotel room—but she figured *Image* could do that—and this time she would check that there were no screw-ups landing her in Russell's penthouse apartment.

The cab passed right by the Hampton Records building, and she thought fleetingly of Mike. She had no hard feelings toward him anymore. She felt exactly nothing in that direction.

Russell was waiting anxiously to greet her. He wore a new Italian suit, and pink striped shirt. "Welcome back!" he exclaimed. "Here—you like it?" He thrust the next issue of *Image* at her. A picture of Butch and Vinnie adorned the cover, and a yellow star proclaimed—"Cleo James—special exclusive story on Butch Kaufman and his sister."

"Well?" questioned Russell.

"I like it." Cleo grinned. Name on the front of the magazine—she had never had *that* honor before.

"This is just the start," said Russell happily. "Remember that piece you did last year on Senator

Ashton. As you know he's running as a presidential candidate in the next election—and guess who will have an upfront exclusive? It's all been arranged."

"But that's so far ahead . . ."

"So what? Now you're back in action you don't plan to fade away again do you?"

Slowly Cleo shook her head. Daniel was just going to have to accept the fact that he was marrying a working girl.

So much happened in such a short time, that before Cleo knew it a week had passed. Russell wanted her to do an on-the-spot interview with a deposed foreign king, and she could hardly turn *that* down. Then a top book publisher requested a meeting and offered her a hefty advance to do a book of interviews on prominent people. It was an offer she could hardly refuse. Then *Women's Wear Daily* wanted to do a story on *her*.

Everyone loved the Butch and Vinnie piece, and publicists were calling *Image* saying that this celebrity and that celebrity would like to be interviewed by Cleo James.

It all just seemed to come together at once.

"My celebrity reporter," Russell grinned. "Someone on the magazine will have to interview *you* next."

She called Daniel to explain. Each phone call his voice grew colder and colder. After three days she felt a bit silly telling him every day she would be back the next. So she decided to just ride with what was happening and make it up to Daniel when she got back. After all, when he heard about the baby . . . well she just knew he would be as thrilled as she was. Meanwhile New York was such fun.

Visiting old restaurants, new shows, boogieing at Studio 54 with a young gay copywriter from the magazine.

Russell drove her to the airport. Her book contract was signed and sealed, and a six month contract with *Image*. She felt great. But she missed Daniel, and couldn't wait to surprise him with all her good news.

At the airport Russell suggested magazines and candy, and that was *all* he had suggested the whole trip. It was a relief. At last she could really relax with him. A newspaper headline caught her eye. It caught her eye because it was accompanied by a photograph of Daniel. He was not alone in the photo. He was with Swedish Ingmar from the Bahamas.

Calmly Cleo purchased the paper—the headline was enough to give her the whole story.

ENGLISH ACTOR DANIEL ONEL WEDS
SWEDISH HEIRESS IN SECRET CEREMONY

Silently Russell took her arm. "Shall we forget about the plane?"

Dumbly she nodded.

Goddamn Daniel. Was he that insecure that he couldn't have waited a few extra days?

Chapter 54

Karmen was more excited about *The Girl With the Golden Snatch* than any of the multi-million-dollar epics she had starred in. The film was her baby, and she nursed it carefully through every stage.

The finished product was everything she had hoped for. It had comedy and humor, an interesting story, and the best looking cunt in Hollywood. Muffin was sensational. When she opened her legs for the close-ups every man in America was going to fall instantly in love.

Karmen was delighted, only sorry that she was unable to attach her name to it. A porno movie directed by Karmen Rush would guarantee disaster for her public image. Of course it was not exactly a secret, people in the business knew—Natasha Mount—credited as director—was Karmen Rush. It was a well-known fact. Only no one could prove it.

Diana and Jon were at a producer's house for dinner one night. About twelve people were present and it was a convivial meal. For once they had not argued before coming out, but Jon knew his time was almost up. He had already spent a couple of afternoons photographing April Crawford—and he felt that if things got desperate he would find a bed in that direction—more than a bed, but it wouldn't be the first time he had obliged a lady in the older age group. Diana was treating him as nothing more than an unpaid lackey, and he wasn't going to hang around for the final kick out. If nothing else turned up ... well April *was* a star ... had been a star ... and with him to guide her. ...

"Movietime, folks." Their hostess was clapping her hands excitedly. "We have a preview tonight."

They all trooped into the screening room.

Diana was paying too much attention to an aging writer. Jon had a nasty feeling the man would be his successor.

Their host was passing round brandies and laughing. "You're not going to *believe* this film," he announced to all and sundry. "You just will not believe it!"

The lights dimmed, and a golden sunset flickered onto the screen. Very beautiful.

Jon was trying to see if Diana had physical contact with the aging writer seated on her left.

A roar of laughter went up and Jon glanced back at the screen. James Bond-type music was blaring forth, and spelled out in girls naked bodies sprayed gold was the title, *The Girl With the Golden Snatch*.

In a busby Berkeley routine the girls changed position, and starring "*Muffin*" appeared on the screen.

"Oh my God!" laughed Diana. "Don't tell me wifey has become a movie star!"

Muffin strolled across the titles, naked and gold. She lay down on the sand, opened her legs, and the camera panned in.

"Christ!" said Diana reverently, "whatever made you divorce *that!*"

"He's here again," said Keeley.

Muffin grinned, It was the fourth time Jon had attempted to see her.

"I think it's about time we had the shit kicked outa him. I know a coupla of dudes get their jollies doin' that kinda thing. What ya say?"

"I say today I'll see him." Muffin jumped up and surveyed herself in the nearest mirror. "Show him in, Keeley." She fluffed her hair a little, licked shiny lips. She had just completed a photo layout for *Macho* magazine. She knew she looked adorable.

Muffin loved her new notoriety. Karmen had been right, as the movie started to take off all over America, her fame began.

Karmen, away on a location trip, called her daily. They had a wonderful relationship, warm and caring and very, very sexual.

Muffin giggled at the thought. The only bad news in her life now was that she would have to move out of the Rush mansion. It didn't look right her staying there. Now that she was famous (well nearly) separate abodes were the order of the day.

Keeley walked back in, an anxious Jon behind him.

"Shall I stay?" asked Keeley.

"It's O.K.," said Muffin. "He won't be staying long." She stared at Jon. "You look ever so skinny," she remarked. "Your old lady not feeding you?"

Jon ignored her question. "My little Muff!" he exclaimed admiringly. "How about *you* then?"

"How about me?"

"I saw the movie."

"Somehow I thought you had."

"It seems that all our plans for you worked out."

"What plans?"

"The singing, dancing, acting lessons I made you have."

Muffin yawned. "*You* made me have them. I paid for them."

"It was our money."

"What's up Jon? What do you want?"

He ventured closer. "Nice greeting."

"Almost as nice as your last goodbye. Remember? Leaving me stuck in that house with all the bills and no car."

"You can't drive."

"I can now. I can do lots of things I never did before." She walked over to the bar and opened up a can of Seven Up.

Jon followed her. "Can I have a drink?"

"Help yourself."

"You're being very cold."

"I can be what I like. We're divorced, or did you forget?"

"What did they pay you to do that film?"

"None of your business."

He sighed. "You never did understand money. You're probably getting taken for the ride of your life."

"Oh no. I *had* that ride already."

He slid his arm around her wiast. "You need looking after. I've missed you like crazy. I was nuts to go—I just had this stupid idea that you'd manage better without me—and you did."

"And I still can." She moved away from him, swigging from the can of Seven-Up.

"Listen Muff. I know you're bugged with me and I don't blame you. But I made a mistake—just like the one you made with Little Marty Pearl." He paused, followed her across the room, grabbed her. "You and I belong together." He felt her incredible tits and realized that he *had* missed them. No one had tits like Muffin. "We're a team. I can look after you like nobody else—in *every* way."

She was silent, allowing him to fondle her, feeling her nipples harden.

"Pack up your things," Jon whispered, his hand sliding down the front of her shorts. "I've got some very exciting things planned for you."

She didn't say anything. She was waiting for the amazing jolt of excitement she felt when Karmen touched her. It didn't come. His hand was between her legs and it didn't come. His fingers were exploring further and it didn't come.

She stared at the bulge in his jeans. So what?

Roughly she moved his hand and stood back—hands on hips—surveying him with scorn.

"Piss off, Jon. I'm not the same dumb bunny you married. You're not taking another free ride with me. So just piss off—and don't bother coming back."

Chapter 55

At first, when Cleo had read about Daniel marrying, she had been destroyed, in a state of shock.

Russell had been very kind. He had insisted she stay in his apartment—no strings—and this time there had been no strings, and she had been grateful for that. Somehow he had arranged for her things to be sent on from California—she hadn't asked how— she didn't even want to hear Daniel's name mentioned.

Within a week she threw herself into work with a vengeance, telling no one of the fact that she was pregnant. She found a pretty little apartment, went on occasional one-off dates, and for the first time in her life realized that she was quite capable of managing on her own. She did not need a permanent man. She could get along very nicely without one. It was strangely exciting having to go it alone. And somehow fulfilling.

Russell was very supportive. He was always there in case she needed him, and when it turned out her supposed pregnancy was a false alarm, it was *his* shoulder she cried on.

"But you should be pleased," he stated, after she had confided in him.

She shook her head sadly. "I wanted Daniel's baby."

Russell was very matter of fact. "If it's a baby you want *I'll* marry you."

Cleo couldn't help laughing. "What is this hang up everyone has with marriage? You don't need to be *married* to have a baby."

"I'll be happy to oblige either way," Russell offered nervously.

"Oh, Russ, you're very sweet. I appreciate all your kindness—but find yourself a big tall model girl. You and I can never be anything but the *best* of friends."

"Why?" He was piqued.

"Because it's a question of chemistry. Our chemistry is of the platonic friend variety. We've already discussed it a hundred times and both agreed."

"I never agreed."

"Oh yes you did."

Work was her salvation. Things were going really well, and then suddenly, out of the blue, she was invited to do a television pilot. A fifteen minute face-to-face interview show.

She knew that at least eight other people were being considered for the job, and after the pilot she forgot about it, and got on with the other things in her life.

It came as a great surprise to her when she was picked to do the show.

"I just can't believe it!" she told Russell, and grabbed at the opportunity.

They went out to celebrate.

"I feel I'm at the threshold of a whole new life," Cleo enthused. "Television is such a great challenge."

She threw herself into her new job with boundless enthusiasm.

The show was an instant success, thanks to Cleo. She had a television presence that made her an immediate celebrity.

The loss of privacy was a jolt. Being recognized in the supermarket and street by total strangers who felt they had every right in the world to talk to her.

And then there were all her new-found friends. People she had only met once briefly—maybe with Butch, or Mike, or when she was writing for *Image*. Suddenly, according to them, she was their best friend.

It was all very startling. But Cleo weathered it, accepted it, and eventually began to enjoy it.

A month after the show was screening, Daniel got divorced.

Ingmar stated to any newspaper that would listen that Daniel was an impossible and difficult man. She then demanded a million dollar divorce settlement.

Cleo could just imagine Daniel pacing around his house in his gym shoes and dyed hair screaming about the unfairness of it all.

She did think of him often. Sometimes he came to her in dreams, and they were back together, and oh so happy. Maybe it wasn't such an impossible thought that one day they might be together again. It was a feeling she had.

He was like a magnet. Sure he was difficult. But she could have handled him, if she had been willing to concentrate all her energies in his direction. She understood him. She didn't love him because of who he was, but because of *what* he was. And the moodiness, depression and petty jealousies were a part of him. The timing had been wrong for their affair. She had jumped from Butch's bed to Daniel's with no space in between. She had needed a freedom on her own terms that Daniel hadn't understood.

Maybe now things could be different. Maybe. . . .

Mike followed Cleo's every move. He watched her on television, read about her in magazines, and had vague casual conversations with Russell about her. It irked him beyond belief that his dear friend Russell was spending so much time with his ex-wife. Were they screwing? It was a question which haunted Mike. He didn't think he could stand it if they were.

Russell, of course, was giving nothing away. He was as tight-mouthed and smug as ever.

Eventually Mike knew that he would have to see Cleo, and he devised what he thought was a fiendishly clever plan. Russell had mentioned that Cleo was to tape several shows in Los Angeles, he had even mentioned the date she was going.

Mike had a business trip to L.A. he had been postponing. It didn't take too much detective work to find out what flight Cleo would be taking. Mike booked himself on to the same one.

Perfect. An accidental meeting. Natural and nice.

He didn't even mention to Russell he was going —wouldn't do to give the game away.

Cleo decided she would call Daniel when she arrived in L.A. Why not? Then again, why yes? She *still* hadn't made a firm decision. Yet she had to know how she really felt about him. She couldn't continue in the limbo land of not really knowing what she wanted. Did she still love him? Didn't she? How did *he* feel about *her*?

It was no use pretending, she had to know.

She hadn't exactly been pining for him—there had been other men. Only one she had actually slept with. Her director on the show who looked ever so slightly like Daniel. Now that was sick. She needed to know her true feelings so that she could get on with the rest of her life. It was as simple as that.

On the plane she enjoyed the celebrity treatment. She was travelling alone, her crew had gone on ahead.

The TV show was enjoying excellent ratings, and Cleo had to admit that she loved doing it more every program.

The thrill of each new guest. The research—done for her—but she still read every author's book, saw every actor's film, read up on every politician.

She was meeting so many new and interesting people. It was a job that was never boring.

She opened up her Vuitton briefcase. There was an art book to study, a record by a new girl rock sensation, a folder on *Surf Stud* and another on *The Girl with the Golden Snatch*. She was going to Los Angeles to tape two specials. One on Muffin—current porno superstar—and the second on Butch and Vinnie. *Surf Stud* had become *the* cult movie, and

Vinnie *the* new teenage star. Funny how the Kaufmans drifted in and out of her life.

She wondered how Vinnie was making out with all her new found fame. Probably loving every minute of it, and acting in an even more obnoxious way—if that was possible. So far the Kaufmans had managed to maintain the brother-sister image. It would be interesting to see how long they could keep it up—and *she* wasn't going to be the one to give them away.

She opened up the folder on *The Girl with the Golden Snatch*, and leafed through a series of stills from the movie. Hmmm ... Naked was no longer naughty. It was boring as hell. All those acres of bums and tits, and a few stiff pricks for good measure.

She had to admit though that Muffin was certainly something. Sort of a teenage Marilyn Monroe type—dumb and cunty—the type that appealed to most men.

"Cleo?"

She glanced up. Standing in the aisle was Mike.

"Hey—what a *surprise!*" he exclaimed, availing himself of the empty seat next to her, and shaking his head in amazement. "Of all the places to bump into each other! You going to L.A.?"

"If I'm not, I'm on the wrong plane," Cleo replied dryly, and shut the folder.

"Do you mind if I sit here?" Mike asked.

"It looks like I have no choice."

"Hey," he said quickly, "it's a long time ago. At least we can be friends now, can't we?"

She stared at her ex-husband. Horny-looking Mike—with the come-on eyes and black curly hair. He was a very attractive man. A man she had once loved to distraction. A man she now felt absolutely nothing for. No hate. No recriminations. Yes, they *could* be friends.

She smiled. "Why not?"

He was pleased. He summoned the stewardess and ordered champagne.

"This is a celebration," he told Cleo. "It's been a long time."

They talked casually about mutual acquaintances, what was happening over at Hampton Records, Russell, Cleo's TV show, family.

"It's really *great* to see you." Mike fixed her with his incredibly sexual eyes. "I have missed you more than you could ever possibly believe." His hand reached over and covered hers.

Oh Christ! She had fallen into a trap. She didn't need this. Deftly she moved her hand away and stood up. "Got to visit the john." She squeezed past him. Damn Mike being on the same plane. He never had been a good loser—he probably would only consider their marriage over if he had been the one to walk. Yet it was over. Irrevocably. She had a piece of paper to prove it.

She stayed in the toilet for a while. She knew Mike—knew exactly what the next conversational tack would be. In a way it was flattering that he obviously still wanted her—but not *that* flattering. He still wanted her because she didn't want him. Shit! What bad luck to be on the same plane as Mike. If indeed it was luck. She wouldn't put it past him to have arranged the whole thing . . .

It occurred to her that there was a way of stopping him dead in his tracks, before he said things he would regret. She made her way back to her seat.

He stood attentively to let her pass, making sure there was body contact as she did so.

"Still got the sexiest ass in the world," he leered, the confidence of a successful cocksman deep in his voice.

"Your lines haven't improved. In fact they're getting even cornier."

"Ain't nothing wrong with a sexy ass."

"Yeah. Ass. That's all women are to you aren't they?"

"Hey—come on—I was joking. Can't you take a joke?"

She stared at him, and wondered how they had ever survived four-and-a-half years together. "I'm getting married again, Mike. It's a secret at the moment, so I'd appreciate it if you wouldn't tell anyone. Even Russell doesn't know about it. But I thought you should know."

He was stunned. This piece of news was totally unexpected. Cleo. *His* Cleo getting married again.

He could feel the anger rising within him. She was a bitch. He had always known it.

He attempted to keep his voice steady and light. Mustn't let the bitch know she had gotten to him. "Who's the lucky guy then?"

She was dismissive and secretive. "No one you know."

Christ! She had let him sit next to her for the whole frigging flight making a fool of himself. He tried to think of something that would hurt. Came up with Ginny. "I was thinking of giving the marriage scene another try myself," he said, casually.

"Oh, yes?"

"Well . . . you know how it is. Lonely nights— lonely beds—even if you've got three girls shacked up with you."

"I've never had that problem myself."

She was a cutting bitch. "I've been spending a lot of time with Ginny."

"Ginny?" Cleo couldn't keep the amusement out of her voice.

Not quite the reaction he had expected. "Yes—Ginny," he pushed on regardless, "she's a very warm and giving person. I've always had a lot of feeling for her."

Cleo wanted to say, "Yes—so I discovered in London." Instead she said, "I hope you'll both be very happy."

Then, fortunately, the seat belt sign was flashing on, and their conversation came to a halt.

Neither spoke again until the plane had landed, and they were ready to disembark.

"See you around, Cleo," said Mike. He had already spotted a ripe and luscious redhead moving down the aisle. She looked like she could entertain him for an evening or two. He set off after her.

Cleo remained seated for a few minutes while the plane emptied out.

Mike and Ginny. It couldn't be true, could it? Mike's taste had always been so much more up-market. But then Ginny was probably the perfect companion for him. Two sex maniacs together. What could be better.

She suppressed a smile. Poor old Mike. The same tired old lines. Briefly she felt sorry for him—but only briefly. He was a big boy. He could look after himself.

Once installed in the Beverly Hills hotel Cleo found she had itchy fingers to use the phone.

Daniel.

He was on her mind.

Constantly.

Funny. It was all the other guys that came running. Daniel merely got married behind her back without so much as a word of explanation. It was a *very* shitty thing to do. After all they *had* been living together, planning their own marriage.

It made absolutely no difference to the way she felt about him. She wanted to see him—dyed hair and all.

A woman answered the phone. Young, unfriendly, with a distinct English accent. Coldly. "I'll see if he's here."

A pause. Then Daniel. "How are *you?*"

His voice brought back every good memory. "I'm fine. You?"

"The same."

She laughed softly. "Is that good or bad?"

"It depends."

"I'm in Los Angeles."

"Oh. You finally came back."

"Yeah, it took me a little time. How did the marriage go?"

"Quickly."

His replies were sparse to say the least. "Are you alone?" she asked.

"No."

"Can you talk?"

"No."

"You're not married *again* are you?"

"No."

She took a deep breath. "Daniel, do you want to see me?"

"Of course."

"So call me back when you *can* talk. I'm at the Beverly Hills."

After hanging up she couldn't concentrate on anything. Her director called her about dinner but she hedged her way out of it.

Daniel did not call back. His secretary called at approximately 5 PM and in a very businesslike tone stated that Mr. Onel wondered if she was free for lunch the following day, and if she was he would see her at *Ma Maison* at one o'clock.

Terrific. Lunch. And *Ma Maison* was not exactly the most private place in town.

Disgusted, she took a sleeping pill and went to bed.

Daniel was waiting when she arrived. Suntanned, and about eight pounds thinner. He looked good. He would never be a matinee idol, but he was the best looking man *she* had ever seen.

She had dressed carefully. White. His favorite color. Not too much make-up. She was as nervous as a girl on her first date.

He stood as she approached the table. "Hello Cleo," he said.

She was immediately lost in his eyes. He seemed to be returning the silent signals racing back and forth. She knew at once he was as nervous as she was.

They ordered some food, picked at it. Gulped down the wine.

"Who are you living with?" she asked softly.

"A girl."

She attempted a laugh. "I was hoping you hadn't switched to boys."

"A girl who's always around. Sweet, unambitious, concerned only with me."

"Never runs off to New York. Right?"

"Right. Ingmar was a mistake—but we both know—you and I—we would never have worked things out."

There was a lump in her throat. "We wouldn't?"

He took her hand and held it gently. "You know we wouldn't. Let's not kid ourselves, I am a very selfish man—I need someone on call twenty-four hours a day. I need a yes-lady—and you are a lot of things—but a yes-lady—never."

"What is a yes-lady, anyway?"

"Someone who's always there telling me how wonderful I am. Fucking stupid isn't it? But I need that in my life."

The lump in her throat refused to go. "Yeah, it's stupid."

"You're beautiful, intelligent, and quite rightly, you want a career. I could never handle that. I'd go out of my mind with jealousy."

"I never did anything to make you jealous."

"Of course you didn't. It wasn't your fault that I imagined you screwing your way around New York. At home now sits Jilly. She is twenty years old, passive, and dedicated to me. She tells me I'm the best actor in the world, the best lover, the best everything. I am her life. I don't care about her that much, but I do need her. You—I cared about much too much." He squeezed her hand. "Do you understand what I'm saying?"

Her voice was very low. "I think so."

"Of course if you wanted to give your career up . . ." he trailed off, "but you don't do you?"

"Don't answer for me."

"I've seen you on television. You love it—you come alive. You're like me—you have to express

404

yourself in many ways." He shrugged. "Nothing wrong with *that*."

"But you couldn't take it . . ."

"I'm being honest with you. That's what our relationship was about wasn't it? We *were* always honest with each other weren't we?"

"What about Ingmar?"

"I never had her in the Bahamas. She turned up in L.A. when you were in New York. I was lonely, mad at you. She was around. Getting married was a horrible mistake. I just wanted to get my own back on you."

"For what?"

"For leaving me."

"Oh Daniel." Her eyes filled with tears. "*I* think we could make things work."

A waiter was hovering, pouring more wine. Cleo blinked back tears. This was hardly the place to break down.

"Damn!" The waiter had spilled some wine on Daniel's gray gaberdine trousers, and was now trying to rub it off. "Leave it alone, man," Daniel stormed. "Bloody careless." He grimaced at Cleo. "Just had them made—first time I wore them."

"Try water. It's white wine, won't stain."

Industriously he soaked his napkin in water and dabbed at the offending stain. Somehow Cleo felt that if Jilly was around she would produce an instant solution. After all, a totally dedicated twenty-year-old girl would *never* allow his precious new trousers to remain stained.

Cleo stood up. "I have to go," she said quickly.

Daniel stopped rubbing. "Yes, I understand. It was nice seeing you again."

Only nice?

"Maybe we can have lunch again," he continued, his attention now torn between her and the stain.

"Why not?" Why yes?

She left the restaurant, blinked in the sunshine. Well, that was that. At least Daniel knew what *he* wanted. And it obviously wasn't her.

So . . . she was free . . . all options open.

Daniel was right—a yes-lady she could never be. And if that was the kind of woman he would be satisfied with . . . well maybe he wasn't the man she had thought he was.

She went back to her hotel, slipped off the white outfit, lay on the bed, lit a cigarette and called her director. "I'm available," she said. "What's happening?"

"Nice of you," he replied. "You're sure?"

"You sound pissed off."

"I *am* pissed off. You come to L.A. and vanish. We have a show tomorrow. If you can spare the time, tonight we are dining with Muffin. You *do* want to talk to her before the show don't you?"

"Tell me where and when and I'll be there."

"I'll pick you up at seven-thirty."

"I'll look forward to it."

"And Cleo?"

"Yes."

"It will be nice to see you again. You've been avoiding me since . . ."

"Later." She put the phone down. True. She had been avoiding him since they had slept together.

But it wasn't *his* fault he looked ever so slightly like Daniel. And anyway—he was younger by at least twelve years, and better looking, taller, smarter, and he didn't dye his hair, and he wasn't a fucking egomaniac.

She sighed. Time to start forgetting Daniel. Definitely time.

Chapter 56

Muffin had moved from the Rush mansion. She now lived in a fantasy Spanish Palace of pink brick and tile situated in the very center of Beverly Hills. She did not live alone. Three miniature dogs cavorted through the house, and oriental twin maids tended to her every need.

In residence also was a young man named Buff. He was not unlike Jon in appearance—skinny, blond, boyish. But Buff had no control over Muffin's new found fortunes, he was merely installed as a sort of Keeley figure—just around for the size of his cock.

Karmen and Muffin still shared a more than intimate relationship, but for appearances sake they kept separate houses. Now that Muffin was *the* current porno superstar, she could no longer afford to share a house with Karmen. It wouldn't look right.

People would talk. And Karmen had a formidable reputation to protect.

Cleo arrived at the house in a white chauffeured Cadillac.

Buff came out to greet her. His tight jeans emphasized the reason he was Muffin's live-in boyfriend. "Hi," he mumbled, "good t'see you again."

They had all spent a drunken evening together the previous night. Cleo, with her director and producer. Buff, with Muffin.

Cleo remembered the evening with a thin smile. Her producer and director had been in a nervous sweat at meeting Muffin. "What do you say to a broad whose pussy has been seen on every screen in the country?" the producer had asked, perplexed.

"Hello puss might be good," Cleo had replied dryly.

"Don't joke around. This girl has the most famous snatch in the country!"

"Why does that make you so nervous?"

"Jeeze! I don't *know!*"

This was the same producer who had met heads of state, senators, movie stars, and not flinched at all.

"The male malady," Cleo had said cuttingly, "a terror of cunt."

"You really know how to turn a pretty phrase," her producer had replied, disgusted. Then he had shut up.

As it turned out Muffin had been a delight. Full of girlish giggles and innocence. Cleo had liked her immediately.

Dinner had been at *Trader Vics*, and the Navy Grogs had been flowing at an alarming rate. Everyone had a good time. Even Cleo. She had decided that her director did not resemble Daniel one little bit—and when they were in bed together later, it was only the influence of the Navy Grogs that made her cry out "Daniel!" at her moment of climax.

The camera crew were already at Muffin's house, setting up and getting things together. Her director greeted her with a more than friendly kiss. Apparently calling out another man's name at orgasm was not the kind of thing to put *him* off.

She pushed him away in an offhand fashion, and the make-up girl came at her with a powder puff.

Cleo thought about the interview as she glanced around the living-room—it was all thick pile carpets and huge cushions. Virgin white. Of course. Very predictable.

Muffin was news. *The Girl with the Golden Snatch* was the biggest grossing porno movie of all time.

Cleo had, of course, seen the film. As porno films went it wasn't bad. But as porno stars went, Muffin was sensational. A child woman, with a totally beautiful body. Nothing tacky about Muffin, she lived up to every word in the somewhat crude title.

It was going to be difficult to attack such a sweet little golden bunny. But attack she must. Her viewers would expect it. They knew her opinions on the way women were used in the massive pornography industry. Only three weeks previously she had taken to task the editor of a sick porno magazine. At the end of the confrontation the man had been a nervous wreck. As a crusader on women's rights Cleo had become something of an overnight phenomenon. She came across as witty, sharp, cutting and intelligent. Also beautiful. The combination was dynamite.

Muffin wafted into the room dressed in white broderie anglaise frills from head to toe.

She was a superstar—just as Karmen had assured her she would be.

"Hi Cleo," she greeted, in carefully cultivated baby girl tones, "are you ready for me?"

"Five minutes—they're setting up now."

Muffin walked to the mirrored bar, and studied her image in the pink tinted glass. She licked her lips and fluffed out her hair. *The Prettiest Girl in Porn" Newsweek* had labelled her in a recent cover story. She wouldn't argue with *that*. She had done pretty good for a little dumb English girl who had been abandoned penniless in big bad Hollywood. Pretty goddamned good. And nobody had been more surprised than Jon bloody Clapton.

It had given her extreme satisfaction telling him exactly what he could do. He had not believed that she wasn't the same pliable sweet dumb little Muff. It had taken Keeley and two strong-arm friends to convince him.

Diana Beeson had kicked him out—and for a while April Crawford had kept him. The last Muffin had heard was that his visa had run out, and he had been forced to return to England. Good riddance.

"All set, Muffin," Cleo called out. "Why don't we sit on the couch."

Muffin joined her, and giggled inanely.

"Don't be nervous," Cleo said reassuringly. "Just make believe the two of us are having a private chat." She glanced over at her director. "Ready, Phil?"

He nodded.

Cleo stared straight into the camera, her face alert and sincere.

"Hi, this is Cleo James talking to you from Los Angeles—city of dreams, city of angels—and a city that runs one of the largest pornographic industries in the world. Whatever your kink, you can get it here. Right now I am sitting in the home of Muffin —your average pretty girl next door porno star."

The camera panned to include Muffin in the shot.

Cleo turned to her and smiled. "Hi, Muffin. Welcome to the show."

Muffin dimpled in return. "It's *my* pleasure," she lisped sexily.

"Yes," Cleo said, the smile sliding from her face, "that's exactly what I wanted to talk to you about . . ."

She turned back to face the camera. "Tonight ladies and gentlemen, our subject is pornography. Do we want it? Can we take it? And why the hell don't we get rid of it?"

Cleo was back on the screen. It felt good. Somehow she knew Daniel was right. This was where she really belonged.